Ways of F

Earlyworks Press Fiction

Ways of Falling

Copyright Information

Printed in the UK
by MPG Books Group

ISBN 978-1-906451-30-1

Published by Earlyworks Press
Creative Media Centre,
45 Robertson St, Hastings,
Sussex TN34 1HL

www.earlyworkspress.co.uk

Contents

Reflections of a Guinea Pig

by Diane Churchill Evans

I talk, but few words form.
I cry, but no tears fall.
I sleep, but no rest relieves.
I squint in the mirror, and the reflection of another
grimaces back at me.

Who is this macabre imposter who stole my identity whilst I slept my last rest? I awoke one horrifying day to find that I had become a crude mimic of what I used to be. I have recently worn several faces, each a subtle amendment on the previous but none of them resembling the face I had fallen into sleep with. In short, I have been reborn as a Guinea Pig.

My last memory of me was on a warm, summer afternoon. The somewhat stifled air in her room carried the scent of perfume; the sparse remains in the bottle on the dresser bore testimony to a bygone time. A stocking lay strewn on the floor, cast aside flippantly in the moment but in the knowledge that it would soon after be laid delicately in the drawer. The room itself was sparse but that didn't matter. All that I lived for was between the sheets and the rest was mere subtext. The window stretched open but the bustle and strain of voices in the street below could not touch us for our last half hour of euphoria. Time was treasured and grasped whenever possible. The future was unpredictable so we lived for the immediate.

As she slowly tore herself away from the mattress where I reclined, our fingers entangled in a reluctance to part, then lost their grip at the tips. Our uniforms summoned and we dutifully obeyed. Hers brought comfort and relief; mine, adrenaline and a parched fear whose insipid taste I can barely describe. I had enjoyed Sophie but now others needed her more: men, women and children, all victims of the Blitz. For me, a train would soon be waiting that would take me to my second home – a long, grey strip of concrete that regularly

1

spat me up into the threatening skies but then forgivingly welcomed me back.

Within three hours of leaving the comfort of her arms, I was standing broadly on that very strip of concrete. It burned under my feet in the sun. All around me people hurried about their business with an air of anticipation that was mingled with the antithesis of apprehension and excitement. I would spend the next twenty-four hours preparing for a night sortie over the Reich. I pored over maps and plans and discussed tactics until I could recite them backwards.

I remember as a child seeing an aeroplane fly over our school playground one day, a fairly uncommon sight then for where we lived, and everyone went quiet for a moment as they stared, mesmerised. Some eighty or more jaws gaped in wonder, little heads thrown back, necks stretched up. Even after the aircraft had flown out of sight behind some clouds, my gaze remained transfixed until the sound of her engines carried her too far away. We then charged around the playground with arms stretched wide pretending we were planes. In our minds we were flying over fields and villages, heading to the open seas and finding our way to countries we had read about, like India and America. Robert was carrying wealthy passengers; I was carrying important cargo and mail that was vital to the running of the Empire. The air amusedly toyed with our hair as we raced about trying to avoid the chatting girls. They stood huddled in random pockets that served as islands in our imagination. For the first time my geography lessons came alive; I pictured myself flying through the pages of the atlas, pouting my lips and blowing hard to make authentic engine sounds. That was when I decided I would one day be a pilot. I would fly across oceans, wear a smart uniform and maybe even build my own plane. I would be King of the Clouds.

Taking to the skies in combat was not something I had envisaged at that time. The skies in my games were always welcoming, blue and sunny but now they were dark and foreboding. We had to fly under the blanket of nightfall, no small schoolboys in sight to imitate enviously as I flew overhead. Perhaps the odd pair of eyes would stray out of bed and look up from behind the safety of their window but I felt like shouting to them, 'Close your curtains and your imaginations, the reality bears little resemblance to the game.' Flying, in itself, was everything and more I had ever dreamt it would be but not under the circumstances of war. What goes up must come down. That much alone was certain but the speed and location of that descent was Fortune's decision. 'Russian roulette', sighed my father as he gripped me tightly in an embrace the first time I donned my uniform. I was buzzing with excitement but he had known enough of aerial combat at the end of the Great War to perceive some notion of what lay in store for me. Still, he bore his burden of anguished pride with dignity.

I pushed my dinner around the plate, struggling to swallow the bland food. My stomach was beginning to churn with anticipation of the impending nightfall. How I longed to be back in London with Sophie, another world away now. The mouthful of food gripped the back of my throat as it crawled down. Perhaps the idyllic afternoon with Sophie the day before was making it harder than usual to summon my passion to fly. Never before had I had so much to live for and yet now I was regularly chancing death.

As I sat in the cockpit my hands grew clammy. My heart was pounding ferociously but the adrenaline and excitement that was lacking during dinner had resurfaced and was pulsing through my veins. I felt ready to take on the world again. I put Sophie to the back of my mind because if I were to have any hope of seeing her again I would need to concentrate entirely on the present. I did my checks and the engines began to roar.

The ground started to race past as we whipped up speed. My Halifax tilted her nose to the skies, in much the same way that I had done as that awe-struck schoolboy. I simultaneously sank back into my seat and tipped upwards with her hulk of a frame. My head pressed hard against the backrest. My hands gripped the controls. As we gained altitude we rapidly lost sight of our homeland due to the blackout. It became impossible to distinguish when we had left the land and flown out over the sea. Millions below slept off the strain of the day as we passed unsuspected overhead. It was an unnervingly solitary feeling and yet I was not alone. Besides my crew of six others I was a formational pattern in the clouds, surrounded by further members of my bomber squadron. We moved stealthily through the night, each precious life nervously ensconced within its protective, metallic shell.

I could have gladly flown on until dawn but our target was fast approaching. We had a mission to accomplish before we could return home. In sequence, entirely to the letter, we deployed our bombs over the industrial site. For a short time our cockpits were illuminated by the conflagration that raged below. The sound must have been deafening on the ground, like a decade of November fifths rolled into one. How ever did the world get itself caught up in this mess? It is hard to believe that all the protagonists in this horrific drama had at one time been innocent infants.

I knew in an instant something was wrong when we were jerked off course and into a small spin. It felt as though we had collided with a huge bird. Just moments before, an allied aircraft had combusted overhead, hit by a sidling Ju 88. Debris flew at a tremendous speed and pebble-dashed our windscreen. Almost as quickly it was gone again. German anti-aircraft artillery had opened fire directly below. Flak thickened the air. We had no time to lose in getting out of range. I quickly recovered the plane and set her on a straight and level course again. One of the finely tuned engines missed a beat and coughed.

'Damn it, we've been hit!' yelled my tail gunner in a tremulous tone.

'It's okay, I've got control again,' I called back reassuringly.

This time the engine spluttered and I could no longer hide behind optimistic denial as we took a sharp and sudden dip that left my stomach feeling like it was several feet above the rest of me.

'What's our exact location?' I shouted to my navigational officer. Sounds were deafening me but I couldn't distinguish what they all were.

'The gauge is dropping. One of our engines must have been hit,' I panted. 'I'd sooner be swallowed up by the tide than come down over enemy territory. If the other three engines are okay we might still make it back to England. What's the fastest course for getting us home with this tail wind?'

We limped along for what felt like an eternity but after that my memory becomes patchy. I vaguely recall my engineer putting my chute on and we left via the escape hatch at the front. I fell from the clouds and intuitively pulled my cord. I remember thinking it hadn't opened but then I was yanked. All I was aware of after that was the piercing silence, a sense of weightlessness and a burning heat around my head… then nothing.

It was when I eventually came round that I discovered the imposter who had stolen my face. He had peeled away my skin to reveal little more than a shadow of someone once very familiar. Many months have passed since I first woke up with this stranger and I have subsequently worn a number of reconstructed masks, each one an echo closer to the face which used to stare back at me in the mirror but I have grown to accept that he is gone. He died on the exterior though lives on, imprisoned, in the interior. Nobody sees the man they previously knew. He might have been partly resurrected had Sophie been able to recognise her love for him but who could blame her for leaving this stranger? Though it pains me to say, it is less lonely living without her than it was having her sit by my bed unable to look at me with anything more than pitying glances. If a girlfriend who was a nurse couldn't bring herself to love me then what woman ever would again, unless she had previously loved me as a wife may have done?

So that is how I came to be a Guinea Pig. One of McIndoe's so-named Guinea Pigs, shuttling between the East Grinstead hospital and Marchwood Park in Hampshire where we enjoy long rests from operations and manufacture items for aircraft navigation. Marchwood Park does all it can to help integrate us back into society but outside of its walls we feel alienated from the country we were fighting to save. There is no easy way back in. Such stark reminders of the price of war do not sit so comfortably with a country celebrating victory. The nation's liberation is secured in exchange for our own. The dead will not be forgotten but we cannot be recognised.

Nobody knows what to say to us, how to look at us, or whether to look at us. McIndoe's pioneering plastic surgery will immortalise my new face in the pages of history books where it can be scrutinised without embarrassment. There they will nametag the survivors as 'heroes' but tell me one thing; what schoolboy now will contemplate the photographs of burnt visages and charcoaled, skeletal planes, then dream that he too will grow up to be a pilot?

Five Little Pinkies

by Stephen Atkinson

After six minutes the man in the beige corduroy jacket, traipsing
through small flowers of yellow and violet up the gentle slope of the
meadow, came to the child hunched in the grass. The small boy
didn't raise his eyes although he had been furtively watching him
throughout his approach. He sat cross-legged and chewing a
succulent green blade. A ladybird crawled lazily and unnoticed
across the bare knee below his shorts. Beside him, his plastic yellow
dumper truck lay abandoned by boredom.

"Wouldn't you like to come home now? Tea will be ready
soon."

"Is there Lemon Drizzle?"

"Undoubtedly. And Nice biscuits and bread and butter."

"I'm rather busy."

"Mum would like it if you came back with me." The man
brushed something from the leather patch on his elbow. He had a
kind face creased just a little with concern.

"I'll be down later. Close your eyes....."

The man scrunched up his eyelids so the boy could see he was
playing their game.

"How many fingers am I holding up?" His chubby little hand
was outstretched before him.

"Four." He knew he always held up five.

"Wrong! Five. I win."

The man opened his eyes. "Five little pinkies."

"I can do it with my toes, too." He started to remove one of his
sandals.

"Don't take your shoes off. You'll lose them."

The boy stopped, closed his eyes. "You do it."

The man held out his hand, holding up three fingers. "How
many?"

"Four," said the boy.

"Right! My little genius."

The boy delightedly opened his eyes to see his father proffering
four fingers before him.

"I always win."

7

The breeze rippled the sea of grass all around them, and the boy wondered at the magic of the countryside, the sun warm and caressing against his cheek. He thought of his mother's touch, and listened for the sound of the windmill. He could hear nothing but the trill of the thrush from the hedgerow to his right.

"Come down soon," said his father and turned away.

Later the soft, warm, fine rain dropping gently on his head caused the figure hunched in the grass to glance upwards. It was a pleasant sensation, like little quail yolks splattering onto his scalp, massaging away the headaches. He wasn't a boy any more. Dostoyevsky had replaced the dumper truck.

He gazed at the solitary summer raincloud that briefly interrupted the late afternoon sunshine and smiled. He covered the leather-bound book with a cagoule and tipped his head back, his mouth open to catch the raindrops.

But the shower stopped almost as soon as it had started and he could only savour the tiniest droplet or two on his tongue. It tasted as sweet and pure as elderflower, lovingly warmed by the sunshine.

The passing cloud drifted away and the afternoon erupted again into a bright, blue-sky heaven.

Before him stood a woman. Tall, blonde and good looking with a unique little twist to one side of her mouth that he always found irresistible, even after he found her perfectly resistible.

She stared at him for a moment. "The house is on fire," she said simply.

"Can anything be saved?"

"Gone already. Everything up in smoke."

"Everything?"

"Everything except that awful gilt-framed mirror your mother gave us. Ted managed to pull it out before the flames took hold."

"My books?"

"Everything."

She didn't look particularly alarmed, but she fiddled with one of the buttons that went from top to bottom on the front of her white summer dress.

"Are you trying to seduce me?" He stared pointedly at the button she was worrying just at the level of her lower belly. She stopped immediately, and the hard, dead look in her eye grew even more distant. She looked to him like a human redoubt.

He raised his face again to the skies hoping to perhaps catch another drop of refreshing rain and when he looked back, she was gone.

He removed the cagoule from his book and began to read, taking a cigarette from the packet beside him and lighting it with his gold Ronson. He inhaled deeply, satisfied, and let the book rest in his lap as he reached over with his other hand to the steaming cup of coffee sitting on his right. Also on the tray were a piece of Lemon Drizzle cake and a plate of Nice biscuits.

"A human redoubt," he said out loud to himself before he turned once again to his book.

He was aware that he could hear no windmill. He longed for the windmill.

It was the middle of the night, soft and warm, and the police officer was shaking him by the arm.

"Sir! Wake up! There's been an accident...."

He stirred and sat up, rubbing his eyes to better see the figure in blue uniform before him, his face creased with the imprint of the grass where he had been laying.

"Accident?"

"Your daughter, sir. I'm sorry...."

"What do you mean, my daughter? What's happened?" He tried to stand but could not. The officer placed a thoughtful, restraining arm on his shoulder to urge him to stay put.

"She didn't stand a chance, sir. It was a lorry; came across the wrong side of the road, out of control. Sally was looking in the window of a bookshop. Died instantly, mercifully."

"Died? Sally?"

"I'm sorry sir. I have to ask you to come down to the morgue. Identification. When you're ready, of course."

"I'm listening out for the windmill."

"Of course, sir. When you're ready. Sally's not going anywhere."

Later in the night the headaches came again. He felt as though his brain was going to explode, his eyes about to burst like squeezed quail's eggs.

"Mother!" he screamed, holding his forehead with both hands, desperate for cool comfort in the night. The grass under his body felt damp with dew and tears. "Mother!"

"Shush, baby," she said, standing before him silhouetted against the indigo moonlit sky.

"Mummy's here."

Even through his migraine he could see that she was old, very old. Her hair was wispy white and her face lined with too many decades of pain and worry. But there was a kindness twinkling in her eyes that lent her ageing, aching body a shining beauty.

"How many fingers am I holding up?"

He winced with pain as he shut his eyes tight and tried to concentrate. She was holding up three fingers in the moonlight.

"Four," he whispered softly.

"My little genius," she said and when he opened his eyes she was holding up four.

"I'm waiting for the windmill," he said.

"I know. It'll come."

"Mother."

"Yes, baby?"

"I want to die."

"Shush, baby. Dying's not all it's cracked up to be, believe me. Hang on."

He watched her through a mist of tears as she faded and all he could think about was the pain in his head: the throbbing, the throbbing.... the THROBBING!

It was here! The windmill was here. He listened with pure glee, a stupid grin on his exhausted face, as the windmill blades 'whooshed' through the air, a loud, rhythmic beat that drummed hope and comfort into his very soul, louder and louder and faster and faster until the deafening crescendo drove the migraine to oblivion.

It took half an hour for the circling helicopter to lower a winchman down to the icy precipice where he was marooned. The blizzard, which hadn't abated for two days, was threatening to worsen and the anxious pilot hovered precariously just a few precious metres above the snow covered mountain.

The stiffened snowman they winched aboard was a fragile whisker from death. Icicles hung from every aperture, his nose and eyelids and the corners of his mouth, and his entire face was caked in a thin layer of snow.

Three paramedics gently massaged his rigid limbs, fearing that hypothermia had already got too strong a grip.

10

He was barely conscious but as they struggled to thaw him out they let out a small cheer when they were finally rewarded with the feeble cough of the pledged dead, red blood smeared with black streaks of hot Bovril trickling down his chin.

Miraculously, by the time the windmill blades were again churning the leaves on the hospital roof at Salzburg, it was clear he was going to survive, albeit with the loss from frostbite of all five digits on his right hand.

Falling From the Sky

by Shirley Golden

It was Zoë's idea. We'd meet on the edge of the wasteland where the runway stopped, before the housing estate began; the spot where I smoked for bravado and watched 747s descend.

'God, I'm bored.'

I took another drag and smothered a cough. She was always bored, and it's not like I disagreed – it was boring; but crazy was reserved for when her parents were away. Her dad is this hotshot theatre director and her mum is an actress. They take highbrow productions to America and show off, according to Zoë. They consigned her to a "solid comprehensive" 'cause it's important she "make her own way." She thought them pretentious and riddled with clichés. But she has a love of drama, so I guess there's something she'll take from them.

My parents were far less exotic. They were lame and inconvenient. I couldn't wait to leave home. Dad loved to remind me that if I didn't do well in my exams I wouldn't be able to get a job and I'd not be able to afford to leave. He said things like, 'Believe me, I know what I'm talking about,' in that hard-done-by tone he had perfected.

'You need to study harder,' he said.

'If I didn't have such a mass of chores, perhaps I could.'

And so it would start. We'd shout for a bit – he'd call me selfish and manipulative. I'd call him a control-freak and a bully.

Zoë flipped up her phone.

A plane coasted down the runway, and I shouted, 'Whatta you doing?'

'Gonna vote for those two wankers again.' She jabbed on the keypad, silver nails clicking; eyes black-lined and deadly. Her entertainment for the past three weeks was to keep an act with no talent from being booted off *The X Factor*. Everyone at school said it was unfair, that others with ability were losing out. Zoë said life was unfair. She said if those being dumped were any good they'd find another way. Real breaks shouldn't be given by fast-tracking through a naff TV show. She was on a mission. She reckoned if the losers won they'd be forgotten in a month. But every dog should have its day. I sniggered, and thought her a proper rebel. I didn't dare vote 'cause mum threatened to ground me for a month if another whopping phone bill arrived on the mat. A plane dipped in the sky to land, and its engine stuttered.

She snapped shut the lid of her phone, stretched and yawned. 'Think of something cool to do.' She fixed onto me.

The bottom dropped from my world. I fiddled with my zip and wondered why she hung out with me. She could be part of the clued-in crowd no probs, and date cool boys with charged bikes.

Last time her parents were absent we played chicken on the dual-carriage way – her call.

'You gotta stay for longer,' she said, eyes glazed from her near miss. 'No rush without guts.'

But I couldn't do it, not like she did.

So I stepped aside and cheered her on because she was the best, the bravest, the keenest, and the meanest. The cars swerved, horns blasting, and their headlights glared through spray. It was exhilarating; but I didn't have her guts.

What could I suggest that she might find exciting? 'Dad's got a couple of tins of paint left over in the garage. We could splodge the speed cameras?'

She shook her head and yawned again. 'Been there, done it.' And we had – a couple of times before. It didn't have the immediacy of scaring drivers in the rain.

What could I suggest that could make us equal? 'Security cameras are on the blink at Jackson's. We could nick stuff?'

Her pupils dilated. 'Your mum tell you 'bout the cameras?'

I nodded and kept focused on my zip.

Jackson's was the local hardware-cum-sell-anything-cheap type shop, where my mum worked part-time, but not on Fridays. Zoë was fired up. I was off the hook, but now a different kind of anxiety breathed in tiny jets at my temples. I stamped on my butt end to concentrate on something else.

'Sounds like a blast,' she said.

Locked in my room, I twist the light beam on and off. Twist on, twist off. Jack White's face appears and is gone. He's posed in sepia tones with his band: old-fashioned black hats and buttoned waistcoats, as if from another time. Off and on, poster-sized, he emerges without judgement above my paint-peeled wardrobe and its spillage of black hooded jackets and stressed jeans. Head's bursting with noise and images. Room's good: silence. No planes, no landings, runways or flights, no city cars or headlights. And no accidents waiting to happen.

Footsteps. The door handle's jerked a couple of times. 'Rachel, Rachel. Your friend called again – Zoë. She wants to talk – says it's important, Rachel? Have you lost your mobile? Zoë says she keeps trying but it's on answer phone all the time. Rachel, are you listening? Are you going to open this door? Open this door.'

I keep the point of light off, dark and safe. If I don't answer, perhaps she'll think I'm sleeping.

'Oh, for God's sake! I told you not to fix a bolt to this door. What on earth are you doing in there?'

I can't ignore it. Her voice is high, unbalanced. 'I don't feel well, Mum. Go away.'

More footsteps, followed by muttering voices: 'Not well? Unacceptable, so rude,' and, 'fed up, bad attitude,' and, 'just moping.'

Dad takes a turn to handle-rattle. 'Rach, love, open the door.'

'Go away. I don't want to see her. I don't want to see anybody, OK?'

A pause and voices mutter again, only softer, out of range.

Dad changes tack, his voice hard and strained, 'Rach, if you don't come down for dinner I *will* force the door. Do you understand?' Pause. Louder. 'Do you understand?'

'Yes,' I mutter.

Why can't they leave me alone? It's better this way. If I sit and nod and smile, eat with them, they'll think all's well, but nothing will ever be the same.

'Sweet corn?'

I shake my head; stare at ravioli parcels and packet sauce. It smells of ketchup and vinegar.

'Just a little, Rachel, else you've got no veg.'

14

I roll my eyes and shift the plate towards her. Why does she bother with the pretence that I've a choice?

Once we're eating, Dad pipes up, 'You had an argument with Zoë or something?'

I squirm. They use the dining space like an interrogation room; a bare light bulb and stainless pincers is all it lacks. 'Erm, no nothing like that. I told you, I don't feel so good.'

'You look at bit peaky,' Mum says. 'Did you find your phone?' She reaches for my forehead and I baulk.

'What ever is the matter?'

Parents don't get it: once you're no longer a kid, you can't be handled whenever they've a whim to do so.

'Nothing, just a headache.'

'For a week? That doesn't sound right. You should see the doctor if you're really unwell. Perhaps I'll book an appointment...'

'It's fine, it's kinda on and off. I'm fine, really.' My head begins to pound again.

'Everything OK at school, Rachel? You're not having trouble with that Gemma girl again, are you?' Mum lowers her head to get a proper look through my tangle of hair, as if peering down the burrow of a crepuscular creature.

Trouble with that Gemma girl? No, that stopped once me and Zoë started to hang. Truth is I owe Zoë big time. She let me escape my saddo self and become someone else.

'Back off. I'm fine,' I say. I push my picked-at meal aside. I need to get back to my room.

'Is that all you're going to eat?'

Dad's switching the news on. I start to scrape back my chair.

'Let's not have the bloody telly on for once,' Mum says. Dad gropes with the remote and the screen blackens.

'Can I get down?'

Mum frowns, but not at me. 'Not just yet.'

'Not yet,' Zoë muttered in my ear. 'Don't forget the lasers.'

I nodded.

She kept an eye on the assistant, who gave us sidelong looks from beneath a greasy fringe; eventually he was distracted by a real customer.

'Now,' she hissed.

I snatched handfuls of this and that, not really paying attention. I tried to concentrate under strip lights; I tried to ignore the intoxication of leaked superglue. But then I saw the slender laser lights; it was all that mattered.

Zoë sauntered down the aisle and whistled tunelessly. The assistant fumbled with coins whilst trying to keep an eye on her. I slipped down the next aisle and forced myself not to dash for the exit. I was primed for a voice to shout, 'stop', or to be grabbed and held, or for alarms to screech. Mum only ever mentioned cameras. Were there alarms, like in *New Look*? Nothing. I walked down the road. Nothing. Only the beat, beat, beat of my heart. Then footsteps, running. I tensed.

Zoë drew up beside me, laughing. 'Come on,' she said. 'You did it!' We high-fived each other; nothing had ever felt so good – ever.

On the waste ground I tipped the contents onto mossy grass: hair bands and bracelets, bottle-openers and i-Pod socks, key rings and bolts, and laser lights. We knelt to examine them like a couple of seven-year-olds. Drizzle fell from the sky and plane lights surfaced from broken clouds; it'd be a moment before the sound hit us, and the world rumbled in time with the engines. Zoë gathered the items she wanted. I was left with bottle-openers and bolts; but more than that, I'd earned her respect and I was so damned proud.

'Help me load the dishwasher, then you can go,' Mum says. 'What *has* happened to your phone?'

'It's switched off, is all.' I scowl at the back of her head.

Dad disappears, and we finish loading in silence. I rinse off the worst of the sauce and hand the plates to her. She pushes the "on" button and I'm free to leave.

But when I climb the stairs, Dad's there, screwdriver and bolt in hand. His shoulders sag. He stares beyond the banisters, unable to look me in the eye.

He mutters, 'It's not healthy to lock yourself in like that, Rach.'

'You've no right.'

'It's for your own good…'

'You don't get it, do you?'

'Really, Rach, calm down…'

'You just don't get it!' I scratch away tears before they fall down my face.

'It's not good for you to…'

'It's not to keep you out; it's to keep me in.'

He gapes. I slam the door. I drag my bed to block the entrance. Outside, he stirs to life. 'Rach, Rach? What are you doing?' He rattles the handle. He hammers, and plywood judders against the metal bed frame. Vibrations filter through the worn mattress and into my body. But I plug in my earphones to drown out reality and *Carolina Drama* unfolds in my head.

It was dusk and we were back on the wasteland. I was lost in a baggy jumper. Zoë had called, said I had to meet her, said it was a matter of life and death. I climbed out of my window, knowing I'd never be allowed to hang with her so late in the evening.

'Look,' she said and pointed her laser into the distance; the beam reached far above the dull orange streetlights of the distant motorway, far above houses and civilisation. The cloud cleared and stars emerged in the darkening sky. 'Here, you take one too.'

I smiled and rubbed my hands together. I'd no gloves.

'I thought it was a matter of…'

'Don't be a bore, Rach.' She pushed a laser torch into my hands.

We shone them in unison at first. Two specks of green met in the dying light, and then we pointed them at each other, swiping, as if crossing swords. I blinked. 'Keep it down, you'll fucking blind me.'

'Ooo, wimp!' she said, but turned back to the sky.

I'd never had the courage to boss or swear at her before, but that day I felt I was her equal. I shone the light upwards again and we swivelled the lasers; scribbling unseen messages in the black. Specks of white light grew in the distance. Zoë threw back her head and laughed; she kept laughing and writing invisible messages; faster and faster, closer and closer towards the oncoming lights.

I couldn't see what was so funny, but I laughed too and criss-crossed next to her patterns. It was just a stupid mess about, and I laughed harder as she became manic. Green latticed streaks carving up the sky. The white lights wavered and dropped. She laughed:

criss-crossed. The plane sank further. I paused and lowered my imaginary weapon. The sound of engines was growing.

'Come on,' she said. Criss-crossed.

We slashed at the oncoming lights. With a rush of adrenaline I swiped across her design. I was her equal.

The plane grew louder, the white lights larger. She kept laughing but the sound was lost to the plane. She slashed again and again, across the nose; slit down belly to tail. The wings wobbled and tilted. She was out for the kill.

Cold air blasted me, like a slap. The ground trembled.

'Stop it, Zoë! Not at the plane like that – it's getting too close.'

I was competing with the engines, and I fancied the pilot shaded his eyes. But of course, it was impossible to see. I couldn't hear or focus, or think straight. But somewhere inside, a voice said, this wasn't right. It didn't matter if we were insignificant specks of light to the jet; I just didn't like her intent.

'Stop it,' I yelled. But I couldn't hear my voice.

Her mouth was open, her head tipped back. Her shoulders were shaking with laughter: soundless and merciless.

The underbelly of the plane passed and the noise and confusion shrank with it. She continued to flick her point of light in its direction, but her venom had gone. Wheels appeared from its bowels and it touched the runway.

It was beyond reach and she shrugged, sobered at last. When her lips moved, the words were no longer obscured. 'That's the 6am from New York.'

And my insides flipped and grew as cold as my fingers.

'You think the pilot noticed our little light show?' she asked casually the next day over the phone.

'Dunno,' I replied.

'You think it's possible to cause chaos? You think it's possible to bring down a jet?' Her speech became faster, breathless. 'We need stronger lights, I reckon,' and she laughed in the silence.

A slow build of disgust filled my head. Was I her equal?

I pressed "end call" on my mobile, and switched it off.

I fixed a stolen bolt to my door and that's where I've been holed-up this past week, trying to avoid her and figure it out, trying to take comfort in Jack, trying to forget myself, and trying to become someone else.

I tug out each earpiece and the song continues in tinny tones. Beyond my room, debating in the hall, my parents' voices are fretful.

But I'm not her. And I don't want to be her. I owe her nothing.

So, I line the stolen goods along my duvet, starting with the plastic bottle-openers and ending with the laser light.

Then I haul the bed into the room, release the door, and prepare to crash land.

The Empty Place

by Martin Badger

From where she is now, Anna can see him clearly, though she imagines he is no more aware of her than a fish in a tank would be of a human. He has boundaries which do not apply to her. If she was still thinking in the old terms, she would have said that she had been liberated.

She might have been bored, just watching him, had she not sensed something about him. So she follows him from where she is now, as he follows the trail of where she used to be.

Frequently he stops and looks around, trying to fix the landscape in his mind. He wants to picture the girl, leaning against a tree or seated on a dry stone wall, imagine her wiping her brow perhaps, or murmuring 'Shit!' to herself as she spots another insect bite on her bare leg. He has never actually met her of course, but he has the photographs and a very vivid imagination. Too vivid most of the time, and too often stimulated by sights nobody should have to endure.

As he walks the trail through the wood, he looks about him constantly, eyes scouring other paths, boring into the trees, the plants, the bushes. Always hoping for something that shouldn't be there, something that might tell him the girl did come this way, as they suspect, or even – if he got really lucky – that someone else was here. Nothing.

He knows that twenty men have been this way but he knows, too, they were not twenty like him. His record in this is exceptional, though he has had his failures too. He suspects Anna will be another. He has a bad feeling in his head, despite the bright midday sun and the piercing blue sky: despite the slight yield in the ground underfoot – there was a storm two days ago – and the keen air from the not very distant Pyrenees. It is not going well and that usually means the one he is stalking, the one they are all stalking, was either very good or very fortunate.

He stops and sits on a fallen tree trunk: probably a victim of a lightning bolt. Struck down in its prime, as Anna probably was.

Shakes his head as he remembers the grief etched into the faces of the girls' parents. He is still angry with Boada for introducing him to the parents. He never wanted to meet them. Doesn't want to meet any more suffering relatives: he's had more than enough of all that over the years. Boada strikes him as barely competent. Very likely there were things he did that he shouldn't have and vice-versa. Or maybe he's being a little hard on the Inspector.

He looks around again. Strange, but he has the feeling that he's being watched. He's had it all morning almost, since he set off after breakfast. It is surely impossible for anyone to be following him and keeping a watch – he is just too good for that to happen. And yet the feeling persists. It is one more inconvenience, like the right ankle which he hurt last year and which still pains him if he walks too much. Like the slight indigestion and the worry about his wife, who resents him spending so much time away from home. 'Helping the police again! What have they ever done for you?'

He realises how uneasy he must be when he sees the ant he has crushed on the tree trunk. Just squashed it under his finger. Not normally something he would do. He takes the water bottle out of his backpack and pours a little over the tip of the finger which has committed the murder. He shudders slightly even though it is hot in the sun. His ankle throbs. It is not going well so he turns his face to the sun, eyes closed, and breathes deeply. Tells himself to relax and starts to call down energy.

Anna can see him breathing deeply and charging himself with natural forces. He is very different from the other men who were here. She can picture them easily, moving slowly over the landscape in a line, prodding the ground with sticks, thinking of lottery wins and getting a girl down on all fours. He is much more advanced along the path. A much older spirit. He is in tune with the forces around him, though still troubled at times. He has resources not available to most people and is practised in using them. She is almost sure he can sense he is being watched and is puzzled by it.

She knows the degradation inflicted on the world must trouble him, but here near the mountains everything is fresh and green and the air is still pure. There are no factories or traffic fumes and he is putting filth aside and refreshing himself. He is very still now, a part of the landscape. Like the pine rearing from a deep ditch a few yards from him, or the stream of bubbling clear water where it happened.

21

If she were still counting in his time she would call it ten days ago, but that is no longer relevant. She is no more likely to think of days or hours than he is to imagine how she is watching him.

He strides along the wooded path purposefully. Nothing of the natural world around him, not the sun on his skin or the warm buzz of insects, impinges on his consciousness. His mind is a cavern of blackness.

Ten days have gone by and nothing has happened. He was spoken to once, by one of the officers, on the third day. Just a few questions. Nothing of importance. Nobody suspects a thing.

He decides he will pass right by where he did her. Up till now, he hasn't. Just skirted the location. Today he'll give himself the real thrill. He can recall every detail. Even talking to customers in the bar he owns, or chatting to his wife, he can remember everything. No effort required.

He had been out riding. He had made frequent use of the whip and it had put him in the mood. As he reined in by the stream of Can Deu, he had thought about a girl and ached with need. A dark-haired teenager to savage. Hardly likely out here in the mountains. Not many walkers were on their own and none of the ones he had seen had been worth... And then, just as if his musings had conjured her up, she suddenly appeared. He could scarcely believe it. Even now he can hardly believe it. Almost exactly as he had pictured her: dark hair, long bare legs, late teens. Later on, of course, he had read the papers, discovered what she was doing in the mountains that hot noon.

She had been wearing just a t-shirt and shorts. Standing in the water up to her knees, backpack on the bank. Her back to him. He took in the fullness of her buttocks and he knew he had to have her. There was nobody around; it was perfect. She was perfect.

Not until he grabbed her around the neck from behind and jerked her off her feet did she know she was not alone. She had struggled but he was far too powerful. She had no more chance of escape than a fish on a hook. Thick sausage-like fingers tore at her t-shirt and shorts. He began to pant as he violated her, then to howl. Her face was forced into the soft ground at the side of the stream.

She could not breathe and her horror and terror rose up until it encompassed the entire valley. Her jaw worked futilely at the ground as he beastied her. Her chest burst but he went on until he was finished, not even aware she was already dead. He became his fantasies.

Thinking about it now excites him all over again. He feels his whole life had been a preparation for that one moment. He wonders how he could have lived without doing that before, denying the beast in him. It is as crazy as living without sleeping or drinking. One thing he is absolutely certain of is that he will do it again.

The searchers have all gone, leaving a few signs behind. He doubts they were very efficient. When they were poking around he stayed in the village, only joining in the search when Boada had called for volunteers and not looking too happy about it. Many killers, he is well aware, are caught because they seem too eager to help. He does not know if this area, by the stream, was searched or not. It hardly matters. He believes there was nothing to find. The girl and her rucksack were disposed of far from here. He tells himself that despite all the tools at their disposal, the police catch fewer criminals than ever. He also knows – he knows a great deal about criminology – that unless a breakthrough is made early it is usually never made at all. Ten days have gone by. The searchers have disappeared and even in the village the topic is not mentioned all the time, as it was initially.

Suddenly he stops, staring ahead of him. He sees a man looking around carefully, keen eyes searching for something. Right by the bank. Right by where he did her. Who is he? What is he after? His hands tighten into fists.

Since he came over to the stream everything has changed. Now he feels very close. Very close to where it happened. He looks about him, almost certain there is something here. Something very important. Something crying out to him. He blots out everything. He is totally focused, his breathing shallow, grey eyes glinting. He closes his eyes and tilts his head to the left, unblocking a partially obstructed sinus. When he can breathe perfectly through his nose, he opens his eyes again and sees it at once.

The ground is disturbed. Something has been pushed into the soil a couple of metres from the water. Her bag? No, her face. He sees it clearly now. Her face was pushed down, just here. Desperate for air, she opened her mouth and some of the land bears teeth marks. He shudders, momentarily overwhelmed by the horror in her soul as she died here. Again he closes his eyes and allows the terror to overwhelm him. He does not resist and soon it passes.

Very likely she was distracted by the water. A hot day. She might have been bathing. Might even have been nude. He would have come upon her and thought it a chance impossible to miss. Such a good-looking girl. Alone in the mountains on a hot day.

He sees the horse's prints now. They look fresh, but he cannot be sure. Just a couple of prints, but no doubt about it. Was the killer a horseman? He shakes his head, uncertain.

If she had still been thinking in the old terms, she would have called herself a virgin. A virgin when it happened. The thought had come to her, when she had set off, that one day soon she would like not to be a virgin any longer. She had never imagined... Now she sees the hunter approaching. Silent despite his bulk. Though he is not riding today, he has picked up the riding crop for his walk. He was swishing it through the air, recalling the fierce strokes he had landed on her over and over again. She recalls looking up at him, eyes blinded by the sun, seeing a red film blot out everything as the swish filled her ears. Then the silence, such silence as she had never experienced. Not even here in the mountains.

"Can I help you?"
    "Help me?"
    "You seem to be looking for something."

He looks carefully at the newcomer. Sees at once the psychopath.

He has interviewed too many to be wrong. He sees right through the man, to the empty place where his heart should be. He knows. It is for that reason he is so very good at this work. Everything he could

24

say and everything the monster could reply pass through his head in a second.

She who was Anna knows, too. The man is very advanced along the path. He knows he is in the presence of the killer. She is sure of it. She is aware of his guts, taut as a bowstring. He has seen the riding whip. He knows almost everything.

"I dropped my watch."
    "Oh."
    "Took a dip and now I can't find it. Lucky it wasn't worth much."

He does not want, one day, to talk to this man. Does not wish to sit across the table from another psychopath. And he suspects that he will not have to: the man is making up his mind to come at him. Inevitably he will decide to attack. He is younger, bigger and stronger. Motivated by the terror of discovery, he is as pitiless as a komodo dragon. If he is successful he will dispose of the body as he did the girl. Or perhaps not: he does not have the horse today.

Anna knows it too. The man will attack. He is weighing it up but almost decided. She knows he is what she would once have called strong. Brutal. But the other man has his advantages too. He has resources the psychopath cannot imagine, cannot have encountered before. As she watches, the man who murdered her launches himself, both arms out to tear and rend, to rip and pound and drown and choke.
    By the two men in a death grip, the stream flows clean and fresh from the Pyrenees. The air blows pure down from the mountains, filling the higher spirit with resolve. For what she would once have called a minute, Anna watches, her heart filled with what she would once have called hope. But even from her location now, she cannot see the end before it happens.

No Better Than This

by Jim Bowen

Waiyaki Way, heading north out of Nairobi, was as slow as ever with heavily laden, diesel belching trucks struggling to overtake donkey carts on the inner lane. Matatu minibuses stopped abruptly wherever there was a fare to pick up. Kenyans ran full pelt from the Kanyariri Estate on one side of the highway, leaping the four-foot-high concrete barrier that divided the carriages, and waving down buses heading into the city as they landed unevenly on the cracked tarmac of the southbound side.

Police stood in the mud on the roadside pointing faulty speed cameras at the vehicles. Those in the know smiled and kept driving, but the naïve pulled over and were shown the reading on the speed gun that always said 72 miles per hour. The drivers shook their heads and paid the chai, amazed that their smoky old bangers could ever go so fast. How come it takes over half an hour to drive fifteen miles to Limuru if the car really can go seventy up this steep section of the A104? It really was a mystery.

Mac Benjamin's old Nissan dripped oil and had a dent in the nearside door, but Mac didn't mind. Good cars got stolen but, while old Nissans were targeted by fundis, who broke them down for spares, smart new cars were much more valuable and vulnerable, and so a little dent every now and then was almost welcomed.

'Do you want some water?' Mac asked. He struggled as he reached for a bottle from the cool box on the back seat. His passenger shook her head. 'It's hot now and sure to get hotter later.' He unscrewed the cap. 'It's best to drink little and often.' He took a sip and passed the bottle to her. 'Little and often.'

'I don't want any,' she said, pushing the bottle away. The bottle slipped from his fingers and landed in her lap. 'God damn it Mac,' she spat. 'Look what you've gone and done. I'm soaking wet.'

'Sorry,' Mac murmured, but he didn't look over. There was no need. He knew she would be looking at him with the same hostility that she always looked at him. He kept his eyes on the road as he handed her the lid of the plastic bottle, flinching as she snatched it from his fingers.

Fifteen miles further on, the Rift Valley opened out on the left. 'There's a viewing platform and some trinket shops a couple of miles up,' said Mac. 'Do you want to stop and take some pictures? It's an amazing sight, Mary.'

'A true wonder of the world, yeah you said.'

He steered the Nissan off the tarmac onto the loose chippings of the car park. He pulled up next to a minibus and watched as the white occupants staggered out and waddled over to the gift shops, photographing each other with the Great Rift Valley behind them. Tired and dirty shop assistants swarmed around them like mosquitoes around a flame.

'Come to my shop mzee.'

'My shop, mzungu madam. Howareyoufine.'

'We give you the best price. Very best price.'

'It don't get no better than this, do it Marlene?' yelled a big American with a massive camera round his neck and a tiny video camera, dwarfed by his sausage-fingered hand. He pointed down into the valley at some speck of interest. 'No better than this.'

'Come here Tad, you've just gotta see this etching,' Marlene called. 'You just gotta. This guy says it's done by a genuine Masai chieftain. Oh my Gaaad!' She waved a tatty piece of hide in his direction. 'A genuine chieftain d'you hear me?'

'Get us out-ta here,' Mary said as Mac turned the key. The gravel spat against the Nissan's undercarriage as he pulled back onto the highway. 'We get everywhere. The God damn American tourist.'

'Why ever do you think I left?' said Mac.

He turned the car west off the A104 and drove down the hill into Naivasha. They ate breakfast on the outdoor terrace of La Belle Inn keeping a cautious eye on the Nissan and a pair of vagrants dozing on the roadside.

Mac bought a bottle of water from a miserable woman in the Jolly Café and then they drove off along a potholed, dusty track, the small town thinning out as the ruggedness of the Rift Valley absorbed them.

'Can you smell the frangipani?' Mac asked.

'Mmm,' said Mary.

'I said, "Can you smell the frangipani"?' Mac repeated.

'I heard you. I said "Mmm".'

'You said, "Mmm"? I thought you said "Mmm?"'

'No. I said, "Mmm."'

'Oh. Well, it's gone now.'

'I know.'

The silence hung between them as heavily as the heat that simmered along the valley floor. Occasionally children, who were supposed to be minding goats, ran up to the car, holding on to the door handles as it crawled along the rutted road. 'How are you mzungu? Give me shillingi. Howareyoufine?' Their bare, dusty feet skipped lightly over the baked red ground. After a while the children gave up, their figures disappearing in the dust and sand blown up behind the car.

'How can you put up with this?' Mary asked, and Mac just smiled. He glanced at her as she stared out of car's grimy window. Her jaw was set, her sunglasses jammed on her nose and the muscles in her neck so taut that it worried him. Better this than some junkie flagging you down in the weirdly lit never-land of the Lincoln Tunnel, or a windshield-washing terrorist setting about you while you sat in a jam on Broadway.

'There's no way you'd understand,' Mac wanted to say, 'even if I had the heart or the words to explain.'

Mount Longonot grew larger as they approached it, its volcanic structure strange in the scrubland surrounds.

Mac had done his best to show her as much of the country as he could during her two week visit. He had tried to help her understand why he was there. From the white coral sands of the North Coast, to the red dusty planes of Samburu District and the Camel races at Maralal, hell they'd done some mileage, but Mary had remained unmoved by it all.

She was closed to him from the start.

She knew about his Somali girlfriend, and nothing else mattered.

Mac pulled the Nissan to a halt in the shade of an acacia tree. He'd nearly missed the sign for the Mount Longonot National Park and almost ended up in a ditch as he took the corner too tight. His back felt sweaty as he climbed out of the car and walked towards the Ranger's Station. It was a hot day, but the old car had air conditioning and he knew he shouldn't feel this sweaty. Must have been the shock of that corner.

'Benjamin and Benjamin.' The ranger repeated their surnames as he carefully filled out the forms. Two white people. One of them

28

was a resident; one had a visitor's permit. They were the first visitors to the National Park in a week. Maybe things were getting back to normal after the election. The ranger's brow wrinkled at the thought. With no tourists, Kenya really would be in a jam. He studied their passports and glanced up at them to check the likenesses. They looked a little like each other. Perhaps whites were like people who owned dogs. Perhaps the longer they were together the more they looked alike. Then again, all whites look the same don't they? The ranger grinned at the thought and wondered how whites could possibly think that all Africans look the same. True, Meru and Kikuyu people had similar skin tone, but what could be more different than the facial structure of a Masai and a Luo or the colouring of the Njemps and the Okiek? He passed the forms through the sliding glass, watched the whites sign on the dotted line and then he took their money.

The ranger joined the Benjamins by their car. 'I will call Gideon for you now,' he said.

'Gideon?' said Mac.

'Yes, Gideon. He will be your guide. Do not worry. There is no trouble here now. It is only for the buffalo.' He called a phrase in Kiswahili and a small old man dressed in khaki with a large floppy green hat stood up from where he was sitting in the partial shade of some spindly bushes. 'You will see. It is necessary.' Gideon picked up his rifle and shuffled over. 'This is Gideon,' said the ranger proudly. 'He will be your guide.'

Gideon nodded and ambled away towards the volcano. 'You come, you come,' he called without looking back.

'He'd better wait,' Mary said. 'I need to change my shoes. He's not going to be a hell of a lot of help if he runs off ahead of us.'

The ranger laughed. The thought of old Gideon running anywhere was pretty amusing. Whites are so funny. 'Gideon is a good man,' the ranger said with a smile. 'He will keep you safe. Have a good trip,' and he returned to the shade of his office.

The climb to the summit rim of Mount Longonot took an hour, resting for water half way up. They passed groups of grazing gazelle and zebra and watched a family of weaverbirds building a home on an acacia bush. The path was obvious, with so many tourists having walked it, but both Mac and Mary slipped on the loose stones on the incline and were short of breath by the time they reached the top. At

29

over 9,000 feet, the air was thin and, even with a hat, Mac felt a headache coming. The thought he might have malaria came to mind, but he pushed this notion to one side. He was determined to keep up with Gideon, who wandered on ahead, walking so slowly, but so steadily. He was always ahead, always the same distance ahead.

Near the top, Mary stumbled and scratched her leg on a stone through her skirt. Mac slid his first-aid kit out of his backpack and dabbed iodine onto the cut to disinfect it. You had to be prepared for everything in this country.

'You want some water, Gideon?' Mac called, once they had reached the top. It would take up to three hours to walk the whole way round the rim and he was in two minds whether or not to suggest it.

'Asante sana, mzee,' the old man said with a broken-tooth grin. He wandered over to take the bottle from the deep-breathing white man.

'It's a long way around,' said Mac. The Masai call Mount Longonot "oloonongot", meaning the mountain of many spurs, and the ridged and rumpled flanks looked brutal.

Gideon shrugged. 'Long way, long way,' he agreed. He didn't know whether they wanted to walk it or not. Nobody had said. It was a hot day, but there was more of a breeze at the top than down there at the Ranger's Station where the heat got so heavy it felt almost airless. 'Very high,' he grinned and gestured down into the base of the volcano. 'Elephants, buffalo,' he nodded. He put his hand over his eyes as he peered down into the depths of the crater. 'You look,' he instructed. 'Airplane too. Crashed.' He demonstrated the action with his hands. 'Long time ago.'

The crater was an awesome sight, with its jagged edge and near vertical sides down to the dense vegetation on the crater's base.

Mac peered down into the green and woody volcano. 'I can't see anything,' he said.

'Nor can I,' Mary said, peering around him. A few geothermal steams trickled upwards from the larva canyon walls. She shook her head as she looked for a place to sit, somewhere with some shade, and she spread a kanga on the rough ground. She put down her day-sack and lay down with it beneath her head as a pillow.

'We'll stay here for a bit, shall we?' Mac said, and when she didn't reply, he told Gideon they needed to rest. 'Perhaps we'll circle the rim later, yeah?'

Gideon shrugged and ambled away. He leant his gun against a boulder, sat down with his back to the crater and pulled his hat low. He didn't care either way. It was all the same to him.

Mac looked down at Lake Naivasha to the north and at the steam rising from the geothermal plant in Hells Gate National Park.

'They filmed *Sheena – Queen of the Jungle* in Hells Gate,' he said. 'I met this guy who was an extra in it.' Mary said nothing, so he let the subject drop. Mac put the emptied water bottle back in his bag and took out his binoculars. He peered down on the acres of glasshouses that surrounded the southern shore of the lake where white-owned companies grew flowers, vegetables and grapes for the export market. Some nights, over a million stems were cut and flown north to brighten the flower-sparse European winters. A cabin cruiser pulled out from the shore of the lake, startling a group of Great White Pelicans, which struggled into the air and lumbered away close to the surface of the water. There were hippos down there too but Mac couldn't see them.

He sat down on a boulder and took out a biography of Joy Adamson, who had made her home at Elsamere on the banks of the lake. She was a true pioneer back in the days when a visit to Kenya took more effort than a few cramped hours on a Boeing.

He looked down at the lake again, wondering whether he could make out where Elsamere was. He watched a troupe of baboons move along the northern ridge of the volcano. A few younger ones came closer and sat watching him watching them. Mac rubbed the scar on his arm where one scratched him nearly a year ago in the car park at Lake Nakuru. He'd been sitting in his car getting ready to leave and it had leapt at him, shocked at the sound of the car ignition. He was lucky the scratch hadn't gone septic.

'I visited an orphanage in Kipsano a few months ago that belonged to Kip Keino, the runner,' Mac said. He glanced over at Mary. 'He was orphaned himself when he was three.' Her expression hadn't changed. Mac sighed. 'Kip Keino.' He closed his eyes, tipped back his head feeling the full force of the sun on his face. 'Yeah, he put all the money he made from athletics back into his own community.' Mary reached into her bag for a bottle of water, took a mouthful and continued staring out into the middle distance. She made no sign that she was listening, or that she had even heard him. 'He won two gold medals at the Mexico City Olympics, you know?' Mac said, but he knew she wasn't interested. Nothing he could say would interest her now. It was too late for that. 'He was a great hero,' he murmured as he looked again at the baboons. The group of youngsters had increased in number. They sat picking fleas, chattering to one another.

Libiqsi, Mac's Somali girlfriend, never asked anything of him. She was happy just to be with him, doing simple things like walking quietly during the day and sharing a bed at night. She liked going somewhere nice in Malindi once in a while, but the rest of the time she was happy grabbing a chapatti and a beer in the Come Back Club in Watamu where the other girls gathered. She loved the Palm Garden on Lamu Road in Malindi, and buying milkshakes from the Bahari Restaurant. She'd never had a milkshake before she met Mac, or a pizza, come to that. Mac took her to the *I Love Pizza* restaurant on the day she chose as her birthday. He'd kissed her in full view of everyone afterwards on the Metro Hotel's fishing jetty nearby. She couldn't believe that he'd done that. Not in view of the white tourists. What would they think? She'd asked, embarrassed but delighted. Mac didn't mind. She was his girl, and that was that.

The day he gave Libiqsi flowers was the happiest in her life, she told him. He found them on the beach early one morning, pulling them from a funeral wreath that had washed up on the shore. He dismantled it on the way home, putting the flowers in a vase so she would find them beside a bowl of passion fruit on the table by the bed when she woke up. He still felt cold when he thought about those flowers. It was the wrong thing to do, like stealing flowers from a grave, but it made her cry with joy. No one had ever given her flowers before, she'd said. He really must love her if he could find such beautiful flowers so early in the morning. She took him to bed again; giving him more than any woman had ever given him.

Libiqsi knew she'd hit the jackpot when she met Mac, but she never asked anything of him. She just wanted him, and because of this he was able to give her all she wanted. He knew she loved the feeling of his soft white skin against hers; delighting in the way her lithe body excited his. She scented herself with jasmine and wore her hair in tightly woven braids because it pleased him, and this thrilled her too.

And the henna—ah, the henna patterns with which she decorated her palms. To Mac they were like a magician's hypnotic maze that drew him into her exotic mystery. He was so easy to please, and with Mac beside her so was Libiqsi. He bought her silver anklets and a chain of coral and pearl which glowed against her neck. Libiqsi was made shy by Mac's nervous fumblings, mistaking his tentative touch for tenderness. She felt coy, like the innocent girl she could barely remember having been. And he led the way that first time. She followed willingly as he led her into his African dream. And in the morning he gave her the flowers.

'Did you hear about the Scotsman who got arrested in London for using the ladies toilets?' Mac tried again. He shook his head to remove the thoughts of Libiqsi and glanced over at Mary; nervous of the aggressive angle she held her chin. 'This Scotsman said he was looking for the ladies and got the wrong one. Said he knew people said things differently in the south of England and guessed they spelt things differently too.'

'Is that supposed to be funny?' Mary said abruptly.

'Yeah, I suppose that it is,' Mac grinned.

'Funny guy,' she spat.

'At least I'm trying.' He'd tried the joke on Libiqsi, but she hadn't laughed either.

'And I'm not?'

'I don't know anymore,' Mac murmured. She'd be on the flight home in a few hours, so it was a bit late to hope for the easy humour of the old days.

The troupe of baboons moved nearer, taking up position on a termite mound. Mac picked up a stone in readiness.

'God damn it Mac,' Mary said. 'What's the point in trying to be funny now? It's a God-awful mess you're in and you know it.' She turned to him, leaning up on one elbow. 'You've been a lot of things in your life, but a stubborn bloody fool, never. I've been here what, two weeks, and you've been so busy keeping us busy, making sure we don't have time to talk.' She clenched her hands furiously. 'And when we do you keep making bad jokes. Even now, when I'm going home in what, eight, nine hours' time you're still making bad jokes. Don't you know I care about you, Mac? Don't you know we all care?' Her voice dropped. 'That's why I came. Everyone's worried about you back home. What happened after the elections here was terrifying. It was all over the papers. Trouble everywhere. You could have been caught up in God knows what, and we wouldn't have know until…'

'Ah, the election wasn't that bad…' Mac started, but she cut him short.

'Well we'd never have known what happened, probably, we'd just never have heard from you again.'

'Whites weren't involved in the election,' Mac said. 'We weren't targeted at all.'

'Even before the elections. This place is hardly safe, is it? And as for that girl… Well, don't you get me started on that girl…'

But Libiqsi was everything Mac had dreamed of. Her ancestry gave her the wide, brown eyes, amber skin and long gleaming hair typical of Sub-Saharan coastal women and she had a gentleness he had never seen before.

'Don't you even care how you make us worry?'

Libiqsi knew how to work with and enhance her natural beauty, rather than caking over the blemishes with slap as Western women often do. She crushed flowers to make her own perfume and he loved watching her paint her skin with henna. With her bright, elaborate saris and simple cotton batiks she was elegant and unfussy, and her delicate silver chains with glass beads did more for her than a ten thousand dollar diamond tiara would have done on any number of Boston Brahmins.

'Nearly 10% of the population here have HIV, damn it, Mac,' Mary continued. 'That must mean something to you? How do you know that girl doesn't?' Words came but Mac wasn't listening. He watched Mary with narrowing eyes, wondering how long she'd practised this speech. 'Sure she's exotic with her dark skin, her shawls and that paint shit on her hands, but Jesus Christ! How do you know she's not going extra-curricular on you and catching God knows what from some beach boy while you're up here with me?' She'd probably rehearsed all of this with her friends down at the marina. 'How pleased do you think everyone will be back home if you come back with some disease that's killing you?' Mac wanted to laugh. He looked away, angry as she worked herself up into a fury. 'Family will take care of you, sure. That's what families have to do, but your friends? No way. They'll disappear the way that friends do, and it'll be up to your family to take care of you.' Gideon's head popped up over a rock, wondering what the noise was all about. He exchanged glances with Mac and sat down again. Best not to get involved.

'You bloody fool,' Mary yelled, getting to her feet. 'Either that or you'll die out here, stubborn and alone. You'll die out here alone with that girl, that's all. That Libiqsi.' Mary spat the name. 'And what use will she be dying next to you? Do you really think she loves you, or is it the colour of your skin? You're just one in a long line of white people messing around in Africa. Playing games with Africans. And she's playing you. You know that don't you. You're a meal ticket, Mac. That's all you are. A meal ticket. It's not you she likes; it's the colour of the skin you're in. And you're too much of a dummy to know it.'

'Go to hell,' Mac said brutally. He stood up and called to Gideon. 'I wanna walk the ridge now, you hear? You stay with Madam, okay?' Gideon nodded, bemused. 'I'll see you at the car in three hours.' Mac threw the car's keys to Mary. 'Three hours. There's more water in the cool box if you need it,' and he headed off around the rim.

Fifteen minutes later Mac stopped crying.

He leant against a rock two hundred yards from where he'd left them, and tried to calm himself down. What was he thinking of, storming off like that? Leaving Mary with a stranger; an African stranger with a gun, at that? She'd go ballistic when he got back, and he frowned at the thought of her trying to talk civilly to Gideon. That would be a first. He couldn't remember her ever talking politely to any black man. She wouldn't know where to start.

Walking away from a guard with a gun was pretty foolish when there were buffalo and baboons around too. And what happened if he twisted his ankle and slipped into the volcano? Mary was right about so much. He was a bloody fool, on so many levels.

Mac stood up. He opened his final bottle of water and took a long drink. He looked slowly around the rim of the volcano; his stare following every peek and dip in its serrated edge. Three hours, the guidebook said if you were fit. It was a long time since he could claim to be fit.

Mac shouldered his pack and shook his head. It was a futile idea. Even without the distance and the heat, there were the baboons and the buffalo to worry about. If the ranger was right, he would be the only person walking the rim, which was exciting in one way, but barmy in another.

He stood there turning circles in his mind.

Still, it would be a good way to show Mary that he was man enough to cope out here, and that he was not as useless as she believed him to be.

But he couldn't cope, not really, and he knew it. He spent his days drinking honey wine on the beach in Watamu, sitting beneath the palm trees or in the shade of his little house and then walking in the evenings, wandering around sandy tracks with Libiqsi on his arm. They hardly spoke to each other, just enjoyed the company. That was what he liked about his life in Kenya—the warmth, the wine and the easy company.

Mary's arrival had shaken him. 'If you really had to run away from the States, why didn't you go to Europe?' she asked him early on in her visit when they were still trying to talk. 'Hans Christian Anderson country? Switzerland or someplace like that. You could've found a nice little Heidi girl to shack up with. Some cute mountain girl with curly blonde pigtails and a red and white cotton apron. Why East Africa for God's sake?' and he couldn't find an answer. 'You speak French. At least you'd have been able to communicate in Switzerland.'

Mac couldn't speak Kiswahili and Libiqsi didn't have much English, but they managed to communicate in non-verbal ways. There was a lot to be said for not being able to communicate all that well. You didn't get bogged down with semantics. You conveyed what was needed, and that was enough. So maybe he would never have a soul-bearing conversation with Libiqsi, but what did that matter when she was so beautiful?

When you talk deeply with someone, you find yourself thinking deeply too, and as he thought about it, Mac knew he was out of his depth. He'd hoped Mary's questions would stop as she warmed to Kenya, to the pace of life and the people. But they didn't and he'd started questioning himself more profoundly, finding dissatisfaction where all had been well.

He was rich here, he'd argued. The living was easy and there were few demands. So long as he was sensible, it would be ten years before the money ran out, and the world would be a different place by then. What with global warming, American warmongering, oil shortages and the growth of the Tiger economy, the world was a rapidly changing place. What was the point in thinking long-term these days?

The silent conversation made sense back there on the beach, but it didn't now.

Slowly, Mac retraced his steps. He peered around a rock, looking back at where he had left Gideon and Mary, but they'd gone. The baboons had come over, searching the site for any sign of food left behind. Two were humping where Gideon had sat, while a few others play-fought where Mary had lain.

The books said that baboons didn't like having stones thrown at them. This was the best form of defence if they approached. The books also said that the best way to deal with a charging buffalo was to stand still and throw your clothes away to distract them. They should be more interested in savaging your clothes and leave you alone, the books said, and once the animal had forgotten about you, you should climb a tree and wait up there until it went away. The books didn't advise how you should get your clothes back, or how to behave when you are stuck up a tree in the middle of the African wilderness stark naked. The books said you shouldn't panic. Above all else, don't panic.

Books were great, but in reality Mac preferred to read than to act and he wished Gideon was there with his gummy grin and his rifle. It might not have been much good against a swarm of killer bees – another thing the books warned about – but a rifle would have been a pretty useful deterrent with the baboons right now.

Mac's mind felt tight with a curious fear. He picked up a couple of baseball-sized rocks, hoping he wouldn't have to use them.

'Mrs Benjamin?' the ranger called as he walked over from his office. He'd watched the two people walking down the last part of the track towards the car park. From the white woman's urgent movements he knew something was wrong. 'Mrs Benjamin, your husband is not with you?' The ranger cast a worried glance over towards Gideon who shrugged his shoulders and grinned. 'What has happened?' the ranger asked.

'Mrs Benjamin?' spat Mary. 'Mrs Benjamin?' her voice was raising. 'I'm not Mrs bloody Benjamin. No way would I choose to be related to that dumb ass. You can choose who you marry but you can't choose your family. He's my bloody brother, the fool,' and she started crying the tears that had been building inside her all the way down the hill. Her shoulders rose and fell with the violence of the emotion. 'The stubborn bloody fool.'

The ranger looked over at Gideon, whose grin had disappeared. 'What happened up there?' he barked in English and then in Kiswahili. 'Where is the mzungu?' and Gideon stumbled through a few short sentences ending with '…the mzee, he walk away.'

The ranger took Mary's arm and led her over to the small building. He sat her down on the bench outside and brought out his thermos of tea. 'It is very sweet,' he said as he poured some into a cracked china cup. 'I think whites do not usually take it so sweet?' He smiled apologetically as he passed her the cup. 'I am afraid I do not have a saucer.'

Mary sipped the tea and wiped her eyes, streaking tears across her cheeks with the back of her hand. She watched the old black man with the gun walk back to the rock in the shade of the thorn trees. He rested the gun by his side and lit a cigarette. She smelt the sharp tobacco smoke and heard him cough. The gravel of the car park shimmered in the heat but her furious sweat had chilled her, and she felt cold to her core. She took another sip of tea and looked up at the ranger who was standing by her side. 'It's very sweet,' she said. 'The tea and your help. Both very sweet.' His eyes were so kind.

'Do not worry, mama. Your brother will return soon. He has water and he is a fit man, no?' He watched her nod doubtfully. He was a big man, that was for sure, but whites never really were as fit as they thought they were. Especially not beneath the midday African sun. 'If he has not returned in one hour, I will go and find him myself,' and to show he meant it, the ranger went back into the building and brought out a rifle, which he gave a quick wipe down with an oily rag.

The first stone went wide, but Mac hit the leading baboon on the forehead with the second. The troupe stopped briefly, but their screaming increased and, as he bent down to pick up more stones, Mac realised he was shaking. He threw the stones and shouted, 'Come on you bastards. You've got to do better than that to scare an American boy.'

He threw until his throwing arm ached, but still he kept turning it over. He imagined himself to be Joe DiMaggio, Babe Ruth or Willie Mays. He couldn't remember if any of them were pitchers, but that didn't matter. He just kept throwing. Most of the stones went wide, or landed short, splintering and cascading over the animals in a smaller wave of dusty shrapnel. Still, the baboons kept creeping forward, and Mac kept inching back as he threw more stones and sticks. He imagined the scene from the Stanley Kubrick film where the monkeys start smashing each others' heads in with a branch. He hoped these baboons hadn't learnt that trick. He didn't want to die alone at the top of an inactive volcano in East Africa. It was not nearly as heroic a prospect as Hemingway had described in *The Snows of Kilimanjaro*. As he retreated ever nearer to the volcano's lip, he threw the stones harder and shouted all the louder.

Growing up, Mac had imagined himself dying a quiet death lying between crisp white sheets in the General Hospital on Varnum Avenue in Lowell, Massachusetts, in the same hospital that he was born. He'd envisaged many years of growing old with dignity; joining the Parish Council and taking his turn to read at Mass on Sundays in Saint Margaret's Church on Stevens Street, the same church that Monsignor Raymond L Hyder had baptised him in and the same church that he had served in as an altar boy in his youth. Monsignor Hyder died in the long winter of 1975, but the church was still there, and Mac felt cold as he grasped the fact that he might never see it again. But then, after nine years together, his wife told him she loved someone else, he laughed with relief and almost kicked the door down in his haste to get out. The fresh air of freedom smelt so sweet. Don't look back he told himself as he packed his bag and boarded a plane. Don't ever look back

Gradually the baboon's progress slowed and they sat back chattering. 'Shit,' Mac whispered, and hoped that was it. He looked down at the near vertical sides of the crater just yards behind him, and then back at the baboons. 'Shit,' he said again and wiped sweat from his forehead with the back of his trembling hand.

The ranger scanned the top of the volcano through his binoculars. 'I cannot see the entire rim from here,' he said to Mary, 'but do not worry. I am sure your brother will be down shortly.'

The hottest part of the day had passed and the early afternoon clouds were banking up in the west. The ranger was not happy. The likelihood of finding the white man was good so long as he had stayed on the track. If the white man had left the track, or fallen or jumped over the edge of the volcano, then the chance of finding him was small, and with the Kenya Wildlife Services cutbacks, Gideon was the only other ranger on duty. They had no radio to communicate with each other, and the phone hadn't worked since the elections, so he couldn't call for more help. If the two of them couldn't find Mr Benjamin quickly, they would have to call out more rangers, and that wouldn't happen until the morning at the very earliest. By then the chances of finding the white man alive were miniscule.

If he sent Gideon back up the way they had come down, while he headed up the opposite way himself, then surely one of them would meet the white man on their way round, or they would meet each other at the top. Either way they should leave now to be sure they were back by the time it got dark. 'I am sure he will be down shortly,' the ranger said. He walked over to the long-drop pit latrine to prepare for the climb ahead.

Gideon lit another Rooster. He knew what was coming. He had watched the white woman sitting in the shade and the ranger's attempts to keep her spirits high. He had seen all this before – unfit whites arguing as their petty grievances came to the surface as they tired climbing the hill. Some stormed off the way that this man had done, but they tended not to stay away for long. Gideon sighed as he watched the ranger buckle himself up as he closed the door of the pit latrine and walk over towards him. He ground his cigarette out in the dirt, and picked up his rifle. 'Let's go,' Gideon said, getting to his feet before the ranger had a time to say anything. 'Let's go.'

Mac slipped on the loose gravel and slid on his backside twenty feet down the scree. He brushed the dirt off his trousers and poured some water on the cut on his arm.

In the end, he had run from the baboons, skirting round a volcanic outcrop and heading down a near vertical slope on the hillside above Naivasha. He came to a stop in a thorn tree, on which he had cut his arm. He imagined the baboons way back up there at the top of the hill, killing themselves with laughter at his undignified flight. What did it matter though – he was still alive.

Sitting where he was, he could see the car park and the Nissan, no longer in shade, parked near the Ranger's Station. He thought he could see Mary sitting by the car, but the rest of the place was deserted. He hoped she'd calmed down. If she hadn't, she'd be so furious that he'd probably have been better off up there with the baboons. He took a mouthful of water and stood up. He'd ripped his trousers, and his arm was scraped, but he was okay.

Twenty minutes later he tried to walk tall as he pushed through the acacia bushes and out in to the car park. 'Mary,' he called and his sister ran to him.

'I thought you'd come the other way,' Mary said through her tears. 'I was looking up that way.' She clung to him. 'I'd thought you'd fallen. Jesus Christ, I didn't know. You were so angry. You took so long,' and she shook as she cried into his chest. 'I'm sorry Mac. I didn't mean… I'm so sorry,' and then he was crying too.

Mac's tongue ranged for a way to express the thoughts that muddied his mind, and then the words ran away from him. 'It's okay,' he stammered, unsure where he was going with this. 'I am. I'm a bloody fool. You were right. And I needed you to point it out to me. But it's okay now. It's all okay now.' He looked around for the ranger and for Gideon, but there was no one there.

'They've gone up the mountain to look for you,' Mary said. 'They left about half an hour ago.'

Mac nodded and frowned. 'Well,' he said. He licked his lips carefully. 'They'll be gone for hours, and we've got a plane to catch.' He watched his sister's eyes widen and her face soften. 'Listen Mary, I'm coming too. I'm going home with you.' Mary's hands rose to her mouth, disbelieving. 'This time of year there're sure to be spare seats on the plane as far as Amsterdam.' He patted his backpack. 'I've got my passport and I can get a ticket at Jomo Kenyatta airport to get that far. I don't mind waiting in Schiphol for a couple of days if it takes that long to get a ticket home to the States.'

'Really?' Mary whispered, and more tears came as he nodded his confirmation. 'What about the girl?'

Mac looked at his feet. He'd forgotten about the girl. 'Ah, she'll be alright,' he murmured. 'Like you said, she'll find someone else.' He glanced up at his sister with a sheepish grin. 'Some other white dummy who doesn't know any better, eh?'

Mary smiled and nodded. 'And what about the ranger?' she asked quietly. 'The ranger and Gideon? They're up there looking for you?'

'We can't wait, Mary,' Mac urged. 'They'll hear the car. We've got to get your stuff from the New Stanley and have a wash. I don't need anything else but we don't want to sit for ten hours in a plane this dirty.' He showed her his cuts and ripped clothing. 'I'll blow the horn on the Nissan. They'll hear it and understand. It'll be okay.'

Gideon heard the sound of the car horn and he smiled as he turned back. He looked down the hill and watched the trail of dust as the little car sped along the rutted track. He lit another cigarette and sighed, wondering whether they'd have left him a tip.

The ranger had run up the first part of the incline and didn't hear the horn. His mind was filled with the image of the white woman crying as she sat on his bench, sipping sweet tea from his old china cup. What if her brother had fallen and was clinging to the side of the volcano with his strength failing? He took a mouthful of water from a bottle he carried as he ran; slinging his rifle over his shoulder so it was out of his way. The gun banged against his hip, but he didn't care. He wanted to be the one to make that white woman smile again. He wanted to be the one to bring her brother back alive, and he ran on faster up the hill.

At the same time as KLM flight KLO566 was lifting gently off the runway in Jomo Kenyatta International Airport later that evening,

42

circling above Kenya's capital and picking up a direct line to Amsterdam, Libiqsi finished cleaning the kitchen in the small house not far from the Indian Ocean in Watamu.

There was nothing in the fridge, but she scrubbed it anyway smiling at the beauty of the new white appliance. She and Mac went down to Mombassa to choose it at the new Uchumi superstore. They drove all the way home with it sticking out of the back of the Nissan with the boot lid open. Slowly, she opened and closed the fridge door, grinning as the light went on and off, and then she wiped the handle. This fridge was another amazing thing that Mac had brought into her life.

Libiqsi had already swept all the sand out of the house, wiped the surfaces and dusted all the corners and she was nearly satisfied. Mac would be tired when he got home in the morning. He would be tired with a deep-set weariness after dragging his sister around for two weeks. Libiqsi wanted everything to be perfect when he got home. In the morning she would buy some fresh fruit and milk from the market, bake some bread and get some nyama choma ready to roast on the ghiko for when he arrived. There was some beer in a box in the cupboard that she would put in the fridge later on so that it would be cold. It was a shame to put it in now and spoil the beautiful clean thing.

Libiqsi smiled as she folded some of his shirts and put them away in the drawer. She had washed and pressed them twice. She wanted to be sure they were really clean and ready for him.

She stood beneath the shower and smiled as she washed herself with his imported scented soap. Then felt the label with her thumb. Imperial Leather. Even the name felt clean. They hardly ever had soap back on the Benadir Coast when she was growing up. With the war, you couldn't guarantee enough fresh water to wash in on a daily basis. As she let the warm water flood over her body, she thanked God for taking her out of that poverty.

Libiqsi thought about her mother, who was killed in a street battle between supporters of Ali Mahdi and Farah Aidid shortly after Said Barre's government collapsed in 1990. She'd gone to Mogadishu to visit her own mother, who lived above a Moslem café on the Green Line, and she'd never come home. Libiqusi's brothers joined Aidid's faction shortly afterwards, and they both died in a skirmish with UN troups. Her sister died in the famine the following year, as, along with thousands of others, they tried and failed to grow enough to eat in a land with no rain.

Libiqsi and her father left their family's shamba then, and began walking south. Her father got dysentery and died in Baraawe, and once he was buried, Libiqusi moved on again. She worked her way along to the coast and, in Kismaayo, got a lift in a dhow down to Malindi on Kenya's north shore where she started working the bars using all she had left as a means to survive.

And here she was, three years later, washing herself in the home she had set up with a white man who loved her. She smiled again as she washed her belly, her fingers lingering over the taut and extending stomach, and she wondered if she was showing enough for Mac to be able to tell.

Libiqsi smiled again as she patted herself dry with the white man's towel. It was true what the tourists said – life don't get no better than this.

Apollo Falling

by R J Allison

'The instructions are very clear, Maximus. The statue is to be destroyed. In fact, I believe you had these instructions three months ago. Why has the Augusta Galla Placidia had to send me to enforce them?' Valdric laid a slight emphasis on the last phrase, and was pleased to see it was not lost on the estate manager. Maximus tried to cover his agitation by going to a chest at the back of the room and searching through the scrolls stored there.

'Yes,' he muttered. 'Yes, I remember something of the sort... Here it is!' He held up one of the scrolls triumphantly, but Valdric could see his hand trembled. Maximus scanned the document and looked up.

'Certainly, the statue is to be destroyed,' he said. 'But there seemed no great urgency. There are so many other things to attend to. Does it really matter if that job is put off for a while? It will not affect the harvest. The vineyards prosper as they have done for all the centuries the statue has stood there. Why the rush?'

Why indeed, thought Valdric. Still, he was a soldier, and he had his orders.

'Maximus, you sound as if you're afraid the harvest will fail if we destroy the statue.'

'No, no, not at all!' The estate manager was definitely flustered now. He waved his hands in the air, as if warding off the implicit accusation of pagan beliefs. 'I am well known to the church here. I was baptised years ago. The statue means nothing to me. The trouble is, it means a great deal to many of the people who work on the estate and in the surrounding countryside. They won't tell you to your face, of course, but they do believe the god is in the statue watching over them. They still think it raised the storm that destroyed the fleet of the Visigoths.' He broke off, suddenly remembering who he was talking to.

Valdric let him sweat for a moment, then waved his own hand dismissively.

'Oh, yes, Maximus, I remember that storm. I damn' near drowned trying to cross to Sicily that day. But the war's over now, so you need not fear. I'm not here to settle old scores. Certainly not with a statue. The Visigoths are Christians, and we have no time for that nonsense. Anyway, I've seen too much disaster from one source or another. I've seen – ' Now it was his turn to break off. 'Well, never mind what I've seen.'

Seen too damn' much, he thought to himself. Twenty-five years of wandering and soldiering across the Empire, as his leaders switched allegiances back and forth, until he had lost track of whether he was supposed to be a warrior of the Visigoths or a soldier of the Empire. Still, he had one constant loyalty spanning those divisions, and he took refuge in it now.

'Galla Placidia was here the day of that storm. We brought her out of Rome when we took the City, and she travelled with us for many a year. She saw the fleet wrecked that day. Aye, and she heard the legend of the statue too. She married our King in the end, and I entered her service then.' He laughed bitterly. 'But fate takes strange turnings, and now that King is dead, and she has returned to the Empire. Now she is Galla Placidia Augusta, wife of the Emperor Constantius. Yet I serve her still.' He rounded suddenly on Maximus. 'More to the point, you also serve her! She is a good Christian, and she will not permit this pagan thing to remain on her estate.'

'Of course,' said Maximus. 'Of course. As soon as I can manage'

Valdric shook his head.

'I have not come here to nag you about doing the job. I have come to do it myself. In the courtyard below I have a working party of my men, well versed in the arts of destruction. I require nothing of you, except that you lead us to the statue. But that I do require. Now.'

Valdric stood, signalling the end of the discussion. Maximus scuttled through the door ahead of him, and led the way out into the estate.

The shrine was at the top of a low hill. It took the form of a slender tower about twenty feet high, with a niche at the top holding the statue. A little larger than a man in size, Valdric reckoned, peering up at it. From that vantage point it could look out over the countryside. Not that it can look at anything, he reminded himself. It's just a statue.

He turned his back on the tower and surveyed the scene below: the fields, the vineyards, a few small villages, the glint of the sea in

46

the distance. For most of the country people, never straying far from their homes, the landscape visible from this spot was most of the world. No wonder they felt the god watching over them from the statue. Which god, anyway?

'Which god, Maximus?'

'What?'

'Which god? Who is the statue supposed to be?'

'Oh! He is Apollo. The sun god.'

Valdric peered up again.

'Ah, yes. Well, his sun is about to set.'

He issued crisp orders to his troopers. Young Gainas clambered up the tower and fastened a rope round the base of the statue. He tossed down armfuls of decaying flowers as he worked. Valdric glanced at Maximus.

'These were garlands not long ago. Is the statue still adorned, then? That's against the law, you know.'

Maximus shrugged.

'There are no official ceremonies, of course. But I'm sure some of the local diehards place their offerings from time to time.'

Valdric nodded, unsurprised. Christianity prevailed in the cities, but out in the country the old ways lingered. For the past quarter-century the law had forbidden pagan worship, but in the country this was impossible to enforce.

'We're ready now, sir!' The young soldier called to him from the tower.

'Good! Get yourself down here then. You others, catch up that rope!'

Gainas scrambled down and joined the rest of the squad pulling the rope taut. They looked at Valdric, ready for his order. For a moment he paused, strangely reluctant to give the command that would bring the statue crashing to the ground.

He turned and looked again at the landscape, peaceful and sleepy in the late afternoon sunlight. The scene was spread out at his feet like a picture set in a mosaic floor, and the moment seemed just as fixed – eternal, removed from time. A man could gaze at it and not sense the passing of things. But Valdric had no leisure to gaze. He turned back to his duty, and cried out the order.

The soldiers heaved on the rope. Nothing happened. Again. The statue quivered slightly. A third time, and there was a loud crack from the top of the tower. Apollo leaped into the air, and for a moment he seemed about to ascend into the heavens. Then the statue came crashing down towards the soldiers. Too close to the tower, dammit! They all scattered as the statue smashed into the ground – all except Gainas, who was too slow off the mark.

The marble figure shattered and Valdric saw the fragments bounce high into the air and hit the ground and roll and slide across it. The hand of Apollo skidded to within a pace or two of where he stood, and spun and lay still. It seemed to point back towards the tower, to where Gainas lay sprawled beside the fallen god.

The soldiers rushed to the young man, but there was clearly nothing to be done. From the angle of his head it was obvious that his neck had been broken instantly. Like a sacrificial victim, Valdric thought, and grew cold. A sudden rising wind drove clouds across the face of the lowering sun. The warmth faded and the light grew dim.

Maximus came up, and looked from the smashed statue to the dead soldier; bitterness and satisfaction struggled for control of his face. Valdric felt like punching it, but bit back his own anger. Maximus spoke, and his voice was suddenly more confident than it had been before. He seemed to draw courage from the fact that the god had not gone quietly.

'There's a storm coming up now, sudden, like we have in these parts. You remember, of course. Like the day the fleet was wrecked.' The faintest hint of a sneer flickered across his face. 'You'd better take your dead and get under cover before it breaks. My men will clear up this wreckage later.'

No doubt, thought Valdric, and they'll put the bloody thing back together if they can. Aloud, he replied calmly:

'Thank you, Maximus.'

The horses were brought up and the squad mounted, the body of Gainas tied across his horse's back. Just as Valdric was mounting, he paused and said:

'We'll take the head, as proof we've done our errand.'

He heaved the trophy into his saddle-bag and mounted. Maximus stood there, suddenly grim-faced. Valdric smiled down at him, glad to have out-manoeuvred the crypto-pagan. There could be no remaking of a headless statue.

A moment later the squad was hurrying back towards the base in the nearby town of Rhegium. Valdric had thought originally they might spend the night on the estate, but he'd have none of that now. The men were disappointed, for they had hoped to become better acquainted with the local peasant girls.

'Never mind, lads,' he told them. 'There are plenty of good Christian whores in Rhegium.'

Near the town, the road ran along the coast and across the top of a sea-cliff. Valdric halted his men near the edge and dismounted. He took the head of the statue from the saddlebag and looked at it in the last gleams of the setting sun, red and angry on the horizon.

The painted face stared back at him, impassive, aloof. The god's head felt heavy in his hands. He carried his burden to the edge of the cliff and with a sudden loud cry threw it hard – two-handed – up and out towards the sea. It rose and fell in an arc, and the dying sun made it red as blood. The head of Apollo struck the sea with a loud noise that echoed off the cliffs, booming like an angry shout. As the head vanished beneath the water, the sun disappeared below the horizon. All was dark and silent. Valdric turned back to his waiting troopers.

'The sun's gone down,' said one of them, a hint of superstitious fear in his voice.

'Don't you start,' said Valdric, remounting and leading the way towards the welcoming lights of the town. 'He will rise again in the morning.'

The Deserter

by Daniel Gustafsson

I

It was a chill, sodden day, the rain fell in jabs from the leaden sky and the men on return from drills had trudged in single file for a mile or more along the muddy road; their bodies soaked and heavy, their foreheads down against the lashing wind, they stalked or ploughed a ragged mass behind the horse-bound Captain in front. This was George Sutton; a heavy body held erect upon the dark, glistening horse, he strained to pierce the driving rain with stern and squinting eyes, his stiff collar drawn up to the bristly ends of his moustache. His horse was tired and traced the obscured road with a sluggish, irregular movement of its bulky form.

In amongst the rain-beaten band of young men was one, John Burrough, raked up in conscription with the rest, whose dissent was well known to his superiors and to the men; some murmured in sympathy, others openly shunned him. He walked now along the battered road not far behind the wet back and bright helmet of the Captain.

As they were crossing a turbulent stream on a rickety wooden bridge, the Captain's horse, disturbed by the lashing gale or blinded by the rain, jerked its head in a spasm, its weary hoof slipped upon the wood, and horse with rider fell through the brittle railing into the water; the animal first struck its front legs against the muddy bank, then its twisted heavy head struck the wet clay, before it fell back and bore down with all its weight upon the Captain; his body was half submerged, his face beaten by the cold waves as the horse kicked and kicked against the flood of grey, before it ceased and its body stilled, dead from a broken neck.

While the remainder of the company stood paralysed, unable to act, they could see how John Burrough sprung forward and let himself down into the freezing brook; he pulled at the man while spurning and pushing with his back against the dead weight of the horse, and managed to draw the bruised and choking Captain from his trap. As Burrough dragged Sutton onto the black earth of the bank, the company crowded around the heaving body of their

50

superior, who had escaped with only a crushed leg; or they watched the dead animal, whose dark form sunk beneath the pale waves.

In the confusion that ensued, John Burrough slipped away, peeled off his uniform and rushed across the grey fields in the cloaking rain.

This last act came to overshadow the first; in his absence he was branded a deserter, the gratitude owed him, for the life of George Sutton, soon all but forgotten.

Two years passed.

II

He emerged a solitary figure from the scarlet front of autumn trees, and crossed the burnished fields beneath a sky of pale blue; the sun was stark upon the cut stalks of wheat and rye, and bright in strokes upon the cold soil of the furrows, where he walked with his bare feet. His boots he had removed at first light, having walked all night, his steps now faltering, now speeding to a fitful run; the boots hung now by the strings in his left hand, and but for this he carried nothing with him.

These were fields not tilled or harvested by human hands, and the soil bore the imprint of no human feet but his own; he trod with his bare skin the tracks and scars left by large machines, the stalks at his sides cut by a single motion, clinical and uniform, and strips and stumps of pale straw lay tossed and scattered upon the clay. Here poppies grew along the ditches and the churned up tracks, and some in clusters among the crop, a scattered horde of fickle fires among the stubble of pale gold.

Now, as the sun rose higher above the browned and crimsoned woods, as he could see his shadow upon the coarse fabric of the brightened field, he stopped, to rest his wearied body, and to sleep. He made for himself a bed of tall, yellow grass; for his pillow he found a small log, around which he wound some dry straw, and put a bundle of fallen leaves upon it to soften the roughness of the wood; then he stretched out upon the ground, his coat wrapped about him and the collar turned up, and he felt the sun warm upon him, beating firm upon his breast and falling softer upon his brow, the ridge of his nose and the sprouting hair of his beard.

He slept long, until well past midday, and as he awoke and walked on, the lowering sun shone full in his weathered face; he walked without encountering a single soul, skirting the wooded edges of the flat fields to keep out of sight of the few houses he passed. At one point he approached a derelict farm and presented himself, but the man whom he encountered at work in the garden turned him away; and so he trudged on across the fiery patchwork of wood and fields, at times having to cross ditches, climb stiles or ease himself through fences of barbed wire.

As the sun was reddening above the crests of maroon trees, and the shadows lengthening upon the bronzed fields, he was forced to cross a railway. Here, too, the poppies grew, clustering close to the railway and breaking in red bursts through the rusted ribs of the tracks. As he climbed the slight bank of the elevated track, the sharp pebbles cut into the rough skin of his soles, and he sat himself down upon the stones to put his boots back on. Sitting there, looking down along the track, he saw he was close to a small town; he saw, too, a farmhouse in among the trees, at the fringe of another field and cut off from the town by the railway and a small wood. Before he had time to put his shoes on and fully catch his breath, the earth trembled where he sat and he was snatched from his rest by a coming train; the metallic mass screeched past him almost close enough to tear his skin and beat across the fields with brute insistency, disappearing out of sight, leaving only a trail of smoke and a shudder behind. As he staggered to his feet, he saw how the poppies shook and fluttered in the fierce rush of air, some stripped of leaf or petal, some in their frailty persisting.

He approached the farmhouse from the adjacent field and stepped through a grove of aged apple trees onto the lawn in full view of the house; he took his position by a small pile of chopped logs next to a wooden shed, and waited. Only one window at the back of the house was lit, the rest reflected the smouldering colours of the sky behind him. From where he stood he could see the gravel drive leading from the house towards the railway and the town; shortly there came up this path a young boy, his back burdened with books, who stopped to peer at the strange man but passed into the house; where he soon appeared in a window and resumed his study of the stranger.

Not long thereafter, however, two men were driven up to the house and immediately sighted the intruder, who raised his hand in a greeting. As they came towards him, he saw how they were father and son, the former past middle age, the latter barely a man, but both clad in uniform; the grey, moustachioed father walked first, the clean-shaven son trailing behind him with a practised swagger and stopping out of earshot. The father was of strong build, but his bearing was somewhat hunched, possessing little of the rigour and assurance of the military man; the straight back and the firm stride were now his son's.

The old man walked with the limp of an injured leg, but held himself erect as he approached the man; he let one hand hang freely in a loosely knit fist at his side, while the other firmly tugged at the lapel of his greatcoat. He lifted the hand from his side to smooth his moustache before he came close enough to address the man and view his young but weathered face, with its dry lips and beard unkempt and its quietly defiant eyes.

'Can I help you?' he asked, but as he was scrutinising the visitor his words nearly stuck in his throat.

'Good evening. Please forgive my intrusion, I am looking for a place to lodge, temporarily, and will work hard for it', the young man responded, his words hastened at first.

After the first look at the young man's face, the old Captain kept his eyes from looking straight at him; his furtive glance noted instead the threadbare state of his coat, and the faded leather of his boots, before it fell upon the ground strewn with red and brown leaves.

'You are on the run?' he managed to mutter. The young man's voice had now grown assured as he replied;

'I need food and shelter, that is all, a couple of weeks is all I ask. I work hard. I'd be very grateful, it is near impossible to find someone willing to open up their doors to one like me.' He spoke gently while studying the grey furrows of the man's lowered face and noting the slight tremor of his shoulders beneath the thick uniform.

'I can't refuse you,' the latter confessed while stroking his bristly jaw with a cold hand, but still did not look up.

The matter was settled in few words; the old man lived alone with his two sons, but a housekeeper came regularly from town to help. He pointed the young man to a cottage at the back of the house

53

where he could sleep; he would collect his meals from the kitchen, he would work on whatever needed doing in the grounds, and he would not reveal himself to anyone but the family.

As the Captain walked back to the house, he shrugged off the inquiries of his son, who expressed his bewilderment at not having seen the drifter shown off the land. The young soldier looked hard at the unwelcome guest, before calling after his father,

'Did he give us his name?'

'His name is John Burrough,' came the brusque reply.

Retiring to the little cottage he had been offered, Burrough found it plain and comfortable, its only conspicuous feature the large stag's head mounted above the fireplace. It was cold and damp as he entered, but soon, John having lit a fire, the room came alive with the warm scent of burning wood. That night, eating by the roaring fire, soup warmed his lips and throat, and bread, withheld for days past, tempered the pains of hunger. Through the window, John could see the last embers of the waning sun lingeringly glow upon the rim of the field, and slowly fade.

III

John rose early the next morning; in the pale light the air was still, the ground touched with cold beads of frosted dew, as he proceeded immediately to carry and chop wood. He lifted the first log calmly, its weight rough in his hands, and firmly placed it upon the block, then raised the blade of the axe and with a clean, strong motion cleft the wood in half; then raised the warm, ringing steel to cleave the log again. He went about his task intently, invigorated by the muscles of his sinewy body working, and he inhaled the clear autumnal air in large draughts.

He had been out for an hour before he saw the first lamps lit in the house, and the young boy watching him from the window over his breakfast. Shortly he stepped out onto the drive and was off for school, and John watched after him, a lean boy with sandy hair, before he resumed his work. Soon thereafter George Sutton left the house with his eldest son, the young recruit donning a new uniform, starched and sharply cut. It was not long before the Captain returned, however, and he immediately went over to speak with John, who was busy on a ladder picking apples from the old trees with coarse bark and cold leaves.

'The garden isn't what it used to be', Sutton began; standing beneath the man at work in the tree, he told how he rarely laboured himself these days, as little remained of his original land. During the cold season he would retire indoors, and except for what the elements could accomplish themselves, the grounds fell into disrepair; John could himself see the plots and patches overgrown with weeds in webs of brown and pale green, and the fruit in droves rotting beneath the plum and apple trees.

He worked slowly as the old man spoke; as he stopped, John sat himself upon a rung and assured his host again of his gratitude for being allowed to stay.

'That's nothing,' Sutton shrugged; and after a few approving remarks about the young man's work, added impatiently, 'How is it you live? You have had nothing, nowhere to stay, all this time?' He looked at John's feet, level with his own face, as he spoke.

'I walk from place to place. I work for my board and I ask for little else. I am not alone; there are those who are sympathetic, either to my vision or simply to my plight, who will house me for weeks or even a month. But sooner or later I am pressured to move on; the word, it seems, gets around, and some people get too curious.'

'Yes', the old man murmured, 'it is difficult...' He shifted before looking the deserter in the face; 'And you are content? You are determined to stay like this, not to turn back?'

'Yes, as long as necessary', Burrough answered firmly before Sutton went on,

'And loyalty to the nation there is none? You will walk without order and without allegiance?'

'I believe that I bear my allegiance with me, you will understand.'

'I may understand your inclination, if I try, but I doubt I shall understand your priorities; there are duties, I believe, above all others, especially in circumstances as these... but let us not debate,' he added; 'I have things to see to.' And so he lowered his head and began to leave; but John halted him briefly with the question, 'When is your son leaving for the front?'

'Paul is leaving in a few weeks,' Sutton replied and then returned through the grove and across the lawn to the house. The leaves, orange or scarlet still upon the dark boughs, dyed deeper upon the grass, burned brightly in the noonday sun.

After a break for some food, John resumed chopping the wood. In the afternoon the boy returned, walking slowly in his stuffy school-uniform, dragging his feet in the gravel before sitting down upon the steps of the house; from there the boy observed with interest the new man, the rhythm of his solitary movements, quiet and contained as he raised the axe or as he bore and stacked the logs against the shed. He saw, too, how John at one point put the axe aside and knelt upon the ground beneath the stack; his hands were folded, and raised to touch his lowered brow.

As evening fell George Sutton was sitting at a window of the house, a drink in his hand, watching the man at work; the old Captain's countenance was grave, chin heavy in a grey hand, and his uneven breath was visible upon the cold pane.

The following morning, Sutton joined his guest at work, pulling the last beetroots from the frosted soil; nodding a greeting to the young man, but staying at a distance too far for intimate speech, George crept out of his jacket and rolled up his sleeves; as he worked, the pale skin of his arms was pricked gently by the early, red sun. He moved methodically, yet dug his fingers with a fumbling eagerness into the cold earth, and he stopped at intervals with one hand upon his hip, the other wiping his perspiring face, bearing the ancient scent of fresh soil upon his coarse fingers. Thus the two men worked somewhat in tune and sympathy as they dug and pulled at the earthy fruit, both breaking sweat and both crouching beneath the burnt sky, filling bucketfuls with the dark and blood-red root. As they finished, John's lower arms and his shins, between the battered boots and the tattered flags of his trouser-legs, were dusted black.

Resting against the trunks of some trees, Sutton finally addressed the young man;

'The kid is taking a liking to you, I believe.'

'Is he?' John asked, pleased. 'He hasn't introduced himself.'

'But he has been watching you, and I am sure he welcomes a new presence.'

'He seems a nice boy. How old is he?'

'William is seven.' Then the father added: 'You may accompany him for walks, little excursions, if you like; I know he is eager to, in summer he roams the woods and fields like a reckless little savage,

56

he is insatiable, and happy in his ways. But I am cautious to let him off by himself, now it's colder and the days shorter, and I can't go with him. On account of the leg.'

'I would be happy to get to know him,' John affirmed. 'It would be a pleasure.'

'Very well,' George concluded; at that point his oldest son had appeared on the drive and George made haste to take leave of John and join him. John watched the awkward figure cross the grass, limping slightly while getting into his jacket again and dusting the soil off his trousers.

John approached William that afternoon as he came trudging back along the drive; the two spoke awkwardly at first, before the one overcame his awe and the other the impulse to patronise. Both by nature and circumstance quiet and solitary, an inherent sympathy quickened between the young and the older recluse; each happy to walk apart as a stranger to all, soon a friendship sprung up between the two.

For the next week John would meet William as he walked back from school, waiting for him where the boy had to cross the railway tracks that severed the house and surroundings from the town; each day William had to stop as the heavy train grinded past and shook the ground where he stood, looking up at the pallid anonymous faces shooting past with no volition of their own. John, as he waited, could see above the roof of the train the jutting structures of the town; the towers of the court and steeple-house, the livid smoke of the many chimneys of the red-brick rows, and the looming smokestacks whose sooty fumes perpetually smote and speckled the blue sky. Then William would appear, John would take his book-bag, and they would stroll homewards between the hazel and the blushing chestnut trees; and they would go for longer explorations into the nearby woods.

Now with the changing colours and the stripped landscape, William's actions were quieter, his pace pensive and reverent, as his clear eyes peered across the frosted fields or deep into the stark woods; he stopped to listen to the rustling and whispering sounds of the glade or vacant grove, of hidden steps upon dry leaves, of wings unfurled unseen; he scanned the ashen trunks and the twilit spaces between with a watchful and inward eye. And John followed as the boy moved stealthily within a wood of silver birch; with tingles and shivers upon his own skin he touched the soft white of the trees, and traced with young fingers the pale veins, or the fissures of weather and age. In the cold glare of daylight, these trunks shone ethereal or rose in flickers of smoke, while in the lowering scarlet of nightfall they stood cast in fired steel; and their presence would weigh and brand itself upon the two walkers, their cautious steps made heavier. One evening, walking home between these trunks, the boy was about to say something to his companion when a sudden roar stunned and silenced him; overhead, an aeroplane shot swiftly past, its dark metal flashing in the furnace-glow.

IV

John Burrough laboured diligently, ever finding new tasks, pruning trees and bushes or clearing away stone and dead wood, to the rhythm of the rise and sudden fall of the brief autumn days; in the afternoons he walked and spoke with William, while in the evenings he would read and write by lamp or firelight in his hut.

One morning after a stormy night, as he was gathering bark and sticks for firewood from beneath the storm-tossed maples, he stopped short at the fringe of the trees to see two men, their faces indistinct but their uniforms evident, come up to the house; they spoke outside in the drive to Paul, their glances and stern gestures directed at John's hut. John watched intently, but they stayed only for a few minutes before Paul escorted them back down the drive out of sight, and returned alone; he stepped into the house without seeing the man among the trees, and without a further glance at the hut. As John bent to resume his work, his hands fumbled in distraction and some sticks fell from his grasp onto the bed of dry, decomposing leaves.

Immediately after this he set to clearing a large potato-patch of the intrusion of weeds, nettles sickly green and pale, ghostly thistles; he worked fiercely, resting little, bracing his fired body against the cold air to exert his entire strength. Scythe, rake and other tools stood leaning disorderly against the shed; John found there the rusted blade of an old plough, fastened temporarily to a wooden shaft, both metal and wood ruined by years of exposure to storm and sleet. This he took, and struck and dragged to break and shift the freezing soil; as tiny splinters lodged one by one into the skin of his palms, John removed the plough from its handle and worked, kneeling and crouching, with the metal straight in his bare hands; scales of rust flaked off on his skin but did not cut him, and the tool grew firm in his grip, fast in tune to his regular and forceful motion. After hours of fervent toil beneath the cold sun, he had unearthed a mass of the stony, indomitable fruit, some cast in a near-human mould, but sightless and deformed, others scarcely distinguishable from the clods of clay of their dark bed. The flesh of John's arms and neck were hardened red from his exertion and the firebrand of wind and sun.

For several days after, John suffered from a cold and from brief attacks of fever; he laboured still, but was often forced to stop as a cough grew in his throat, or as the cold sweat pricked his skin, creeping up along his spine or gathering in a thin film upon his brow. Instead of going for long walks, he would sit contemplatively in his hut, between the frosted windows and the cracking fire; here William would bring his friend hot drinks in the evening and sit and listen to him speak. One evening, however, John was instead visited by George Sutton, in company with his firstborn son. They had come to check on his health.

'I will be better in a few days I am sure. Thank you,' John said.

'It is a precarious life you are leading, spending yourself like this,' George suggested.

'I try to live the only way I know how to,' John replied.

'And you don't feel that you are staking your health for a life that is too much removed from the other, some might say, more important, affairs of the world?'

'Circumstance has forced me to live apart like this, and choice has kept me here. What is important, I believe, is to live life straight from the source, without fear of effort or misfortune. This is all I attempt to practise.' George took the words in, before continuing in a measured tone,

'And this faith of yours leads you to renounce your bonds with your fellow citizens at a time which calls for unity of purpose, at the risk of the safety of the nation, or so it seems to me.'

'What the times call for, and what I ask of my fellow citizens, is to cast their weapons aside, or to turn their swords inwards and die to this outward war,' John declared.

'You are evidently a man of ideals, how accurate they are is not for me to say; but don't you feel that you may and should contribute to the preservation of this country, and the efforts of thousands to keep our shores safe from the serious threat of our enemies? These are times, I am convinced, when our first duty is to our nation, to its military command, and the primary loyalty of any able man is unquestionable. There.' As he finished, he leant against the wall to listen to John's response.

'Our only duty, for lack of a better word, is to live truthfully and in peace; this is the moral judgement I feel upon myself, and this is all I ask of every other man, yourselves included.' He paused to look into the eyes of the others, but George's face was turned to the fire, and his son's were full of impatient derision. 'I see bonds between men where you see none,' John went on, 'but where you see loyalty, I see only death, and where you see a structured effort for victory and preservation, or whatever you call it, I see a chaos of men, men fickle and moth-like driven upon a dark breath.' He rubbed his face as he stopped, and stared fixedly into the leaping flames.

George stepped towards the door, his actions groping and hesitant, and he spoke falteringly.

'You are very eloquent, I give you that; no doubt you will persist in your vision, as we must persist in ours. It remains to see what we will gain.' With this he pushed open the door onto the cold, metallic evening, and left. Paul stayed behind, however, and soon engaged his combatant anew.

'We had a visit some days ago. You are well known in these counties; it seems you have a habit of upsetting our highest institutions, yes?'

'I do not seek to quarrel, but I will make my voice heard if I feel strongly and truly impelled.'

'And you are prepared to interrupt and disturb the efforts of this nation?'

John rose from his chair and went over to the window; as he replied, his tone was determined: 'If and when I do choose to speak up, I do so under the conviction that I am speaking on behalf of what little life remains in this nation of yours.'

'There are plenty of brave men who risk their lives daily for the life of this nation, and what it represents, and their countrymen.'

The young soldier was sweating in the close room; his uniform was too warm, his fresh skin visibly stung by the lashes of heat from the fire; his stride back and forth across the wooden floor was irregular and petulant, his speech impetuous and abrupt.

'They breed nothing but death,' was John's reply, at which the fresh-faced and sweating soldier blustered back,

'Death? Death, we all understand, is what awaits us all if we do not fight back!'

'On the contrary,' claimed John, also inflamed now, 'death is perpetuated here behind our own lines. He who goes with weapons in hand to kill another is dead already.'

'Ha!' the young soldier shouted.

'Dead to their fellow men, dead to God,' John insisted.

'I am dead then, you say?' Paul moved closer to confront the traitor, who firmly replied: 'There are many kinds of death, and your imbecile patriotism is one.'

At this last response, the furious, unrestrained soldier struck him in the face. John staggered back, his cheek burning and his entire frame trembling, and stared at the other man; Paul met his eyes, but as the struck man didn't speak or move, he turned in frustration and dashed out of the room.

John stepped slowly out of the cottage and grimaced in pain as the cold wind kissed the bone and skin of his bruised and swollen cheek; he took a few deep breaths and sat down against the wall, peering across the pale fields beneath the dusky blue.

V

The next day a rain driven by a fierce wind crowded the skies and pierced the earth at a sharp angle; the brown and crimson leaves were torn in tatters from the trees, and as the onslaught receded the woods stood stripped of their late splendour, while the soil, saturated with water, glowed a deep purple in the evening light. As John went for a solitary stroll, the sunset was copper-coloured, and what little red remained on the skeletal trees flared, unearthly, while on the ground the odd poppies broke the dusk in pale, flimsy fires. William came to John that evening, suggesting they go for a fishing-trip to a nearby lake the following day, if the weather was clear.

First thing in the morning they set off, bringing fishing rods and for bait some worms dug up before they left; the lake was an hour's walk away, and they reached it by a meandering path between dense thickets of bare, sprouting trees. The lake itself was stripped of its covering of water-lilies, the surrounding reeds browned and hollow; yet it was a crisp, tranquil day, and the two friends eagerly pulled the old wooden boat into the water. William, who had been there before, pointed out to John where he had stood angling from the rocks, and where he had lain flat on his belly upon a branch reaching out across the lake. They spent hours on the lake without getting any fish, before they ate their packed lunch and simply enjoyed the movement of the boat upon the mirror-surface of the water; each stroke of the oars and each forward motion of the wooden vessel dipped simultaneously into the still lake and the bright skies above. At one point John stopped rowing and hoisted the oars into the boat to let it float quietly upon the clear surface and bob slightly upon the smooth undulations of the lake; man and boy both sat in silence for a period of suspended time, eyes upon the delicate rings of the water, their bodies now gently lifted, now gently lowered again.

'Do you like the silence?' John asked.

'Yes, I do,' answered the boy. 'Sometimes, don't you think it sounds like voices, like many people singing far away?'

'Yes, you have a good ear,' said John, then, 'Look!'

A crane, invisible at first, had stirred by the waterside, and now stood upon its thin legs and spread its vast wings in full sight of the boat, before it took flight solemnly from the shadows of the shore; as it rose above the top of a weeping willow, it startled a whole group of crows to scatter their black forms across the steely skies.

John and William were still on the water at sundown; they sat in the boat to see a sky of crimson with purple clouds, deepening to the colour of bruised plum, and then to grey; soon the moon rose full above the lake. They remained on the darkening water until they were sure of not getting a single fish on the hook, then rowed placidly to the shore, where waves mercury and moonlit lapped the quiet earth. John pulled the vessel under the arching trees and then, rods and empty net in hand, they walked away from the lake, talking in cheerful tones to dispel the night. Having wandered for some time, the boy's feet getting tired and his tread less sure, John lifted him up onto his shoulders; William sat thus beneath the moon and the trees, his face occasionally touched by drooping leaves, while John kept his eyes upon the ground so as not to trip over stone or root, cautious of the turns and slopes of the path. As they neared home, an aircraft passed high above their heads; William could see, through the intricate silhouettes of the branches above, the grey machine crawl across the leaden sky, and he could hear the distant, muted roar; no echo stirred, and no twilit shadow fell upon the murky ground.

Soon they reached the cottage, but as the earth slept the two stayed awake. John spoke as William sat on the hearth in the firelight, whittling at a stick he had picked up along the way; his work took no definite shape, but the rough bark was parted and peeled off, the white flesh revealed, glistening with the sap that seeped out at every cut of the steel. Their limbs and eyes grew tired, but they remained awake; and then William saw the dawn arrive, breaking the stony covering of the long night; he saw how the east brightened from its first embers of amber to a bright yellow, how the west awoke in waves, the billow of dark clouds giving way to a surge of pale blue. William saw the brick and wood of the house glow with still warmth, while on the trees each twig and veined leaf was distinctly seen in the morning light; and in that light without shadow the boy was stripped of his body to his bare heart. And then at last he slept, and John watched over him; and he turned his vision to that inward heart, and there he saw such promptings, such wondrous fiery openings; and he sat rapt in stillness as the sun rose.

VI

That day was spent in rest, but the next was the day of Paul's departure for the front. It was a foggy morning as father and son appeared on the drive; the young soldier was pale-faced but proudly erect in his immaculate uniform, the old Captain quiet but unstill. As George drove off with Paul to the station, William said farewell to his brother before joining John; they climbed a wooded hill behind the house to reach the fields on the other side, where Paul's train was to pass. Standing on the ridge they could see through the ashen trunks of the trees the railway tracks crossing the deserted field; this was an old pasture, now out of use, and the tracks were lined intermittently on each side by barbed wire used to keep off the cattle. As the fog filtered through the yellow light, the entire sky above the mustard-coloured field took on a sickly, sulphurous hue; yet William and John saw in the midst of this, grazing on the dried grass, a group of deer. The boy expressed his amazement at seeing these graceful creatures, and they began to slowly descend the hill to get a closer view. Just then, however, they also noticed, upon glancing back, that two uniformed men had appeared at the house and were crossing the gardens toward the field; John swiftly led William in among the trees, and they carefully made their way down the hill upon the rusted, crimson shards of dry leaves. At the bottom, at the fringe of the field, they had a close and full view of the deer; the animals of the quiet gathering were eating gently of what the field gave, barely moving their legs and only slightly lifting or letting fall their smooth heads; behind them, the train became visible at the far end of the field, soon to pass this part of the pasture. By now the two officers had rounded the hill and come into the field, the other side of the animals from William and John; as one raised his voice, every one of the deer stirred and turned their heads, and sighting the two intruders began stepping towards the hill – but there being startled instead by the presence of William and John, they shied in fright and rushed the opposite way, towards the track. For the moment ignoring the two men, John and William were struck to see the deer getting through a wide gap in the barbed wire and clustering around the railway as the train was fast approaching; they froze to see the animals scatter in panic and rush frantically from the track, some escaping through the openings in the fence, but several running straight into the barbed metal, smooth breasts and soft brown flanks torn and run through by the sharp spikes, slender legs and bodies buckling under their own weight as lifeless heads bent over the wire. William ran instinctively towards the carnage, but halfway there he broke down in tears and flung himself to the ground. On the train, meanwhile, Paul pressed his white face against the glass, his features contorted at sight of the slaughtered animals and his brother running towards them; after a few moments of sitting down, his eyes staring at the table in front of him, his tongue and lips dry, he rose upon weak legs and reached with a trembling hand for the emergency brake.

Yet John, kneeling by the side of William, saw the train, cold, insentient, beat relentlessly on across the sallow fields. The two officers had stopped at a distance; as George Sutton shortly returned, he told them in a tremulous but commanding voice to be off; this was no time and no place for their purpose, he insisted, and they obeyed and left. After George had comforted William, he and John both set to work pulling the dead deer from the wire; William saw them wring and lift the heavy, lifeless bodies and pull them by the legs away from the track into the pale bed of the field; and he saw them against the sepia sky, coming towards him, clutching the dry grass to wipe their bloodied hands.

George spoke to John afterwards, saying how he felt certain the two officers would come back in the morning if not sooner, and he advised him, regrettably, to become itinerant once more. John resigned himself to this, saying it was not the first time, nor the last, and after a warming supper he bade a reluctant farewell to William, whose eyes remained reddened by tears; and so he left.

They found his body in mid-winter, frozen fast to the cold soil of some field neither trod nor tilled; he lay on his back, eyes open beneath a thin sheet of snow.

The Chose

by Sarah Evans

Rachel walked down the wooden steps, her arms full of the shifting shimmer. At the bottom she shook out the dress. Eliza's eyes shone wide; Mina's mouth gaped.

'It's beautiful,' Eliza said, her lips remaining parted. 'The most beautiful ever.'

'The one I wore,' Rachel said. The village had kept this tradition through the ages. Dresses passed mother to daughter, remaining pristine, worn only once every twenty years or so. Rachel didn't know from when this one dated, not precisely. Only occasionally was a new one made.

If Eliza noticed the emotion in her mother's eye, she showed no sign. She hugged herself, holding in her glee.

'This year,' she said. 'This year I'm going to be Chosen.'

'That you will,' Joe said. 'None's going to look more beautiful than my Eli.' He ignored, or perhaps didn't see, the look cast over to him by his wife.

Rachel sank into a seat, the gossamer dress spreading out around her. Within the multi-layered folds, elaborate flowers grew in gorgeous colours. The strands of thread seemed to shine all the brighter for their long internment in the heavy chest kept in the attic. The bodice was designed to fit close, and intricate lace would veil over shoulders and neck. The full pleats of the skirt glistened in the last rays of sunlight through the open window. Today had seen the best of this year's warmth, filling the air with the fragrance of early summer. Tomorrow promised to be a fine day.

'It just needs taking in a tad,' she said. She plunged her hands into the silk, letting it slip between her fingers and catching a faint scent of decay layered with the lavender and camomile which had been carefully wrapped with the dress. She could remember the slippery feel of it against her skin, the finest thing she ever wore, so different to the daily scratch of raw cotton. She remembered the laughing, breathless thrill of the day all that while ago, the giddied up excitement mingling with something deeper, more feral and unnamed. Seeing the rapture relived in her daughter drew her back into it. Almost. Not quite.

Her hands clenched.

'Mum,' Eliza said. 'You're creasing it.'

'Nonsense. Just needs an inch or so in at the waist.'

'She'll look beautiful,' Joe repeated. 'My Eli.'

Rachel looked over at Joe. She had lain beside him for seventeen years now, had born his children, cooked and cleaned and laboured alongside him in the fields; she had offered consolation, and shared joy. Sometimes she looked at his weather-flayed face, his wide eyes – those same eyes as Eliza's – the square line of his shadowed jaw and felt she didn't know him at all.

Sometimes she felt that she knew nothing.

Rachel stayed up after the others had gone to bed. The dress seemed to have a life of its own, refusing to stay put and yield to her seamstress skill. Eliza was more willow-slender than she had been, her waist turning inwards, accentuating the gentle curves below and above. Rachel took her time in stitching, taking care that the dress might be let out again. Mina would wear it in her turn. Eliza's daughters, were she to have girls, would wear it too.

Unless…

Dismay jolted. It had started dull; more recently it keened. She felt a swift urge to rip the dress. Stop this! She slapped her unruly thoughts away.

Later, fingers sore and mind tired, she hung the dress up outside the girls' room before retiring to her own. She shrugged out of her day clothes, retaining only her roughly woven shift, grey with wear and washing. She rustled into the bed beside Joe. Usually she would shuffle close, moulding her contours to his, interweaving their limbs, so their body-warmth mingled. Tonight she kept herself apart, feeling her skin tight and cold, her body rigid, as she listened for Joe's breathing. The completeness of his silence left her wondering if his sleep were as deep as his inert body seemed to say. No reason to suppose not. It's unfair. Her protest mouthed silently. But it was unfair to blame him. She knew that. Knowing didn't make it stop.

They had been through this two previous years. Except younger girls tended not to be Chosen. It tended to be those in their four

67

square – their sixteenth – year, those on the cusp of womanhood. The other years she had been comfortable in the knowledge that, if she pushed aside the softening haze of motherhood, Eliza was a leggy foal, her limbs too long and gangling for her to use them gracefully. Only in the last few months had Eliza blossomed as surely as a rose in early summer. Like a slowly opening bud, each layer of unfurling seemed more perfect and fragrant than the last. Only in the last months had Rachel begun to narrow her eyes more sharply, comparing her daughter to those around and deducing that this year Eliza had a chance. She really did have a chance. She had tried to voice this to Joe, cautiously, unsure how it would affect their luck – Eliza's luck – if she said it too strongly.

'Chance same as all of them,' was all he'd say, refusing to be drawn, his face as blank as stone.

She woke with the first rays of daylight. Resisting the draw back into sleep, she moved to sit. Flicking a glance behind, just for a moment she thought she saw a glint of light reflecting off the moisture of Joe's eyes. Except his body was still and he was not one to linger once awake.

Today was the longest day of the year. They would need sustenance, all of them, to take them through. Breakfast was to be special. She'd saved small sweet berries, honey freshly drawn from the hives, eggs newly laid, the best of the remaining flour. A feast she knew she'd have no appetite for. She braced herself. Just today. She just needed to get through today. Her thoughts wandered round the village. Mrs Dauber's girl, Meg, had grown up tall and fine. And Jayne too and Charlotte. Foolishness to think Eliza's beauty would surpass them all. It was only her mother-love that made her see Eliza's skin as smoother, her features finer, her emerging womanhood more alluring.

Mina scurried down the steps, like a mountain goat, to join her; she was often the first up after her mother. Rachel smiled at the blunt features and clumsy figure, the type of plainness that would never blossom, not fully. She'd join her sister today, dressed in gingham, appropriate to her age. But even in a couple of years she'd never achieve her sister's exquisite loveliness; that dress in gauzy folds would never become her so completely.

Rachel handed over the bowl with flour and eggs for Mina to beat, and only half listened as she chattered like a morning sparrow. She heated the flat-bottomed iron pan, stoking the fire with the poker. She should have branded her daughter as a baby. The furious thought crossed her mind. Too late now. Besides there were risks to that. Rona Williams had always claimed it was an accident that left her daughter with an angry stroke of red puckering across her pale cheeks. Whispers now were that no man would have her, no family would welcome in such an ill-luck bride.

Rachel sighed. The old ways had served the village well. It was what Joe would say. He was right. Usually Joe was right.

Joe, who now clattered down the steps and sat at the long oak table, leaning back, smilingly at ease in his clean blue-check shirt, saved for days like this. The one he'd married her in. Eliza followed close behind, a yawn interrupting her smile. Rachel placed the pile of pancakes in the middle. Joe beamed round at his family. 'A grand spread,' he said. 'A grand spread indeed. It's going to be a glorious day.'

Unease continued to agitate; butterflies multiplied in Rachel's stomach, preventing her from eating. Unease bred unease, as if her mutinous thoughts might somehow affect the outcome, might influence the Breezes said to whisper their choice to the Chosen. The Breezes that kept them safe and fed and saved from drought and flooding rain and plague.

What good did it do them, she wanted to ask, why was this required? Was she the only one who asked?

'Mu-um.' Eliza's imperious tone drew her back. Normally she'd chide the girl for impertinence. Not this morning though. Not on this special day. She let her gaze fall on her daughter's perfect petal cheeks. She reached a hand across to tidy back a stray wisp from her skein of hair.

'You're not listening,' was Eliza's complaint.

'I am love,' she lied. 'Say again.'

'Will you be proud of me?' Eliza said.

'Course we will be. Who wouldn't?' Joe answered for her, but Eliza's eyes remained on her mother.

'Yes,' she said. 'Of course.'

'And you are wanting me to be Chose?'

'Yes. Of course.' She said it mechanically. What alternative was there? What would be, would be. She had no power to stop it.

The alternative.

There was none.

Except…

She had heard vague rumours whispered behind hands, only semi-believed, rumours that said this was not the only way to do things. Elsewhere the old ways were being challenged.

Mina was pestering Eliza with questions: 'But what happens? What?'

Eliza faked annoyance and impatience as she answered.

Rachel remembered the words from her own girlhood. The tales started early; she had heard them from her mother at an age when she was too young to understand. Later she had done the same with her daughters. By the time teachers at school took the tales up they were already known, absorbed into knowledge, as surely as the knowledge of which berries were good to eat, and when to sow then gather wheat. The promises had always felt so real; only recently had they seemed to wither to cobweb shreds.

Mina's eyes glowed with longing. 'If Eliza's Chose, can I be too?'

But the rule was only ever one daughter from one family. Besides, it was never going to be Mina.

The sun shone unencumbered by the least wisp of cloud. It would be a good day for a good Choosing. Light glinted like wood-fire sparks off the finest fabrics, the summer cheer a world away from dawn to dusk muscle-ache labour. It was the only day in the year when no work was done by the men. The women still cooked and cleared up of course, though that hardly counted as work.

Eliza took her father's hand, like the child she still was, and Rachel felt an awful jealousy at this having to share her, wanting to take her aside, to tell her not to smile, not too much, to look down, not forward, at the crucial moment.

They stopped to talk with the Daubers. Meg was dressed as vibrantly as Eliza and the two girls took hands and stepped back to admire the other's dress. Was Meg's hair a little duller than was usual, Rachel wondered. Had her mother sneaked a little ash into the lard and lye solution used to lather hair, instead of the vinegar that added shine? She had no reason to suppose others thought that way.

Eliza seemed to glow from the inside. It was impossible for Rachel's heart not to swell with a mother's pride. Joe's face beamed a smile. It was an honour, she knew that, to have brought up a girl so full of bloom.

The Chosen – the male Chosen – gathered in a corner. They were dressed all in white, standing pale amidst the colourful crowd.

Too soon the moment came, of parting. Just temporary, Rachel told herself. Joe wrapped his arms round Eliza in a bear-hug. 'The very best of luck,' he wished her.

Rachel found her voice frozen and her body frozen too. She focussed firmly on not letting her tears form and fall. Just for a moment she caught a look in Eliza's eye, a small girl look, looking to her mother for reassurance. She tried her very hardest to smile.

'Go on. Off with you.' Joe's voice seemed unsullied, reflecting nothing but the summer brightness.

As Eliza skipped off, Mina following close behind, Joe tried to take Rachel's hand. She kept it for herself.

The white-clad Chosen led the procession. Rachel didn't know who had chosen them. It was confusing to have the same word used for two such different things. For the men it was a closed ritual. Even Joe knew nothing of it, or so he claimed. She had no objection to the selection. They were the elder members of the community, those who commanded respect by virtue of accumulated years and assets. The father of a Chose girl would join them for two years; sometimes he would be asked to stay on. She wondered how Joe would appreciate the task. She had tried to ask him once. It wasn't for him to say, he'd replied. It would happen or not, no point anticipating things.

The girls came next, the flouncing, agitating mass of them. The plain gingham for the younger girls, there more for the practice of the thing than to compete; the glossy brightness of the older girls. It had always been this way. It always would. But why? Rachel wished she could quell the question pulsing in her mind. She tried to picture feeling the surge of pride that Mrs Mahoney had professed last year as her skin turned death-mask pale. She remembered tears cascading down a blood-drained face and Mrs Mahoney claiming they were of joy, before she had collapsed into the muscled arms of her husband.

Somehow the men took it more easily.

The path started steady along the valley. The river twinkled in the light and diamond sparks were thrown out by the rocks. Green pasture lay to either side, newly grown and vibrant.

The path started to steepen, becoming rockier under foot. Rachel's face was sweating under the glow of the sun. Joe's face was ruddy beside her. She wondered about Eliza, whether her face was blushing with exertion and whether it would enhance her flowering.

It felt like hours later that they came to the opening. It was hard not to feel awe at the tranquil, bubbling beauty. Water fell from above in white cascades, tinkling into a green pool, frothing up in snowy peaks at the point of meeting. Green glistened all around, impossibly lush, so many different shades it hardly felt another colour could be needed, so varied was green in all its forms. The moss and ferns covered the surface of the rock; if you didn't look, you needn't know what it was they disguised.

It would soon be over. The thought washed through her. After all the waiting, it would be over. Soon they would return, the four of them, Eliza disappointed, but she was young, and youthful hearts bounce back. Mina excited, knowing she had another turn. Joe, how he'd really feel, Rachel had no idea. He would feign not to be disappointed. But whether it was the feigning or the non-disappointment that were real she didn't know. Rachel would not feign. She would be practical with her never-you-minds, and Eliza would think her uncaring. Until perhaps, she had daughters of her own.

The families without daughters of age all mingled and chatted merrily. Those whose girls formed part of the bright, young throng, kept themselves a little apart, flustering with excitement, or something else, it was impossible to tell. Mrs Mahoney was there, right at the front. Her cheeks had never quite recovered their colour. Her features had tightened over the year, become more unyielding.

Rachel's eye caught the quiver of white as those ritually clad men, their faces turned stern, fanned out, the water rushing in white arcs behind. There was a brief flurry of drums.

The head of the Chosen started to speak, explaining how they would proceed. His words felt less protracted than when Rachel had been a girl. Or was that her imagination? Was it that her younger self had been more impatient? She tried to remember what it had been like all those years ago, standing there, in the same finery as her daughter, keyed up and excited on all those promises, fevered by the prospect of being shown special, awed at the attention, not believing, not really, that it would be her. She had been pleasant looking, never stunning.

Not like Eliza. How had she and Joe been so lucky? Except just now lucky didn't feel the right word.

The head of the Chosen turned a little to the side, back towards the bank of green, pushing the drooping foliage aside, revealing the grey stone that seemed all of one piece, until you looked close and saw how one boulder could be drawn away. It took two of the Chosen, two strong men, to do it. She watched as the lump of rock was removed to reveal the slender entrance to the caves. It gaped back, black and implacable. Implacable like the faces of the men before her dressed in white. White for the celebration they would all enjoy back in the village. All of them there. All except one. All except the one the Chosen would Choose. The most beautiful of the girls between their thirteen and four-square years. The Chose.

She felt a chill, as if the sun's warmth had momentarily been absorbed by the black cleft, except her eyes were still squinting under the glare of light. The silence of the crowd, broken here and there by foot shuffling and the occasional infant's cry, broken by the continuous gushing of the water, left space to hear the echo of the caves which seemed to speak in some unknown tongue. Perhaps it was just the passage of wind, just the movement of air through the complex paths, which were said to be unknowable, said to change and shift. Perhaps it was the hungry whisper of the Breezes.

The girls were lined up, faces serious now, giggling forgotten. The men walked slowly past. Seven of them passed the thirty or so girls. A one in thirty chance. Except you could discount the younger ones. Ten of the right age. Some of them noticeably plain. Rachel counted five. Five who shone with artless, pure beauty. Each took the hand of each of the Chosen. Each looked into his eyes, bobbed down politely and smiled. They had been taught to smile. Big radiant smiles. Rachel remembered standing there, how suddenly it felt difficult to raise her lips for Mr So and So, the father of someone, the man who owned such and such a field and had a given number of cows, and of children. She could see Eliza only in the pauses between the passing of the men. She couldn't see how her unblemished face shone hope at each of them, willing herself to be picked, or perhaps in the last moment, not to be.

It seemed to take an unconscionable age. All around was quiet and still, except for the rushing collision of water. Rachel's skin sweated and turned cold. Over. It would soon be over.

Having walked the line the men then wrote on squares of paper and cast votes into the small embroidered sack. The method of voting was somewhat complex, trying to ensure a single outcome and avoid disputes and multiple rounds. Three votes cast. Each vote with a name and number. Three for a first choice, two for a second, one for a third. It was rare not to have a definitive result.

Rachel was finding it hard to breathe; the green scented air seemed to choke her. She gazed at her daughters. She could see Mina fidgeting. But Eliza stared ahead, steady and unseeing.

The head of the Chosen took the pieces of paper from the bag, careful not to let them flutter away on the light currents of air. He started jotting down figures on a pad, so pedantically slow in his adding up that she felt like rushing over to offer help. His seconder repeated the exercise, independently, so there'd be no mistake.

And then the head Chosen raised his hand.

'We have a result.' His voice was firm and strong. 'We have Chosen.' Time stopped and even the water seemed to hang suspended in the air. And then he spoke the name, the name that Rachel had spent near on sixteen years dreading to hear.

'Eliza.'

Rachel could no longer see clearly. Blood was draining from her face and Joe was gripping her hand tightly. Every fibre of her was wanting to rush forward, to cry out no, except she seemed to be statued to the spot. She saw, she thought she saw, a smile rise on Eliza's face in triumph.

And then...

This part was always conducted quickly. The seven men closed in around the newly Chose, and the other girls fell back, their faces fallen with disappointment. The grouping headed into the caves. They disappeared one by one, bending their bodies into the crevice left by the rock, lighting candles as they went. Two remained, backs to the crowd, covering the entrance, turning it white.

The girl would be led inside the wandering maze of caves. It was mid-winter cold, moonless-night dark, filled with age-old whispers, so they said. She would be taken, eyes hooded, along a winding route, the way back marked with an unspooling line of thread, through into the chasm, lightly tied to a rock, just enough to retain her a short time, while the men slipped away, winding back along the threaded line.

She must then wait. The tales, told before an age of understanding, told so they were part of what simply was known, were full of fabulous detail, though how anyone came by such knowledge was not clear. It was the collective wisdom of the ages. Rachel tried to bring it all to mind. The girl would be spirited to the depths, embraced by the Breezes, showered with finery and gifts and the best of foods. It had all seemed so vivid, so real, when it was explained, year by year, throughout her growing years at her mother's side, throughout her years of schooling. She'd received it without question, without reflection. A life of unimaginable ease. Being reunited, they said, with those earlier Chose. A lifetime free of day to day cares and woes. The tales crumbled now into decaying dust, just as she was crumpling down.

When she came back to, it was just her and Joe. His eyes were gazing at the entrance, covered once more in the soft green across the replaced rock. She'd hardly know it had been disturbed, if she didn't know where to look.

'We should join the celebrations,' he said, his voice as flat and dead as stone.

And surely there was much to celebrate. The family would be honoured, showered with gifts from the village throughout the year. This winter there would be no finger-freezing cold, no belly-aching hunger. Joe would take his place among the Chosen.

She looked at Joe, the same question in her eyes that had been there since the day her baby was declared a girl, that had never found an answering response.

He gazed ahead. 'What would you have had me do?' he asked.

Unspoken

by Pam Eaves

'Ileana. Is it true you're the daughter of a Count?'

'Is your father rich? What's he Count of?'

'Ileana, Ileana – how did you meet Sir Archibald?'

Why are you going to marry a wealthy industrialist who's fat, bald and forty years older than you?

My question remains unasked. I stay hidden behind the pack of curs lusting after the bitch – the latest 'celebrity' in this country of whores.

Later I shall telephone my 'cousin', Ileana. The Romanian receptionist, one compatriot who has found work, gave me her room number.

Dare I move nearer? No. I look rough, shabby, could be hustled away, questioned, but even from this far I can smell the fragrance of her hair, feel my fingers running through those glossy black waves, and... Stop, Constantin. Don't try to catch her gaze. Look, look again at that slender body draped in silk and jewels, and think – imagine where it's been since it was yours; what it has done to pay for that scarlet gown. 'Scarlet is my colour,' she said when I gave her the cheap beads. She was grateful, then.

This farce is sickening. I slink away, back to my squalid room to stare again at the photograph in the newspaper picked from a bin. The only record I have of my lovely Ileana, so warm, sweet and grateful for scarlet beads before we came here to make our fortunes, together.

'Hello?'

Her voice is the same. Breath leaves my body, I'm choking. Gather yourself, Constantin.

'Hello, who is this please?'

'Constantin.'

'Oh, how are you?'

She sounds wary.

'You've done well for yourself.'

That's weak. I must be strong.

'Yes. Archibald is so kind to me, he…'

'So, what tricks have you done to be kind to him?'

I shouldn't interrupt but my anger is rising.

'No tricks, Constantin. I'm in love with Archibald; he's so sweet and generous.'

'I bet he is, but does he know your background?'

'Of course.'

But she's lying. I always know when Ileana's lying.

'Does he know about all the others?'

'There have been no others, apart from you.'

'There must have been. How else…?'

Gather yourself Constantin, bitterness is not the way.

'I did a little modelling, went to parties, then we met…'

She is lying again. I try and collect my thoughts but the memory of her fragrance is clouding my brain. Concentrate on the need for money. She must pay for my silence.

'Does he know you're a bastard?'

'He wouldn't think that important.'

'Ah, so you've not told him.'

Silence.

'Would he still marry you if he discovered you're not the heir of a wealthy nobleman? Remember the scandal it caused in the town when they discovered the Baron's daughter is his bastard by a common gypsy woman who ran off and left you in a ditch. I offered to marry you then, even though I had just been elected to the judeţ[*], but you wanted to run away – to England.'

Suddenly words pour out. I had almost forgotten my own language but it flows sweetly now.

'You lied when you promised we would support each other whoever got work first, so what lies have you told him?' I ask, '…that man who thinks he is marrying into aristocracy?'

I hear the click of the receiver being replaced. Ileana always ran away from unpleasantness. She ran away from our cold little room. All pretence of love disappeared, and so did she, but to where, and with whom?

---

[*] County Council

I telephone again that evening but as soon as she hears my voice, she puts the phone down. *He's* there. I can imagine her, turning with that bright false smile on her beautiful face. 'Wrong number,' she says, or, 'The press again, but we do not want to be disturbed, do we darling?' And he leers, leans forward, his fat belly wobbling as he reaches for her breasts. I gave her paradise – or so she said.

The following morning:
'No reply from room 202.'
Ah, Romanian girl. I ask when my 'cousin' will be returning.
'Miss Ionescu has beauty treatments in afternoons.'
Do I detect a note of malice? Miss Ionescu! The name of an actress. How apt.

I try at 2pm and Ileana answers.
'What do you want?'
Ah, she recognises my voice. She's been expecting my call so now we're down to business.
'Money, what else? And British status so to work. My English is good now. There must be opportunities with all your lover's connections.'
'Telephone after I'm married. I can't help you now.'
'I need money now.'
'Go back to your hole in the wall.'
The line goes dead.
I ring again, but there's no reply. Anger boils in me. I've been used as a stepping stone; a lump of rock to lean on, to climb above. Rage envelops me and I want to kill. Kill Ileana, whom I love; kill all the whores who tread subservient men into the dirt, making a ladder to reach the pot of gold they've set their greedy eyes on.
But the mood passes as I pace the dingy streets outside my 'hole in the wall'. It always does, and I'm in thrall again. I want her.

The following day I telephone again and she answers, but sounds guarded.
'My manicurist is with me.'

I smile, imagining a woman tending those long fingers, sticking false nails onto bitten stumps.

'False nails, false everything,' I say.

'Five hundred pounds you say? Yes, that's alright. Shall I send you a cheque?'

She knows I have no bank account.

'I want cash,' I tell her. 'You'll have to meet me.'

'OK.' She's trying to sound off-hand. 'Tell me where.'

'You know where I am. Tomorrow at eleven in the morning, and bring cash.'

'I will.'

That's what she wants to say to him, that fat, greasy... but she's said it to me. I take hope because she's frightened. Tomorrow...

Peering from the dirty, rain-streaked window of my room, I see the cab draw up two doors down. Good. She is being careful, and she's not dressed up – casual clothes, but those trousers and sweater are not those she came to this country in. The doorbell rings. I make her wait before I go downstairs to greet her.

'Welcome home.'

'Don't be stupid, Constantin. This is not my home.'

'It should be. This is where you belong.'

'Not any more.' But she follows me up the endless flights of stairs.

The wrinkled nose, the look of disdain as she glances round our love nest hurts. Does she not see the daffodils I stole from the cemetery? There is a supercilious straightening of her shoulders as she hands me crumpled notes.

'Now go away, out of my life. You have no place there any more,' she says, but I move close to her, touch her hair, let my fingers slide down her neck, then lower... It is enough. Ileana was always weak, unable to control her body which responds involuntarily to... Does it respond to him, that fat, old man?

Waves of heavy musk emanate from her – expensive perfume – not the delicate fragrance of old. It sickens me, but the soft, pliant body moves in all the remembered ways under my touch, so easy – too easy now it is pampered, silky smooth. Even her hands have lost that slight endearing roughness, and the false talons scratch deeper

79

than bitten and torn fingernails. When finally she lies passive and sated I take her hand to look at her nails. As I thought – long, perfect and scarlet, set with sparkly glass pieces. No more housework for Ileana. I remember how her father used her as his skivvy, and worse.

A stream of afternoon sunlight creeps through a gap in the torn curtains setting fire to the diamond on her finger.

'I must go. I have an appointment.' She begins to rise, but I grab her hand; inspect the ring. She snatches her hand back.

I turn away, rise and dress silently. Silence unnerves her. She cannot bear silence.

'When I am married I can give you regular money and I'm sure Archibald will help you get a job, nationality…' Her voice trails away as I walk over bare boards and drag the ragged curtain from the window. She blinks in the sunlight, but doesn't move. She looks so beautiful lying there, her pale body appearing replete, satiated, but Ileana was always greedy. I can see a faint quiver in those long white legs; they are ready to curve, enclose again. Stop, Constantin.

'Haven't you got an appointment?' I ask.

She gets up reluctantly, the languid movements as she dresses stir my senses and I long to grab her, tear the encumbering clothes from her, possess her now and for always, but remain stiff and silent, waiting…

'Perhaps, after I'm married…'

I could happily drown in those mystical black eyes when they are turned towards me pleadingly.

'Yes?' I say, as coldly as I can, trying to control my shaking body in the shadowy corner of the room.

'Perhaps, if I give you money on a regular basis, we could meet and…'

'Talk over old times?' I laugh at the confirmation of my guess. Archibald cannot satisfy her and she wants, what do they say here? 'To have eaten her cake and still have it.'

'Perhaps,' I say. 'I'll telephone you when I need more money.'

The room turns cold and dark when she has gone. I lie on the bed and sob, sob for past happiness, lost hopes, but perhaps to share is better than nothing at all – and there's the money. I need money to eat – and drink. I want to move to a better place but for now here is all she knows so I buy myself a small radio and don't look for work so I'm here if she comes. The bait is set so I think she will, but when…? I shall not telephone. She must come to me so I know she is mine completely.

Time stretches endlessly, but it is only two days and I leap to the window at the sound of a cab. Different clothes; still casual trousers but the leather jacket slung round her shoulders is conspicuous in this area. I see men eyeing her as she walks towards my door – for her beauty, or her coat? I rush downstairs and drag her in, regardless of showing my eagerness.

'I heard the cab. You are stupid to wear such clothes in this place. You'll get attacked.'

'I would fight back.'

'And have it all over the newspapers? Sir Archibald's fiancée attacked in Whitechapel. They'd think you were a whore.'

'You think that, so…'

Those eyes, sparkling ebony, challenging as her head tilts, the scarlet nails flash against soft, cream leather as she flings the coat carelessly towards the only chair. She's in my arms, sprawled across the bed, black hair spread across the pillow, her face flushed with desire as I strip and take her roughly.

A moment of peace afterwards. If it were not for that musky scent I would be lost completely, but wait, wait, Constantin. Let her marry the fat oaf, stay with him for – how long? I must study the divorce law. Does it make her a whore, and me – what? A survivor if that is the only way. I raise myself on one elbow and look down on her beautiful face; the face of a whore, but I love her.

'Again?' she whispers. 'I have brought more money.'

My Ileana is so greedy but I can at least give her love.

Much, much later we talk, make plans. She has brought me a mobile telephone.

'Your wedding is in only two weeks. We must be very careful until then,' I say.

'But I must see you again before…' She clings to me. If I forbid her to come, would she try and do these things with him?

'I will stay here until your wedding day,' I tell her. 'No more money in case the old man suspects something. I can wait; so must you.'

'I can't,' she whispers, so I urge her to be very careful or else I shall disappear and she'll never see me again. I'm lying, but Ileana believes me.

That night I drink a bottle of cheap wine to celebrate, and another the following morning, then go out to buy more. Ileana will not come today.

But she does. As I stagger back she's paying off a cab. She looks up, her face radiant and, arms outstretched, runs across the road to greet me. I try to shout a warning but my throat is dry. A white van; a flash of scarlet flying and sprawling in the road, black hair spread in the gutter, dark eyes blank and lifeless. A crowd gathers, chattering, shaking threatening fists at the back of the van speeding away as I stand motionless, wishing I had, just once, told Ileana I still truly loved her.

How to Impersonate a UFO

by Trevor Hopkins

It all started with a chance remark last year, a question I put to my father.

My old man was a pilot in the Royal Air Force for many years, in that interesting period of world history after the Second World War known as the Cold War. He had flown all over the world, in an age where this was very unusual. He had even dropped bombs on Suez during that ill-advised political embarrassment.

Dad is, or was, I should say, a great raconteur, a pillar of the local Rotary Club and very much in demand for his after-dinner speeches. He had a great fund of stories and anecdotes, often based on his flying experiences. But there was one tale which I had not ever heard him tell, one which I discovered buried in the draft of his autobiography when I was reading the proofs. He had written that he "felt sure he had caused a UFO scare on one occasion."

So, here's how to do it – how to provide a convincing imitation of an Unidentified Flying Object. Don't try this at home, kids.

For this trick, you need a night with completely clear skies – no cloud to form a visual reference – and with no moon to provide undesirable illumination.

Pick a time of year when the jet streams are blowing strongly – you know, those fast-moving stratospheric air currents that the pilots of commercial airlines like to blame for their late arrival. Wintertime is preferred. Oh, and you'll need a military jet. My Dad did this in a Canberra, but I dare say that any modern jet fighter would work just as well.

So, off you go. Fly up to 45,000 feet over some major conurbation, and head into the wind. Now, the jet streams are probably running at around 150 knots, so you throttle back until your airspeed is about one-fifty. From the ground, you are now more or less stationary. If you're equipped with a radar ground speed indicator, you can fine-tune your direction and airspeed until you are completely stopped, just hanging in the air.

Then, you turn on all the landing lights. These lights are typically distributed fore-and-aft, and on the wing-tips, and around the undercarriage. So, from the ground, you look like a disk with illuminated portholes, or engines, or whatever, all around the circumference.

You sit there in the jet stream for ten minutes or so, chuckling with your co-pilot about the stir you're probably causing on the ground. What a wizard wheeze. Then, you turn about and throttle right up, so that you are streaking through the skies. Then, just when you've reached your maximum speed, turn the lights off again. Your observers have just seen a hovering object suddenly accelerate from rest to a phenomenal speed – "no known aircraft can fly like that" – and then disappear.

Now you're a UFO. Good, huh? With a bit of luck, your appearance and sudden disappearance will be reported in the more sensationalist newspapers with banner headlines, and some no-doubt anonymous government spokesman will be quoted in the small print explaining that this was a just "an ordinary unscheduled military training flight."

Now my old Dad has something of a reputation as a prankster. He's always ready with a joke or two, often highly politically-incorrect and downright filthy, but usually irresistibly funny for all that. He was the editor of the Rotary Club newsletter, which also gave him an outlet for his personal sense of humour and, since he was a bit of a Silver Surfer, he had taken to trawling the Internet for humorous material. I would occasionally send him 'funnies' in the electronic mail which I feel sure became newsletter material and I would often get something hilarious in return.

Having re-read the words from his book, I had simply assumed it was a practical joke, a lark. I tackled him on the topic during one of my inexcusably infrequent visits.

We were sitting in the small but well-maintained garden at the back of the house last summer, basking in the early evening sunshine and enjoying a glass of sherry before dinner. My wife was occupied elsewhere in the house with our children. My mother was busying herself in the kitchen, producing one of those splendid roast dinners I remember so well from my childhood, but which I feel I must resist most of the time these days, if only to keep my weight and blood pressure down.

Dad went uncharacteristically quiet for a few moments. Then, in low and serious tones, he told me what actually happened on that night back in the fifties, an episode which occurred before I was even born. He made it clear that this was not a prank, a whim, but that he had been specifically instructed to go up and perform this trick.

I already knew that, for many years, my old man was a pilot instructor and flight examiner, flying Canberras. He had countless old comrades and acquaintances that he had met in the service, many of whom he had actually trained at one time or another. Night training flights were a standard part of the instruction programme, an essential part of the military role to be able to be airborne at any time and under any weather conditions.

He reminded me that there was a three-man crew for these early-version Canberras – a pilot, a co-pilot and a navigator-bombardier. The aircraft were equipped with twin controls, highly suitable for pilot training – indeed, Dad had done his own jet training in one of these aircraft not so long ago.

My father explained that, on the night in question, the routine pre-mission briefing for what was originally a standard night training flight was unexpectedly interrupted by the Wing-Commander himself. The Wingco was a RAF officer of the old school, right the way down to the ginger handlebar moustache. He had served with distinction during the war and was widely regarded as one who did not suffer fools gladly.

On this occasion, the Wingco seemed extremely annoyed at the disruption and the sudden change of plan, though my father thought he had detected an undercurrent of nervousness uncharacteristic of the Old Man.

The Wingco was accompanied by three other men, two of whom were not wearing any kind of uniform but nevertheless had the bearing of military men. Dad never did discover the origins of these two men, but he strongly suspected that they were from the US Central Intelligence Agency. At that time, CIA pilots were required to resign their military commission at the time of joining the Agency, a process wittily known as "sheep-dipping".

The third man was in the uniform of the US Air Force. This in itself was not unusual; the RAF maintained a close collaboration with the Americans at this time. In those Cold War days, there were American airbases all over Southern and Eastern England, many of which were reputed to house air-delivered strategic nuclear weapons. As a child, I clearly remember disparaging remarks being make by my father, when passing by in the car, about the bra-less anti-war protesters at Greenham Common with their "ban the bomb" slogans and CND posters.

Of course, in spite of the close collaboration, there was a certain amount of friendly (and occasionally not-so friendly) rivalry between the air forces. My Dad summarised it thus: the Americans considered the RAF tiny and under-equipped to the point of irrelevance, while the Brits found the erstwhile colonials both arrogant and unwilling to take risks.

The USAF officer took immediate charge of the training briefing, leaving the Wingco fuming at being required to do nothing other than to lend his authority to the instructions being issued by the American.

The trainee pilot was quietly but firmly instructed to return to barracks. His place on the mission was taken by an unsmiling man my father was instructed only to refer to as Rex, one of the officer's near-silent companions in mufti. The navigator was retained, although it turned out that his role was very limited, since they wouldn't be flying very far. Dad said that he was killed a few years later in a freak accident, one which was never satisfactorily explained.

At the time, the Canberra was one of the few aircraft capable of flying extremely high – well above the heights achieved by modern commercial jets. My father pointed out that this aircraft was designed as a Cold War bomber, capable of delivering nuclear weapons to foreign capitals whether they wanted them or not.

Early versions of the aircraft had a service ceiling of 48,000 feet, but in the late fifties, Canberra variants set a series of height records, in one case in excess of 70,000 feet. In fact, I understand from Dad that the official maximum height for late-model aircraft is still officially restricted information.

Of course, there were a very few other aircraft then capable of reaching these kinds of heights. Dad had heard rumours of a classified aircraft he later discovered to be the Lockheed U-2 spy plane, which was by then in service with the CIA, flying intelligence missions over potentially hostile foreign soil. The U-2 could travel higher and further than the Canberra, but had a reputation of being tricky to fly and with difficult – even dangerous – handling in poor weather conditions.

The point is that there was very little else up there – still isn't, really. All modern subsonic commercial traffic is at 40,000 feet or below and, now that Concorde has been grounded, anything you see at that height is likely to be military in origin.

Dad's first thought, given the haste and obvious secrecy surrounding this mission, was that there was some military emergency, some reconnaissance that was urgently needed, and that for some reason the U-2 could not be used. But that aircraft was not equipped with cameras – although Canberras were used as flying camera platforms well into the twenty-first century – and, from that height, the human eye is more-or-less useless as a way of spotting anything on the ground.

The mystery man Rex was clearly familiar with modern military aircraft. He also made it clear that Dad was to concentrate on flying the crate while he gave directions over the intercom to the navigator, confirming the directions to set a direct course to over-fly central London, climbing to 48,000 feet and making best possible speed. He also instructed my father to keep a close lookout.

My father was a very experienced pilot, having spent at least thirty years of his life flying various craft around this planet. He also had exceptionally good eyesight. Even in later life, well into his sixties, he was more able to spot objects in the sky and to provide an instant aircraft identification much more quickly than I could ever manage.

So it was no surprise that it was Dad who first spotted the multi-coloured lights in the sky, flying on what he thought was a roughly parallel course. The laconic instruction from the mysterious American came over the intercom: "Head towards the object at eleven o'clock."

At first, my father thought the other aircraft was only a mile or two away, but the true size of the other craft soon became apparent after some minutes flying towards it at 600-plus knots. As Dad described it, it was as large as an ocean-going liner, circular in overall shape and smoothly rounded at the periphery. The bodywork was a deep black, but there were lights streaming from multiple openings or windows all the way around the disk.

It was completely unclear how the strange craft could possibly stay in the air at all. It was making no attempt to get away from the following Canberra. Despite flying at nearly full throttle, Dad reported that he got the strangest sensation that the mysterious flying machine was merely ambling along, deliberately allowing itself to be observed.

Now, it's difficult to see any kind of facial reaction inside a flying helmet and oxygen mask. Looking around at his companions, Dad reported that the navigator's eyes were wide in shock. By contrast, Rex seemed unsurprised but his eyes seemed to have a slightly manic gleam of exultation, reflecting the lights from the instrument panel.

The mysterious American had come aboard equipped with several cameras and a powerful torch. As Dad flew in formation with the giant craft, under and over – 'like a tom-tit on a round of beef', as my old man put it – the American shot off reel after reel of film. He also shone the torch through the canopy; they were flying close enough so that the beam of light could clearly been seen passing over the smooth black hull.

After a few minutes, the other craft dimmed its lights to almost nothing, with just an eerie blue glow remaining around some of the orifices which Dad took to be its engines. Rex's twang came over the intercom, breaking into Dad's thoughts.

"OK, I've seen enough. Break off and descend to 45,000. Head west."

Dad complied immediately. Looking behind, he could see that the mysterious craft seemed to darken and then recede into the distance. It was only after a moment that Dad realised that the machine was going straight up. It disappeared after only a few seconds.

There was an instant of strange stillness in the cabin, despite the ever-present roar of the engines. The moment was broken by Rex's voice, instructing my father to perform the strange manoeuvre I described earlier, the significance of which he did not appreciate until he heard about the reports in the those 'sensationalist newspapers.'

Why? What was the purpose of the ruse? Dad wasn't sure, but I'm convinced it was what these days we would call 'plausible deniability.' It was a provable matter of record that, yes, a military aircraft was flying over London on that day, on a course which corresponded to any sighting which might have been reported, and which had genuinely been practising 'unconventional manoeuvres' which might have confused an observer.

In the post-mission de-brief, it was made very clear that the RAF crew were not supposed to tell anyone about this, not now, and not ever. There were appeals to patriotism, which rankled a bit in the presence of so many Americans, and there were vague threats, not least of which was a blunt reminder of the provisions of the Official Secrets Act.

Just at that moment, Mother appeared at the kitchen door to summon us for dinner, effectively terminating the topic of conversation. Dad and I never spoke of the UFO incident again.

Dad had continued his flying career for many years, first with the RAF and more recently with a number of commercial organisations before heart problems detected by the stringent tests that are required of all commercial pilots forced him to retire. Since then, he has lived the quiet life, cultivating his garden and his little circle of cronies, and occasionally acting as a chauffeur for funeral companies.

As far as I can see, his only rebellious act was writing that autobiography, laboriously typing up his stories and anecdotes for what is likely to be, I'm afraid, a frankly miniscule audience. I don't suppose that the book will actually be published now. But I do know that he also vaguely mentioned something about lights in the sky in the same chapter where he reports his antics, although he notes that there was probably a "mundane explanation to this phenomenon." It was probably a huge mistake to write this stuff down at all.

My father died very suddenly, only last week. The funeral is tomorrow. My mother is distraught, inconsolable. I'm pretty upset about it myself, as I'm sure you can imagine. I'll miss him.

In one of her more coherent moments, Mother expressed her surprise at Dad's sudden death. She said that he had remained fit and active, walking the dog twice a day and keeping the kitchen garden in good order. (I remember those runner beans lined up with military precision.) He had been watching his diet after his open-heart surgery, and stimulating his brain by contributing to his Rotary Club meetings, engaging with his circle of friends, and tackling crosswords and puzzle books.

So, despite his age, his death came as a considerable surprise, especially to his GP. I spoke to his doctor while I was helping to tidy up his remaining financial affairs. The quack said to me privately that he could see no reason why he should have passed away, but there had been some subtle but distinct official pressure to avoid an inquest, so he felt he had to enter 'death from natural causes' on the death certificate.

Which leads me to a really important question – does anyone know that he talked to me about the UFO incident? Now I'm looking over my shoulder all the time. Are they out there, coming for me too?

Diary of a Deserter

by Annemarie Neary

They are taking Oskar to Ireland. To visit his granddaughter Ute who makes pots, and sometimes cheese. Oskar has always liked Ute, an awkward customer like himself. Even as a kid she was a spiky little thing, a thorn in Sophie's side.

At Frankfurt airport, he slips away while Sophie and Karl argue over which perfume to buy Ute, who never wears the stuff. Oskar knows exactly what he's looking for. Writing would take too long and besides, he has always liked gadgets. He likes them even better now they're smaller, smoother, steelier. He lets the dictaphone sit snug in his palm and tries to remember the last time he used one. The young fellow who sells him the machine is patronising, disinterested.

When he rejoins them at the departure gate, Sophie is biting the corner of her lower lip the way her mother used to do. Karl has his precious Tag Heuer clapped to his ear. Oskar pats the breast pocket and, inside, the dictaphone. It gives him a pinch of satisfaction to have a new secret.

Once they're airborne he thinks he might weep for joy. It was a grey day down there in Frankfurt, but up here it's radiant. He smiles at the hostess when she hands him a paper cup of hot tea, then a waxy pyramid of milk and some rectangles of sugar. Sophie and Karl are reading thick paperbacks with gold embossed titles. He offers chocolate from his inside pocket, but they shake their heads and return to their books. The drone of the engines is like a lullaby and soon Oskar nods off, his tea undrunk. When he wakes they are clipping back the tabletops already, and he is suddenly sad. The descent always had that effect on him, in the old days. He always hated to leave the sky.

In the terminal, the carousel starts, then stops again. By the time the luggage chugs past them, Oskar is tired. He sits in the back of the hire car as they drive along winding roads flanked on either side by high banks. He tries to guess how far they are from the ragged inlets that trail off the end of the map. When at last they arrive at the cottage, he allows Sophie to help him out of the car. He goes straight to bed, and sleeps without dreams.

91

In the morning, he wakes to wan light and birds; more birds than seem possible. He gets up, but there is nothing to see past a line of hedge under a scrap of sky. There is no sound from Sophie and Karl, so he starts to unpack. He takes out the present he bought Ute in a Turkish shop around the corner from his apartment; a beautiful little clay pipe. Sophie will disapprove, but no matter. He places it on the window, then removes the dictaphone from its box and inserts the batteries. He sits back on the bed and closes his eyes until the pictures start to form again in his head. When he has decided how to start, he takes a deep breath and begins to tell the story he has kept for Ute.

That lunchtime, they go to the pub where she is working part-time behind the bar. She comes bouncing out the moment she sees them. Makes straight for Oskar. That's my girl. When she speaks, he notices that her German is a little off-key. Just a little. He wonders how soon his own would have faltered, had he stayed.

'How are you, you old rascal?' she says, punching him in the solar plexus.

'Careful, Ute.' Good old Sophie.

'Oh, he's solid steel,' Ute says, punching him again. Not so hard this time. Her hair is purple. She likes purple, he remembers. She is brown and purple, peat and heather like her pots. He catches her hand and gives her the present. She rips off the paper and waves the little meerschaum at her friend behind the bar. Then she takes his face in her hands and kisses it. One. Two. Three. A man with a crumpled mouth looks up for a minute then dips his head back to his pint.

'So, Ute,' Oskar asks, 'what have you planned for me?'

'I'm taking you for a walk this afternoon. I'll call for you when I finish my shift. Take you up on the cliff.'

'That would be lovely,' Sophie says.

'Oh, I'm not taking you two.' Ute squeezes his hand. 'It's just me and the old man.'

Tape One – May 14 1999

My name is Oskar Muller. But, of course, you know that. Born Berlin 1919, in the autumn. You told me that made me a Libran, whatever that is. I have been married twice. Generally speaking, I don't count the first time. It was brief and corroding, like an efficient poison. I first got married a year or so after the war ended. To a girl from Bremen. It lasted no more than a month or two and I remember her no better than the others for having married her.

I met Rosa, your grandmother, a couple of years later. She would have hated your hair, by the way. In those days, we tried not to think too much about the past. By the time we were able to cast the occasional glance over our shoulders, it was too late really to come to terms with it. We left that task to your generation. As for our own children, they showed surprisingly little curiosity about how life had been for us during the war. Rolf jumped to his own conclusions. He never asked anything. He just assumed I must have done something dreadful. Maybe that's why he went off to Africa. To flay himself for what he feared I might have done.

Oh Ute, you were always trouble Poor Sophie was in despair most of the time. You were incomprehensible to her. No sooner had she told herself that she'd found a tree that you would never manage to climb, than you'd be stuck at the top like a wild kitten. I've always liked you for it. After two earnest children it's satisfying to find a chip off the old block.

I wasn't surprised when you told them you were off. Opting out, that's what you said. What were you, sixteen? Sophie almost managed to catch up with you, then lost you again on the edge of an autobahn just as you hopped into that lorry. Off to make pots in Ireland. Poor old Karl, he didn't know what to tell the boys at that place he went riding. All their kids were thinking of sensible careers, war-proof things like physiotherapy. 'Luckily, she's not without talent.' I heard him telling some banker chap one day. Not without talent.

You know I'm turning eighty soon. The biggie, Sophie calls it. 'For your eightieth,' she said, 'let's go somewhere completely new. Somewhere you've never been. Why don't we all go and visit Ute in Ireland.' I almost laughed out loud. Sophie loves so much to control everything. Just look at what she did to the honeysuckle. Sometimes

I just can't resist leaving her in the dark. So, here we are in Ireland and your mother has not the slightest idea that I've ever been here before.

Later, Ute leads them to her house, riding on her bicycle in front of the car, weaving all over the road. Sophie is clutching the steering wheel with her driving gloves on. Karl is asleep. The place is below the level of the road; half hidden behind a high bank of nettles. She shares it with a young man with a beard and a fisherman's sweater. She says he's a poet and maybe the eyes do look a little mad, always flicking up to the clouds like he's lost something up there. His name is Finn and he touches her a lot. Even the sharp prickles on her head seem to relax a little when he is there. Oskar's little sparrow is in love.

Tape One – Continued – May 15 1999

I notice that paint has come into fashion in Ireland now. The village has a pink house next to the yellow one, which rubs shoulders with the blue. None of that when I was here. No colour in the man-made things at all. They left all that to their God, to whom, I must say, they were most attentive. Ireland back then was grey, hazy, undefined. It was so strange, after Germany, where everything was sharp and crisp, all black and white and red.

Oskar is walking on the cliff road with Ute. They don't say much. Then, just as he's wondering if she has listened to the first part of the tape yet, she leads him off the usual road. They cut off at the crossroads and take the low road to the beach. Ute sits on a rock skimming stones while Oskar props himself up beside her on his shooting stick. He thinks how they must make for a strange sight. Ute all cropped and dyed and himself bald as an eagle. That's when she asks him to tell her more.

94

I was interned here for over four years with other airmen, a few mariners too. We were in a place called the Curragh. G-Camp. The day I was brought in, they drove me there in the back of a car. I was dressed in civilian clothes and it felt like a Sunday outing. When we arrived at the camp, I was shown into a room where an Irish officer with a ruddy complexion told me to sit myself down. Even though I hadn't planned to, I told him the truth. That I'd jumped.

"Good lad," he said to me.

To him, it seemed a reasonable thing to do, I think. To desert from the Luftwaffe. I wondered at the time how neutral he thought he was. He just licked his pencil and wrote down what I said.

"We'll keep that under our hats," he said then. "Best to keep the other German lads in the dark on that one."

So, throughout my time in the camp, I wasn't Oskar Muller at all. They signed me in as Konrad Ritter. Just in case by any chance someone there had heard of a deserter with my name.

The camp wasn't so bad. There was plenty of food, although not a lot of variety. Potatoes and meat and eggs and bacon and cabbage and tea and sugar and milk and bread. And that was it, really. Time out, yes. Tennis matches, a little gardening. The cinema and dances in the local towns. But I was never really at ease there. I always worried that someone would guess the truth. Or, worse, that someone knew all along and was waiting for the right time to pounce.

At the end of that first week, I was told that I had a German visitor, an official fellow from the Embassy in Dublin. I was barely inside the room when the voice came at me like an assault. I couldn't see him very well, the sun was in my eyes and he was just a shadow at the window.

"A pity," he said, "you couldn't have managed to stay out of trouble a little longer. You must have the Irish fooled or they'd have sent you to Athlone with the other spies."

I played along. If it was politic to be a spy, then that's what I'd be. I told him I came from Dresden. My friend, Joachim, had told me so much about Dresden that it was easy for me to talk plausibly of life there in a superficial sort of a way. I lived in Joachim's house, went to his school, met my girlfriends in the same parks and cafés. I was just lucky, I suppose, that there was no one to contradict me.

All the same, there was always the chance that someone would recognise me. In my nightmares, it was always a member of my own crew. I'd barely given the crew another thought until arriving at G-camp, but now I thought of them every day. Every day, I wondered if they'd made it home or if I'd left them vulnerable. Caught in some spotlight over England, had they missed the extra gunner?

I formed comradely enough friendships with some of the men in the camp but at heart there was always a gulf between us because, of course, everything I pretended to be was false. The airmen took me under their wing on the basis that, whatever else I was, at least I was better than the sailors who had to be dragged from the sea by the Irish like drowned rats.

Oskar tries not to show how delighted he is to be free of Sophie and Karl. Ute has arranged a cookery course for her parents at Ballymaloe.

'Now we'll have no disturbance,' she whispers to him. 'I want to know everything.'

She drives him out beyond Kinsale and they sit in her little car, munching on Sophie's hummous sandwiches with those irritating bits of weed that get stuck between his teeth.

'I haven't told you about Elsa Frankel,' he says. 'My lovely Elsa.'

By evening, Oskar has said all that he can say. He talks about Elsa and her music. How she loved Chopin. Elsa by the lake, in the woods. Lovely, Jewish Elsa. He explains how Elsa is sent to Belfast on a Kindertransport. He talks of the last time he saw her, a year before war broke out. He talks of his conscription. How he loved to fly, just not for them. How he couldn't help imagining what happened in the dark places below when they dropped their bombs. Couldn't block it out. And then, the day he jumped. The moment he realised there would be just enough time to reach the hatch before anyone could do anything to stop him.

That night, he sleeps badly. This time, it's not his shoulder or the grinding of his heart. It's that he simply cannot remember Elsa's face. The young man he once was would never have believed such a thing possible. He would have been horrified to lose that face.

The next day, Ute doesn't go to work. She doesn't say much at breakfast, but he notices how she is gentler with him. Quieter. She packs a picnic and they go off in her little car. After a half an hour or so they turn inland from a little harbour. A little further on, she stops and they walk a half kilometre or so off the road through a tunnel of fuchsia. At the end of the tunnel, there is a stile and, beyond that, a field where wild flowers surround a stone circle. Ute seems to find the profusion of wild flowers to be evidence of some spiritual richness in the land itself. It amuses him, this faith in nature.

The fact that Elsa was Jewish is everything to Ute. It seems to absolve him of the responsibility of his generation. She refuses to believe that, when the war ended, he simply went back home to Berlin and made no further effort to find her. She cannot accept that he allowed that to happen.

'But I knew,' he says, 'that I must leave that all behind me.'

'After it all came out about the things that had happened, did you not have the urge to tell people about how you tried to find her?'

'Tell them what?'

'Well, tell them that you didn't agree with all that, that you wanted to change things?'

'Change things? By running away? I did nothing to change things.'

'You wanted to, though, didn't you? I mean clearly you didn't support what they did.'

'Perhaps, if I hadn't known Elsa, I would have been the same as the others. Have you ever heard of a hausjude, Ute?'

She shook her head.

'Even the most rabid anti-semite would have known someone they considered not quite as bad as the others. Not quite typical. A kindly shopkeeper, perhaps. Who's to say that Elsa Frankel was not just that, my own personal hausjude?'

'But you stepped outside it all. You threw yourself out of a plane, for God's sake. Just after bombing Belfast. As soon as you knew they were travelling back over neutral airspace, you jumped. You couldn't stand it. You had to find Elsa Frankel.'

'Maybe I just didn't like war. Maybe I wanted to sleep in a soft bed for a change. Get away from the smell of men cooped up together. Don't assume that I was any better than the others. Perhaps I was just more fortunate because I knew they were wrong.'

She looks glum. 'Let's go,' she says.

For a moment he wonders, too, what explanation there could be for the profusion of wildflowers in this meadow. Flowers don't grow like this in Germany any more. Not these days. They've been crowded out by supermarkets and petrol stations. Suddenly he feels rooted to this place, with its ancient stones and stubborn wildflowers.

Sophie and Karl are late back from their day at the cookery school. They are curious as to what an old man could have to say all day to his granddaughter. Sophie seems a little unnerved. That night, Oskar hears Ute downstairs, tapping away on her computer. The noise of it keeps him awake so he gives in to wakefulness and takes out his dictaphone. He wonders if they can hear him, mumbling away to himself. If they can they'll probably think he's finally lost his marbles.

Tape One – Continued May 17 1999

It was just after Easter. Just after Joachim was killed. My mind was turned inside out by his death. The bus picked us up at the hotel at about 7.30 or so, to bring us out to the airfield for the final briefing. We didn't know for sure until then whether we would go or not. Whether it would be Belfast. The Etappe, we called it, the staging post. I don't think I really made my mind up to jump until the very last moment. Years later, I was watching something on television with my grandchildren. You may even have been there yourself, Ute. It was a comedy film and they had a way of making a drink seem to pour itself back into a glass, a custard pie fly back off a face. It came back to me then, sitting on a couch in Sophie's house watching television with her children. As soon as I jumped out of that plane, I wished that I could fly upwards again and land back where I had started.

98

The next morning, getting out of bed is an effort. When he arrives downstairs, Ute is already there. She is like a little current of electricity energising them all. She has already been down at the pottery and has dropped by to leave them in some fresh bread and milk and a copy of The Irish Times. In the kitchen, Sophie is mixing a variety of grains into some natural yoghurt. She might feed that bilge to Karl, but Oskar is having none of it He pours himself some coffee and carries it into the front room that overlooks the sea. Ute follows him, and closes the door behind her.

'I have such exciting news for you,' she says. 'You're not going to believe who I've tracked down.' The girl is speaking as though it was all just a soap opera.

'Why?' he asks, but Ute ignores him.

'Wouldn't you love to know how her life turned out. Where she went. Did she marry? Were there children? Oh, a hundred questions.'

He places his hand on her forearm. 'I jumped. I didn't risk my neck in sabotage or revolt. I jumped. I don't even know now whether I did it for Elsa Frankel. I did it to get away. What had I hoped for? I hadn't even thought about it. Besides, I was arrested almost as soon as my feet touched the ground. I had no chance of finding her anyway.'

Ute ignores him. 'I'm sure it's the same person. Got to be. A pianist. Right age, give or take. German Jew, ended up in New York.'

'No.' he says. 'No more.' She flinches, and then he regrets being so firm with her. 'I'd rather leave it be.'

Tape Two – May 18, 1999

When the time came to leave, they gave us next to no notice at all. Even those who had local girlfriends were marched onto the train and sent packing as soon as the war ended. Of course, I still wanted to find Elsa but there was no chance of that.

It was a long way home. First, a boat across the Irish Sea, then a sealed train through England to the coast, then another ferry across to Ostend. From there, we got a train to Brussels where they held us for a couple of weeks. Everyone said there was no point in going back to Berlin, that there was nothing there. But I had to see it again.

It was utter devastation. Little huddles of people hid in the ruins of bomb damaged buildings, just trying to survive. I am so glad now that Joachim didn't live to see what happened to his beloved Dresden. I had no idea where my family was. I did find one or two school friends, girls who had stayed at home. Our own place was completely destroyed. It was a long time before there was any system set up to try and find relatives but eventually I did find Vati, sleeping rough. Mutti had been killed in an air raid, he told me. He didn't know what had happened to Emmi. You know who Emmi was, Ute? My sister. My only sister. The last Vati heard, she'd gone with her husband Reinhard on a family posting to a KZ over in the East. She hadn't come back. Vati was cagey about it all, said he'd had no idea what was happening in the KZs. I wanted to believe him, for Emmi's sake as much as for his own, but I couldn't. I saw him once or twice only after that. The last time I went to find him at his usual spot he had disappeared.

Elsa, she ran through my life like a red thread, Ute. Like a red thread. I would love to have seen her one more time. Even just once. From a distance, even. All my life I've been looking for her. Running away from her pale copies, choosing the women who least resemble her. And now you find her in an evening.

It's the day of their departure, and Oskar has taken his final walk here. Stiffly, he walks, the same route each day since he arrived. He closes the front door quickly to keep out the wind, then takes fifteen paces to the base of the hill. A sherbet green field angles sharply to the left like it's propped up against the sky. Plump black and white cows clutch at its surface. To the right, long grass slopes to the sea and, all around, the hedgerows are rippling with flowers. He doesn't know many of their names but one flower is everywhere. It is red with purple droplets and it spots the hedgerows like some spectacular affliction. He's been told that it's the fuchsia.

Oskar walks close enough to the edge of the cliff to see the spray tease the rocks below. The voice in his head that is Sophie, says stop this now. After that, the walk loses its charm and he turns around on the pivot of his stick and heads back towards the cottage where Sophie and Karl will be waiting. His absence will make them anxious about missing their flight. Sophie will flap. Karl will examine his Tag Heuer. Ute, though, will understand. She understands everything now.

Outside the rented cottage, he sees the car that Ute uses, the Irishman's little car with the battered red number plate. Ute has been to the city. She has brought something for Oskar to take back to Germany with him. A record. Never came out on CD. American. Old recording. They wouldn't have it only it's Field's Nocturnes. Irish people like their Field, and when you boil it down there aren't that many recordings. So, yes, they told her, as a matter of fact, they do have it. A minor label. Elsa Frankel plays Field. 1960. New York. The poet has a record player and Ute has brought that too.

She watches him as she puts it on. He doesn't recognise the music. He just remembers Chopin. It's like Chopin, he thinks. She hands him the sleeve and he reads the few lines printed on the back. "Elsa Frankel was born in Berlin on 27 April 1922. An only child, her parents perished in the Nazi holocaust. Elsa herself escaped to Belfast thanks to the Kindertransports. She lived briefly in Dublin after the war before emigrating to the United States with her Irish husband."

The music drenches his prune of a heart until the loss of her seems too much to bear. Her face is a crisp snapshot in his head and then it fades again. Can an old man cry for the young man he was once? Then, Ute's voice in his ear, her arm around his shoulder. 'You see. It was for her. You tried.'

Sophie is there now too. A look of horror when she sees his face like that. She offers pills for pain, pills for the heart. Karl is checking his Tag Heuer. Oskar is thinking of the sky and how soothing it will be to be to soar above the clouds, the young man he was once, with Elsa.

Late for Work

by Carolann Samuels

Only one of the CDs in the pile appealed to her, and she had already played it twice. On the radio were a breathless announcer talking about failing standards in schools, reports of death and corruption in Zimbabwe, a repeat of a programme she had listened to earlier in the week while driving to meet a potential new client, and soothing classical music. She did not want to be soothed, she did not want to be jolted into saving the world; she wanted to move from this place, to drive to work, or to go home again. How long had she been sitting in this traffic jam? No mention of this one on the radio – only the M25 and the M4 and important roads around London seemed to matter.

It was remarkable how calm people were staying; around her were lorries, family-filled cars towing caravans, and commuters like her. A few drivers and passengers left their vehicles and walked about, making instant friends with others on their way to the ferry, before the long drive to the south of France, or Italy, or Germany. She could see that some families were in convoy, and they ran up and down the road importantly moving things from one caravan to another, or locating urgently needed boxes from their boots, belongings from their baggage.

Greyness hung over the landscape, painting everything with subdued tones. She noticed that the favourite colour for cars these days seemed to be grey, too. Caravans tended to be white, though, with names like Sprite Surfer, Pennine Pullman, Eccles Elan. Bicycles strapped to the back reminded her of childhood holidays when they would pack up picnics and head off for the day on their bikes. She remembered the freedom they felt as they rode along country roads and farm tracks, feeling as though they were miles away from their parents and discovering places for the first time; feeling daring, but not without a touch of fear. Most times they would have eaten their lunch by eleven o'clock and be home in time to eat another with Mum.

Never before had she had the opportunity to examine the central reservation so closely, the grasses and the low growing plant with an insignificant flower, and she wondered how many insects braved its inhospitality. The roads of her childhood did not have central reservations, but there were grasses and insects a-plenty. She was conscious that this sort of knowledge now belonged to others, no longer to her. She tried to take a mental photograph of the flower, to look it up when she got home, to re-learn what she had once known.

She had been watching the black cloud moving closer and closer, and wondered if it would empty its rain onto the snake of vehicles in front of her. It did; sending mothers in thin T-shirts and men in baseball caps scurrying back to the shelter of their cars.

She resolved to clean her car out next weekend. It was strewn with sweet papers, old lists of directions, a London A to Z with a bulk of pages missing, and bedraggled notes from the university course she was taking. The interior was dusty, too. The car was a method of going from one place to another: there were always many more urgent things to do than clean the car, and once she had cleaned the house, there was little time or inclination to start on the car.

The drive to work took about thirty minutes. She calculated that the earliest she would get to the office today would be midday, and she would have to leave again at two-thirty to collect Eleanor from school – not enough time to complete the report that she had been asked to submit a week ago, and catch up on her to-do list.

She found a chamois leather, stiff with disuse, in the shelf under the steering wheel, and, releasing the seat belt, she moistened it with water from a plastic bottle and leaned over and cleaned the inside of the windscreen. Some of Eleanor's fingermarks had been there her for some time, annoying her, and she never noticed them until she was driving.

An empty carrier bag had been irritating her for about a week, it seemed to have a life of its own as it roamed about the interior of the car, like a zoo animal in a cage. She wondered what was in the glove compartment. In its depths she found a sandwich whose sell-by date she chose not to read. There was also an old pair of spectacles from a holiday in France, which must have been two years ago (French law says drivers must carry spare spectacles when driving their roads). Eleanor's library book that had been missing for three months emerged from its depths; that had involved fines amounting to more than the cost of two new books. She found some money-off supermarket vouchers – again out of date. More promising was half a packet of crystallised fruit that looked edible. They would give her a sugar lift.

The car in front was rolling forwards; she did the same. Rain hammered on the roof. Was this what being in prison feels like?

Her mobile rang: Eleanor's father. He could not meet Eleanor from school on Friday as he usually did, and he was going away for the weekend. Could she explain to their daughter? That would mean getting someone else to take Dad to his hospital appointment, and re-arranging the promised shopping trip with Mum on Saturday. They would all be disappointed; but she was not unhappy to be relieved of the hospital run. There seemed to be so many visits to the hospital these days, and although she would never bother her Dad about it, each one reminded her of the time she spent there caring for Eleanor, in the desperate days after her birth.

As soon as she entered the hospital's automatic doors, the world would change. It became a place of uniforms, trolleys with drugs, trolleys with patients' notes, trolleys with newspapers. It became a place of beds and sheets and tests. A place of waiting, waiting for news. A place of bad coffee, cheerful nurses, sombre doctors. A place not always hospitable.

Some sugar dropped onto her suit trousers. She brushed it off absent-mindedly, making the mark worse.

A young man in jeans and jumper emerged from a van a few yards in front, and was crossing over to a wooded area on the other side of the road. By the time he returned five minutes later they had all moved a couple of hundred yards further forward, his companions cheered him on as he sprinted back to their van, trying, but failing, to miss the next rain shower.

She stared at the wood. She had not paid it much attention on her drives to and from work, and she wondered how far it stretched and what was on the other side. Mature oak trees grew alongside ash, sycamore and dogwood. A sparrowhawk was diving and bouncing across the treetops. She recognised a lapwing, surprised at how the name came to her. For a moment she remembered herself in the woods with her Girl Guide friends, listening to Captain pointing out the birds flying around the scenery of her childhood.

A movement at ground level caught her attention; a glint and a flash, eyes catching the light; too low down for a person. She glanced away, then another movement made her look again. As her eyes focused on the woods, the darkness drew her mind inwards, telling of mystery, of sanctuary. A fox came into view, his brush held straight out behind him; he stopped and looked directly towards her, before turning and trotting back into the woods.

She switched off the radio, to which she had not been listening for the past ten minutes or so; emptied her handbag of rubbish and put it into the carrier bag; tidied up all the bits of paper and sweet wrappers into the bag; dusted across the dashboard and instrument panel with an old tissue; took out her lipstick and applied it, looking in the rear view mirror.

She packed her bag again, zipped it up, and put it on the floor by the front passenger seat.

Then she looked at the road around her – she was boxed in by the traffic and the crash barrier. She did not want to flatten the flowers which had doggedly defied the traffic fumes, so there was no room to move the car.

She felt her breath catch in her chest, and became aware of her heart's beat, which seemed almost audible, almost as though it were coming from somewhere else, someone else.

There was a brief hesitation before she opened the car door, her palm damp on the handle. Closing the door almost soundlessly, she turned to the far side of the dual carriageway and stepped over the crash barrier and the central verge. She made her way across the other side to the wooded area. Behind her rose the sound of car horns and voices above the noise of moving traffic.

She took the path where she had seen the fox.

The Fire in Her Belly

by Adam E Smith

Barely a second after Mary knocked on the door of the hotel suite, a young man snapped it open and bellowed with welcoming laughter.

'Miss Mary,' he proclaimed, ushering her in with a flourish of wide gestures. 'A pleasure to meet you. You are the last interviewer of the day.'

His loose clothes reminded Mary of her last trip to Kenya: her host had worn a billowing shirt and slim trousers which terminated well above his dusty sandals. As the fellow before her now introduced himself as Charles, the bishop's assistant, Mary shook his hand and studied his cheap but polished leather shoes which shone like his teeth. 'Please, Miss Mary, wait here.'

Charles ducked behind a heavy door. Mary glanced around the suite, breathing in the aroma from the fresh flowers and wondering whether she had ever before stood on carpet so thick.

'Miss Park, it is a pleasure,' said Bishop James Ngugi, striding towards her, Charles hovering behind him.

Mary turned and smiled. 'Bishop,' she said, accepting his hand.

Before she could add anything or retract her hand from the bishop's mighty shake, he boomed, 'My gosh – you are tall – like me hahahaha!'

Mary joined him in laughter. 'Somewhere in history, maybe we're related,' she joked. The bishop's laughter vaulted around the luxurious room like a wild animal.

Following Charles's exaggerated directions, they moved into an anteroom.

'I have to tell you,' the bishop said, easing himself into an armchair, 'after speaking with all the journalists, it is a relief to speak with a student.'

Mary jostled herself into the armchair opposite his, noticing that he had not maintained eye contact once he was seated. Instead, he examined his robe, smoothing it across his lap.

'I'm sure the interview style of an academic will be different to that of a journalist,' she promised. He nodded but seemed a little preoccupied, like a politician collecting his thoughts before an important press conference. 'Not sure which is easier though,' she added.

'No comment.' The bishop exploded with riotous laughter at his joke. His cheeks bounced joyfully for a while but then his face drooped and became sombre. Mary took that as a signal and gave him a brief introduction to her PhD, describing it cautiously as an exploration of Christianity in a post-colonial East Africa. The bishop listened like a doctor, calculating clues in order to make a diagnosis. She liked having the attention of this important man and had to stop herself from saying anything more about her project. As they chatted about her research trips to Kenya, Mary made sure not to imply that, for the past three months, her project had remained still, like a construction site where the investment had dried up.

Her mind felt anything but frozen: daily it swung back and forth between theology and the banality of her life. It was not that she found her life dull, just that the formula of modern existence – supermarkets, buses, boxy offices – fell far behind the grand implications of religion. And now, for the first time, she had discovered a connection between the two. Her stomach lurched as she thought of Stu, who didn't have a clue what was going on with her. He probably wouldn't even notice until she turned up with a baby in eight months' time. And even then it would have to cry loud to drag him out of the cosmos and down to Earth.

But she could not be too hard on him: although she understood little of his academic focus on physics and the universe, she loved him for it. He used his knowledge to 'fill in the blanks', as he put it, between her field and his. Their explorations lasted long into the night. A cosmologist had a lot to say about spirituality, it seemed. But she was not sure whether he would see the fibres that now tied the three of them together. She had not even given him the chance to react.

Mary pushed the guilty thought aside and concentrated on the bishop. As he spoke, she watched his enormous, shovel-like hands shift from the chair's arms to his lap and back again. It was too soon to say whether she liked him as a person but she knew already that he was the symbol her PhD needed. The top edge of his gold-rimmed spectacles obscured his eyes. Although Mary found this diverting, it gave her the confidence that he would inject into her thesis the adrenalin and controversy it needed.

'I love Britons,' he was saying, glancing at the sturdy furniture and inhaling. 'So studious. The British like to think. We Kenyans are the same. Inside, we are all the same. But we are not foolish, you know. We had to kick the British out' – his right hand flipped dismissively – 'but we knew that they had brought us a lot. Jesus Christ was the most, the most important.'

While the bishop orated as if to hundreds, Mary made a few notes about his rapid breathing method. It made him sound not short of breath but as if he could never get enough air.

'How is a postcolonial Anglican Church of Kenya different to colonial Anglicanism?' she asked.

The bishop tilted his head. Tapping his bulging chin with a chubby finger, he gave her question some thought. Then he pointed the active digit into the air and answered.

'The British came to chop up our land like butchers and apply their economic framework,' he said, 'leaving many ordinary Kenyans powerless. At the same time the British set up churches and taught us to read the Bible. The single most important transformative act of colonialism. A postcolonial ACK, then, uses this foundation in order to heal and in some cases reverse those other British policies.'

The bishop's sound bites would have been perfect for a feature writer. Indeed, the bishop looked pleased with himself, presumably as he had done after each of the ten times he had said that very speech that same day. However, Mary needed a more theologically based answer. She wanted to know what God had to do with reclaiming Kenya.

'How exactly is Kenya's church different today?'

'For a start, our clergymen are Kenyan.'

'Earlier, you said that 'inside we are all the same'. What does it matter from whom a follower hears the message?'

The bishop chuckled like an exasperated teacher. 'Oh Miss Park, it matters a great deal. Hearing Christ's message of love from a person who is waging war on your land and your family is very different from hearing it from a person who is loving you.'

This answer satisfied Mary as a point well made. She smiled despite herself, but did not look at the bishop. Her smile would have pleased him too much. Instead, she became solemn and asked him about his personal spiritual background. His eyes sparkled and his

108

lips trembled with anticipation, as if she'd just set down before him a delectable steak.

The bishop painted a picture of a poor farmer's boy in central Kenya, scurrying about at the foot of the mountain and poking goats with sticks. School had enriched his soul – and did she know that he was the only one of his brothers and sisters able to go to school? – but church brought him to life. Every Sunday, Bishop Ngugi explained, his mother scrubbed him and his brothers and sisters clean and together they walked to a decrepit wooden building with the words "Most Gloryous Hause of Our Lord" dribbling down one side in errant white paint. The bishop enjoyed particular delight in telling the story of his eleven-year-old self delivering sermons in the schoolyard to all who would listen. 'That boy,' said my teachers, 'he will be a minister of Christ some day,' the bishop chuckled to himself as if Mary were not in the room. 'It was a small, rural community,' he said. 'And I knew I wanted more – to reach more people.'

'To reach them for what?'

He paused. 'To be influential.'

'About what?'

'Christ's message.' He spoke as if it were a strain. 'I had to became a man of the cloth. I wanted people to listen to me and be guided by me. I moved to Nairobi.'

'Didn't people in your village need spiritual guidance?'

'Of course. My uncle was the local pastor. But it was a congregation that never changed. I wanted more. There is a saying: follow bees and get honey. As a young man, I was attracted to the bright lights of Nairobi and I wanted to live in a nice house and those things. In Kenya, being a priest is a very noble position. I wanted to have that position – I couldn't work on a farm. As my teachers said, I was made for the pulpit!' He tittered again and sat back in his armchair with a sense of achievement.

Unconvinced that Bishop Ngugi ever thought about his congregation, Mary wanted to probe beneath his glossy, self-congratulatory exterior to pick at the sinews of his Christianity and his relationship with God.

'Ah yes,' she said, looking up from her notepad as if the question had not just occurred to her. 'Can you describe how you felt your own developing Christianity aligning with that of the ACK?'

'My dear,' he said, leaning forward and regarding Mary as if he knew better than her where the interview was headed. Absurdly, Mary wanted to wave her notepad in the clergyman's face to show him that their dialogue followed her agenda. 'My Christianity is not developing; it is fully formed and is as much a part of me as my right arm.'

That the bishop had misunderstood did not ease the agitation she felt by his smug response. The bishop's implication that he knew God completely would insult most Christians, she felt. He said, 'God and I are on very good terms. Secretly I look forward to judgement.' Mary was incredulous. Her cynical side wanted to laugh; her academic side wanted to argue, to point out his hypocrisy. She even wanted to enrage him, but instead she shuffled in the armchair, which felt increasingly constraining, to turn sideways. She inclined her head and glanced at her watch.

'Now let's discuss your visit to the UK,' she murmured.

Bishop Ngugi looked across at Mary the way a parent studies the face of a mischievous girl caught pinching a biscuit. Then he indulged her.

'Your media is correct,' he said. 'I am here to stir up debate. It's what I seem to do best, hahaha.'

She was about to ask him to outline his views when the bishop began to cough. He gasped and croaked but did not let it leave his control. 'Your media,' he cawed, before the attack had subsided. He took a sip of water. 'Your media. You will have seen the coverage recently, paving the way for my visit with shards of glass. The journalists who have interviewed me today, they have a plot for their articles before they have even shaken my hand! A theology student is better, I think.' The bishop looked at her sideways with a collaborative glint in his eye.

She nodded respectfully but had to look down at her notepad where she wrote, *he thinks I'm a Christian*. As she scribbled, Mary felt a little unsure about where to pick up the conversation. Most people who heard about her PhD assumed she was a Christian and she usually set them right immediately. But the bishop's intimation had been so subtle – and anyway, she would not jeopardise the interview – that she could not respond; she had to let it go.

'You said you're here to stir up debate. Debate about the UK legal position on a number of issues, I'd imagine?'

110

'Of course.' The bishop pursed his lips thoughtfully as a colonel does before ordering his troops to fire. 'You're right. I have been outspoken about some issues.' He relished his words and his tone seemed to stress their importance. 'There are these things such as same-sex marriage and female ordination, but I believe we will overcome them. The Church will unite against such things. My own personal concern on this trip is to reopen Great Britain's abortion debate.'

Mary nodded once and felt again a surge of discomfort in her abdomen. The sensation could only have been in her mind; it was too faint to be anything else. But still, the tiny embryo inside Mary's belly threatened to expose her to the bishop, the last person she wanted to know about her condition. She looked across warily at him. He took his cue.

'I simply cannot believe that a country as developed as Great Britain can allow this to happen in its hospitals. It is unacceptable for a Christian state. And so I am coming to call on all the Christians here to re-ignite this debate and outlaw the murder for good.'

Catchy, Mary wrote.

'Pro-choice campaigners argue it is precisely because we're so developed that we have legalised abortion…'

'That is a contradiction in terms,' he spat, and then quoted Genesis to explain the Christian notion of sanctity of life. The bishop was now on a roll; she let the dictaphone record his attitudes while she concentrated on remaining impassive. But words like 'barbaric' and 'termination' crept under her skin and pricked her nerves. The bishop's arguments and her own thoughts could not resolve her indecision, while this minute thing curled up inside her. It multiplied by the second; how much time did she have?

Mary needed no calculation to know that her PhD would take longer than the apparent alternative. This new option itself presented two choices, neither of which she could describe. Both lingered in her mind, ready to share with Stu. She just did not know when that would be. Her condition was still unreal enough for her to feel completely in control, that it was her decision. If other people became involved in her personal deliberation, Mary would be unable to keep a clear head. Her own opinions would diverge and split into alternate versions of herself. Wasn't that indeed what the embryo inside her was, an alternate version of herself? If only: then it would be easier to take charge. But she knew she could not do that. It may be her body but the embryo was half Stu, too. Or was it more than half her and half him; wasn't it neither of them, its own being?

And if that were the case, did she have the right to determine its future? Another thought immediately overtook that question, as she realised that she had leapt ahead of herself. Upon discovering her condition, Mary's reflexive reaction had not been joy. Instead, she had asked herself instinctively whether to intervene, to put a stop to it. How very peculiar, she now realised. Mary had inadvertently handed herself an ethically charged question for the sake of intellectual enquiry. The practical consideration – not to mention the moral dilemma itself – had been overlooked in her quest to colour this news.

It also posed a problem: her reflex to consider whether or not to continue the pregnancy was, of course, perverse. How had the simple news provoked the terrible thought she was now considering? Even secular people should be outraged at that. It troubled her deeply.

'I am hopeful we can kick-start the debate,' the bishop was saying. 'I know that some of my senior colleagues in the Church of England have been looking for an opportunity like we have now. I know God is against abortion; He is on our side, so hopefully we can harness that power among the nation's Christians.'

'Don't Christians say, "Hope not that God is on your side but that you are on His"?' She knew it was a mite aggressive but his arrogance had offended her.

'I know He is on our side. He says so in the Bible. And you know, Miss Park, people say it is the woman's choice. Hah!' He slapped his thigh. 'When God has already chosen upon who He shall bestow life? The woman has no say – she is the Lord's vessel and it is a terrible crime to forsake that.'

Mary did not respond; she quickly told him with as much composure as she could muster that she had asked all her questions. The bishop had just taken a deep breath as if to begin a new monologue, so instead he exhaled, blowing a gust between them. Beaming, he shot to his feet and plodded over to the door, without waving her past politely as Charles would have done. Mary stood, but froze to watch him move away, studying the rolls of fat bunched up by his stiff collar and thinking: just a man. He's just a man.

In the all-mirrored lift Mary rode to the lobby; her field of vision was arrested by a legion of Marys. She hoped to remember to tell Stu about this ever-shrinking image of herself, replicated to infinity. Wasn't he studying multiple universes?

Staring down the gauntlet of Marys, she hoped that at least one of them would be free of the weight she carried. This fear of having to prolong the suspension of her project, or seeing it collapse entirely, depressed her. This kind of academic research was all she had ever wanted to do. The suggestion of something usurping that made her feel sick. One of the Marys in the lift could tackle her PhD unhindered, with no competing outside influences. As the idea crept into her mind, it became a powerful gauge. Measuring herself against this luckier Mary, she realised that life was incredibly hard (even for an academic, which was something she had not imagined). Mary felt devoted to her PhD. But in reality there were a hundred other pressures that drew on her energy and time. The very thought of a single, heavy load like that of a baby baffled her as much as the reality would. And yet it seemed, on the face of it, that she would have no choice.

As the lift slowed, Mary glanced quickly at one of her reflections. She pushed her spectacles further up her nose and, in a heartbeat, scrutinised her face, feeling unmoved by its neutral reply. She had never known how her face would look at this time in her life. It did not reveal whether she was prepared for a major lifestyle change.

As the doors parted, she looked at the reflection of her abdomen sideways. Of course she wasn't showing. She exhaled and let her shoulders slump. As she stepped out of the lift Mary wished she could leave behind the pregnant version of herself, that crossing the threshold of the lift would liberate her from the burden. But as she walked through the sparkling lobby she still felt that heavy feeling deep inside her. Then Mary spotted a coffee bar and suddenly desired nothing else but the chance to sit and think in this anonymous hotel existence.

After ordering a latte, Mary began making additional observations on her interview notes. They became increasingly unfavourable. Mary did not enjoy re-experiencing her feelings but found the process of jotting them down somewhat heartening: it was all valuable material, she thought. The bishop had patronisingly assumed that he could answer her questions how he wanted and then was arrogant enough to deliver pompous, ego-inflating answers. His theology was skewed and, furthermore, dangerously obscured by his character. Mary found herself formulating various arguments against the bishop and his opinions – she noted some of them down but they all looked embryonic and unformed. To amuse herself, she wrote the word 'argument', and then swiped a giant circle around it. Argument: the missing heart of her thesis. There was neither a shortage of research or points for discussion but she had yet to entwine them all on a central, cohesive line of reasoning – and it broke her heart.

Mary tried to tell herself that none of this mattered, not in light of her news. But she could not believe that her PhD was just work. Leading academics were interested in her project. It could break new ground. It had grown bigger than any of the characters involved. They were all mortal people. James Ngugi was just a man, with rolls of fat at his collar and teeth that needed cleaning; she was just a woman, with… an embryo – but just an embryo. Christians would argue it was a slice of the Lord; she knew otherwise. At the moment, it was just a collection of cells.

If it did become a person, it would not be born a Christian or a Muslim or a vegetarian or a politician – or an academic.

Mary made a note of that, and then, taking a sip of her coffee, she wondered how anyone ever actually became (or grew into a mature understanding of being) a Christian. If, as a young person, or even an adult, one was subject to as many different voices as she had found during her research, how did one understand what Christianity was? Even in the East African countries she knew most, where Christianity had a relatively young tradition, the blending of New Testament teachings with traditional African spirituality – a different concoction in every community – was one example of how African Christianity was impossible to fathom. Mary jotted that down because she liked the sound of the phrase. It exasperated her but, at the same time, had proved to be the very core of her academic interest. She recalled being completely absorbed in her fragmented religious studies classes at school – her first taste of religion. Unfortunately, she was alone in finding the lessons informative and stimulating. Her classmates mocked religious traditions, refused to take notes.

114

It was not until university – and really her master's degree – that she felt she had academic peers in that regard. Even then Mary had not felt a strong connection with them; her fellow students had come from a certain religious tradition and seemed to question her neutrality. 'It's just the way I was raised,' she'd say honestly, noting how the conversation often stalled there. The name her parents had chosen for her was little more than a cosmic joke, which they had had to explain when she was fifteen. Even now, some days she got the joke and others she did not. 'No,' she'd have to admit, 'I'm not 'even' christened.'

'Miss Mary!' Charles's joyful voice gave her a jolt. As soon as she saw his bouncing cheeks, she smiled and asked him to join her.

'Tell me about your studies,' he asked, sitting down with a coffee. 'As a Christian and an East African,' he grinned, 'I find it very interesting.'

'You are a Christian?' she said.

'Of course! I work for a bishop!' Charles stirred his coffee with childlike interest then said, 'But it is only temporary employment because I am also a student.' His eyes swayed around the table as if he wanted to say more and was searching for words.

'Well I think it must be enlightening to assist Bishop Ngugi,' Mary said, watching for Charles's reaction.

He looked at her with a smirk and then said, 'It is enlightening. Especially because I follow a different path to the bishop's.'

'You're not Anglican?'

'I am Anglican more than anything else. My parish is part of the bishop's diocese – my father is a priest. The bishop... He is a great man, but sometimes I do not like what he says, or how he says it. It is the same with all these priests.' Charles cast his arm out, as if to indicate that all the other coffee drinkers belonged to the clergy. The gesture almost made Mary laugh. They could be, she thought, glancing around at the anonymous individuals.

'My Christianity is more akin to an instinct,' Charles affirmed.

Mary told him she had never heard it described as such, and asked if she could make notes. He agreed, amused. 'To me,' he continued, 'Christ's was a simple message. Common sense. It's easy, straightforward and logical – one moral leads to another. This priest says something different to that priest. I've heard them all. This page of the Bible says something different to the last page. I've read them all. So then, it is a question of absorbing it all into me and my heart' – here he pounded his chest emphatically – 'and hearing the best way through. It's an instinct, like finding your way home in the dark when there is a power cut!'

A practical theology for living in Kenya, Mary wrote, and smiled.

'I do not read the Bible any more. Twice was enough. If I read it again and again I would analyse too much and its meaning would change in my hand. Once you can drive you don't need to keep learning, you just need to keep doing. Christianity is the same.'

Mary nodded, perplexed. 'But what do you say to those who argue that the Bible improves every time you read it, that your appreciation of it – and its message – grows?'

Charles' bright eyes sprung into action, punctuating his energetic speech. 'I tell them that of course they are right – if that is the way they see it. But for me, as for many other Christians around the world, it is different.'

'Isn't it arrogant to assume you've understood everything there is to understand?'

'Of course,' answered Charles. 'I don't mean to suggest that I understand everything, only that I understand fundamentally what it means to be a good person and a loyal follower of Christ. Most people in the world share that feeling – whether they describe themselves as 'followers of Christ' or not – and most people in the world do not read the Bible.' Charles paused to take a thoughtful sip of coffee. 'I have that knowledge in my heart, just as everybody else does. I listen to it; some people do not. That is the difference. Reading the Bible and dressing smart for church is neither here nor there. I simply trust my own God-given instinct to love.' He looked at Mary seriously, and then broke into warm laughter, as if everything he had said was a joke, and he himself the punch line.

Mary finished off making a note and thanked him. It was probably the most honest testimony she had ever taken. They said goodbye and Mary watched him amble down the road with his hands clutched together behind his back like an antiquated gentleman.

Once he had turned a corner, she looked around for a bus stop, reeling with delight: this could be the breakthrough she needed. A whole new focus, a clear path through the disjointed findings of her investigation so far. It had come completely by surprise. Life had thrown it at her; that was not an argument for fate but a simple acknowledgment that not everything happened for a reason. Mary of course knew the biological reason behind the creature inside her but to her there was no practical reason: she did not want it. And yet she had stumbled upon it like she had stumbled upon Charles. His ideas freed her from the knots into which she had wound herself and her thesis. In a sense her project became clearer before her very eyes.

Mary admired Charles keeping his focus. It was the single most crucial thing a Christian had to do. He knew in his heart precisely what Christ's message of love was about – that it is very pure, very simple and very good. Mary did not feel the same way about Christ, nor did she have any other interpretation of love that she personally felt aligned to. For Mary, the fabric of her being was bound with academic inquiry. This was her central goal in life: to ask questions and suggest answers. (She and Stuart, who essentially asked the same questions but searched for the answers in different places, had discussed this through the night on many occasions.)

All day long Mary's heart had pounded with the anticipation of finding answers, of unearthing some kind of truth that she had been searching for, so that she could write about it before anyone else. This was what fuelled her existence. She realised just how crucial this fire in her belly was. The fact that it was entwined with her very essence elevated it to the highest of levels: it put it on par with life and death. This alone was justification for challenging anything that jeopardised it.

Mary now spotted the logical path through her problem. After having met Charles, she saw more clearly the terrible trial to which she would have to subject herself. Before considering whether or not to keep her baby, she had to ask whether she could actually ask herself that question.

But now Charles had taught her how to approach it. Ignoring the pressures of society, Mary knew that her morality permitted her to ask herself the question about what to do with the life inside her. If her instinct allowed her to follow that line of enquiry then she should.

She could at least pose the first question.

Coda

by Sarah Oswald

Sometimes I get up just as everyone else is going to bed and sit through the night listening to the wind whistling around the corners of the house, and the sound of the water that leaks from the gutter as it drips off the eaves down my window pane. Icicles form in the gap between the sill and frame, sharp as the stars in the bitter sky.

I drift off as night becomes dawn becomes day in a subtle shift of greys.

I woke to find that snow had fallen, drifted in through my broken window and dusted my blankets with delicate fractal patterns. The air was so cold it numbed my hands and face. I knew I had to get up, get my circulation going before I drifted off again. Eventually, I reached down on the floor for my fleece, pulling it on under the blankets. My nose stung and my breath turned to mist. Across the room I found my matches, cold fingers struggling to light the superser, standing as close to the glowing plate as I dared, holding down the ignition button and counting off the seconds because the thermocouple was broken. Thirteen, fourteen, fifteen… I released the button. The flame went out. You have to wait a bit before you can try again.

I found some more clothes under the bed and spread them in front of the superser. Click, click, click. The little symbol on the ignition button imprinted itself on my thumb. I sat on the edge of the bed with the heater directly in front of me, so close it burnt my shins, and got dressed. Then I went out to walk.

There is no part of our town in which you cannot hear, simultaneously, the roar of the river that flows through it and the sound of the wind moaning through the peaks of the mountains above. Even in the summer, when the river is nothing more than a rippling silver ribbon, the wind just a gentle kiss on your skin, beneath the noise of tourist traffic and holiday hikers you can hear them still if you listen close, singing to one another.

Mad Mrs Price shambled by, screaming the abuse of her dead father at herself, stamping the foot of a trapped little girl and shouting, 'Stop it! Stop it!'

Just then, the bells of St Mary's Church began chiming the funeral toll, and all the dogs down the street began to bark a frenzied chorus.

Patches of livid green grass peeked through the snow.

In the fields by the river, the fresh snow was criss-crossed with animal tracks. Little bird tracks; two-together, two-apart rabbit footprints; dainty cat tracks, tracks made by stalking foxes. Cutting clean lines across the white fields, intersecting and forming patterns.

Then I realised that there were, in fact, no human footprints at all. I looked all around but no, I was indeed the first person to walk these fields since last night, when the snow had fallen.

Above me the mountains were blanked out by snow, the same colour as the clouds behind, so that the clouds themselves looked like more mountains, far off in the distance. Fairy Mountains, that appeared only once every thousand years.

Looking back toward the town, the battlements on the old Norman church, the ancient graveyard yews, and the rooftops of all the houses were frosted white, making the town look like a picture on a Christmas card. Black and white. For only me to see.

At the water's edge, I noticed one or two rivulets that fed into the river had frozen over. I pressed the heel of my boot against the surface of the ice, but it was a good inch or so thick. I though of Annie, and wondered if her little stream was frozen, too. She might not have any water for herself or the animals. It took a lot of melted snow to make a bowl of water, I knew.

Having made up my mind to go check on Annie, I turned and headed back toward the footpath and home. I would pack a couple of big water bottles, wrapped in dry towels, into my rucksack, with teabags and biscuits. Then I would walk the six miles up to Brnywyn Hill to where Annie lived in her antiquated 1960s caravan.

All through the winter I lived in fear that one day I'd walk up Brnywyn Hill to find Annie stiff and dead from hypothermia, surrounded by baying and now orphaned animals. In summer, I thought she'd die of dehydration. But actually I knew she was tough as the hills, and no more likely than them to perish from anything the elements could throw at her.

What I was really afraid of was that one day I'd walk up Brnywyn Hill and find she'd gone.

When I got up to Annie's she wasn't in and the dogs weren't there. I left my rucksack and walked on up the hill, thinking we would meet on the path, or that she'd be home by the time I came back down.

At the top of Brynwyn Hill there's a heap of stones, some huge, some tiny, piled into a rough pyramid about eight feet across and four feet high. No-one knows how long it's been there, who made it, or why. On the Ordnance Survey map it's marked as 'Pile of Stones'.

Annie says it's an ancient burial mound. She says that some nights she can feel the spirits of the ancestors up here on the hill, can hear them calling. I used to think it was just the wind she could hear. She says the big black crow that sits on top of the Pile is really a Gwrach, the spirit of a witch woman who can change into a crow and fly between the worlds of the living and the dead.

Below the Pile there's an overhang of rock where you can shelter from the elements and watch the river wind its way through the fields below.

Crouched there, I can hear the different tunes made by the wind. Close by and low to the ground there's the soft rattle as it stirs the dried stalks of grass and seed-heads of heather. Above that, the eerie whistling it makes as it whips around the rocks. Higher still are the cries of birds and the distorted noises carried up from the fields; dogs barking on a distant farm, the sound of a tractor engine. And always audible, sometimes above and sometimes below, the constant coda of it howling through the peaks of the mountains, funnelling down through the valley and the sound it makes as it hits your ears.

I hear a great piercing cry from above and look up to see the crow perched on the Pile, just a few feet away. It sounds like it's saying the word 'Gwrach!', announcing its presence. There is something definitely more than animal in the way it looks at me with its jet black eye that darts this way and that, all the clouds and sky reflected in its surface. Not animal, but not human either. When you look into a person's eye it's like looking deeper into them, to see more clearly what's inside. But in the crow's I can only see the world

120

outside, mirrored in that glossy black unblinking eye, curved like the curve of the earth in reverse.

It caws once, spreads its wings, takes one hop towards me, and I'm looking up into a rippling sheen of black feathers. Except that close up they're not black at all, but a myriad of iridescent colours, the azure blue of the ocean, emerald green of the forest, amethyst of the setting sun.

Suddenly the crow cries a mighty 'Gwrach!' that makes me start and almost lose my balance, and with one flap of its great wings it takes to the sky. For an instant, the residue of shimmering colours and earth in reverse seems to hover in the space where the crow was, the way a droplet of water shimmers and pauses before it falls. Then Annie's figure fills the space and the illusion is gone.

'Hey!' she calls. 'Cheers for the stuff. Thought I might find you up here. Talking to the Gwrach?'

'Kind of,' I say.

She steps down to squat beside me, long grey hair blowing about her rosy face, and looks out over the valley, hugging herself against the cold.

'Thought you were gonna jump there for a minute,' she says. Then, 'It's bloody freezing up here. Want a cup of tea?'

Back at the caravan, Annie puts more wood on the burner and fills the big cast kettle with water from the bottles. The dogs curl up in their basket under her bed; Coco the cat jumps on my lap and makes herself comfortable. Annie makes a roll-up and gets the mugs ready for tea.

'I had a dream last night,' I tell her, as the warmth from the stove creeps in, making my fingers ache and my nose run. I find a bit of toilet paper in my pocket, not enough but all I've got.

'I dreamt that I was walking by the river, along the ridge and through the trees toward Nant-yr-Helygn. And the path was white, like a polished piece of wood or bone, and although I knew I was going uphill, the path went downward in a sort of spiral. Like the staircase in a stone tower, or giant snail's shell.'

Annie sits cross-legged on the bed and re-lights her roll-up.

'Where were you going?'

'I don't know. The path just carried me along, and the world was going on all around me, but I was outside of it somehow. I could see it and hear it, but because I was on the path, I was separated from it. I just kept going down.'

A faint whistle starts to form inside the kettle. Steam rises. Annie shifts, reaches over and picks up the drip-stained tea towel, puts it around the handle and lifts the kettle from the stove. She looks at me.

'You'll still be here you know,' she says. 'Even when you're gone.'

I have been to the edge of the Universe many times.

I am standing on a thin ledge and all the Universe is spread out before me, like a black ocean stretching out in all directions, lit by the pinpoints of a billion stars. Off in the furthest distance I perceive the beginnings of a disturbance, drawing nearer. A swirling white cloud, like the twister in The Wizard of Oz, is coming right at me. It comes closer and closer, moving in faster. I know it will spin right through me and take me with it. Then it spins away and I watch it recede for a long time, until it's nothing more than a vague speck in the distance once more, then it will turn and spin back again, faster, more insistent, tugging at me, trying to take me with it.

I almost let go.

Part of me wants to so much that a thrill runs right through me, so strong that it nearly carries me right off the edge. But another part of me will not let go, holds tight as a vice and pushes the cloud away with a desperate, violent fear.

In the lane, I meet the Colonel.

'Morning. How are you?'

'Morning,' he replies, a blank look on his face. The Colonel has Alzheimer's and can't usually remember who you are. He knows he knows you, he just can't recall how or where from.

'It's Miss Blake, from number five,' I remind him.

'Oh yes yes yes, of course. Yes. Has Dai been round to see about that immersion heater yet?'

'No Colonel Eldridge, that's Pete at number three with the immersion heater. Number five is the broken window sash.'

'A broken sash? Window sash? Ah.' He thinks about this for a while. He gazes along the lane in the direction his dogs have gone and swipes the air with his walking stick. I've just about decided that his mind has moved elsewhere and I may as well say goodbye, when he looks back at me and smiles.

'Well well well. A broken sash! Still, don't suppose you'd want to open it in this weather, anyway, eh?' he chuckles.

'Actually it's stuck open – '

But he's already turned away and started off down the lane.

The Colonel has a son who's as sharp as a knife. He 'manages' the flats for him. This means that he occasionally sends Dai, the Colonel's old handyman, round to incompetently repair things if you really nag at him for long enough, and it also means that he knocks on your door at seven o'clock sharp every Tuesday to collect the rent, and he always knows damn fine exactly how much you owe and how late you are with it, and woe betide you if you've not swept your bit of the hallway, either.

The Colonel had a daughter once too, but everyone knows she committed suicide by hanging herself from the balustrade on the landing that separates my flat from the one across the hall, years before I ever lived there. People say the dents in the wall along the stairwell were made by her feet as she kicked her last breath away. Sometimes on the stairs I put my fingers in them and try to imagine how she must have felt at the moment she jumped. But I never really feel anything.

It rained a little later, and that night it froze, so that in the morning the snow had become an icy slush that crackled and crunched underfoot.

Lines of human footprints had appeared across my virgin fields, concentrated along the well-worn footpaths, indistinguishable from one another.

Unconsciously I found myself walking the path from my dream, through woods and fields to the boggy place where the water seeps out from under the mountains to join the river, near the scattered farms and one postbox we knew as Nant-yr-Helygn.

As I left the path and made for the river, I noticed a set of prints, slightly larger than mine, that had deviated from the footpath and headed out the way I normally walked. I tracked them for a while along the ridge, but lost them under the trees where there was no snow. Further up past the trees though, I saw the footprints again, the same ones as before.

Curious, I began to follow, placing my feet in the marks left by the stranger's boots. I noticed how nearly our strides matched. The stranger's path ran alongside the river, the way I'd walked in my dream. I followed. The snow had melted where boot had met grass, leaving a line of clear green crunchy holes along the bank. It occurred to me as I placed my feet in the holes that the stranger must only take a size or two bigger shoe than me.

Then I looked closer. The tread pattern in the bottom of the holes matched the one on my own boots exactly, only melted wider by the rain and frozen over. I felt both disappointed and stupid.

Nobody walks here but me.

On the hill above Nant-yr Helygn was a great oak tree. One night when I was young there was a big thunderstorm and the next day I came up here to find that half the tree had broken off and fallen in just the most perfect spot to sit. With the hedge behind me, I could look up at the mountains straight ahead. Turn left and the whole town was spread out below. Turn right and the bracken-covered hills stretched away to the horizon, punctuated by the hospital at Pen-Y-Craig. If I tilted my head back, so that all I could see was sky, I could pretend that I was sitting on top of the world. I would watch the clouds shift across the sky until it seemed that it was the world that was moving and the clouds that were standing still. And because I was sitting on top of the world, I could slow it down: I could make it stop.

Over the years bits of the branch disappeared to wherever it is that nice bits of seasoned wood go, until there was only a large log left, some five feet long.

As the summers and winters came and went I watched it diminish, slowly rotting away until one autumn the whole log became saturated like a giant sponge and I couldn't sit there any more. From that point on it declined rapidly. Big chunks of it flaked away, decomposing into the earth as the vegetation that sprang up from its rich compost swallowed its remains.

Now there is barely a trace of it left, and I think I must be the only person who ever even knew it was there, the seat at the top of the world.

The grey days drip by. Some things stand out, sharp and clear against the murky backdrop, leering out at me from a damp colourless fog. But they are just stills from a film I've never seen. Vivid, technicolour fakes. Phoney as a back lot film set. Fairy mountains.

The world goes to sleep and I sit by my window, listening to the wind and the drip, drip drip.

I can hear...

An aeroplane passing high overhead; a dog barking down the road; the electric hum of the fridge...

Footsteps, on the stairs.

Life speeds by, a constant flux, a time-lapsed film. If I focus really hard I can make it slow, still, static: like stopping the clouds in the sky. Then I experience the sensation you get just before you pass out, when you hear the hum of blood in your ears. The roar of the wind through the mountains. The rush of the river in flood.

I can put my fingers through it.

Mrs Price is standing in the churchyard, shouting at the graves.

I see the body of the little girl that Mrs Price once was, the purest untainted essence of her Self, contained within the adult body that walks every morning up the High Street, collects her laundry, shops at Spar, struggles home with heavy bags past the church to her council flat to sweep her floors and wash her nets and stare out of the bare windows at the rain-washed concrete that roots her in this world.

Her blank blue watering eye turns on me with a sudden lucidity and for one moment she seems to recognise some kinship between us. Then it is gone.

In the part of St Mary's churchyard where the yews grow together to form an arch overhead, there is a tall headstone with a perfectly circular hole through it, inscribed with the words 'I AM

THE GATE'. Lewys Selwyn Blake was almost certainly related to me somehow, though he died in 1929 and like everyone else in this section of the graveyard, must have died whilst resident at the psychiatric hospital at Pen-Y-Craig.

When I was small I would sneak out of church on Sunday and play here by the graves that no-one visited, where the weeds were far more interesting than the gaudy flowers in the neat and tidy part of the graveyard. Everyone was related to someone buried here, if you went back far enough. Blake and Powell, Selwyn and Price, Morgan and Eldridge and Phillips; they were all here. The Colonel would be here one day, protected by his walking stick and guarded by little yappy dogs. Mrs Price, next to her father, watched over by angels made from shopping bags, veiled in net curtains.

And me.

I am the gate.

I look through Lewys Selwyn Blake's headstone along the path to the river. The edges become blurred and fuzzy. It's as though I can look so deep into the stone that I can see its very substance, and deeper still, through that, to the very atoms from which it is created, all whirling and spinning and vibrating. And they are nothing, there is nothing even holding them together but the fields of resistance created by their constant agitated motion.

Everything, everywhere I look; everything made of nothing but constant motion, like the clouds in the sky.

I can make it stop.

I know that Chaos is at the centre of the Universe. All things exploded from it in the beginning: it is the calm eye of the storm and the seething shrieking maelstrom.

I can hear it in the wind. I can see it in a snowflake. In the crow's eye. At the bottom of the river.

Chaos creates and chaos destroys.

It moves so fast.

Chaos repeats itself. Creates, destroys, repeats.

Delicate, fractal patterns.

At night I dream of the path to Nant-Yr-Helygn. Smooth as a stone polished by the river it takes me down, singing a song of wind and water. The bells of St Mary's Church chime the funeral toll that sounds like the water dripping from the eaves onto my window pane. Beyond the path, the world is lost in fog.

On the way down I pass the Colonel, standing solemnly to attention beside the path. He presents me with his walking stick.

Mrs Price has stopped in the middle of the path up ahead. She stamps her foot and shouts, 'Leave the girl alone!' then fixes me with her mad eyes, blue as the sky, and holds out a scrap of crumpled net curtain in her gnarled, ancient hand. I take it and she steps away.

Down, down, and everything shimmers and fades, all but the path that shines like the river in summer. I realise I'm walking in several inches of water.

Annie appears and hands me a steaming mug of tea. She smiles her knowing smile and whispers something in my ear, and I know it's terribly important that I remember what she's said.

The water is up to my knees. Then I see the boat.

Two women dressed in black are standing in the boat, waiting for me. They look alike, as though they might be related in some way. Although I'm certain I've never seen them before, there is something horribly familiar about them.

And suddenly, I know, I know I don't want to get in that boat. A surge of dread gathers in my cold wet toes and flushes all the way to the top of my muddled head. I turn around but everything is gone. Only clouds and fog remain.

They take me into their boat and in that instant, the calm waters become an angry sea. The little boat pitches violently and water floods in. If I can only keep hold of the walking stick and net curtain, and make sure I don't spill the tea, everything will be all right. The boat lurches and dives beneath the waves. We are no longer sailing over the water, but under it, hurtling downward. I struggle desperately to hold on to the pieces of my self and my world as we are sucked down, faster and faster, in the whirling vortex of water. My arms are thrown above my head and the walking stick slips through my fist. I feel a huge sadness stealing over me. The current tugs at the curtain that flows like seaweed from my fingers. I watch a cloud of light brown liquid float upward from Annie's mug and dissolve into the dark ocean, like hope engulfed by despair. I am losing myself. The sound of roaring chaos is in my ears. Down, down, down.

I grip the mug in both hands and try to pull against the force of the water, straining with the effort, as though all Earth's gravity is against me. I manage to drag the mug down level with my eyes, and I can read the words printed on it:

'You'll still be here, even when you're gone.'

Another cold morning. Or is it the same one?

The gas bottle is nearly empty and the remaining gas has frozen. The little blue spark of the superser's ignition flashes uselessly as I click away until my fingers go numb. I boil the kettle instead, holding my hands over the steam until they burn. I make tea, and press the hot mug against my nose and feet and chest.

The icicles have filled the gap and sealed the window shut, finally achieving what the Colonel's handyman never did. Yesterday's clothes feel clammy. The steam from my breath and the tea fogs the room. My room is full of clouds, obscuring the walls and windows, swirling to the sound of the wind as it whistles around the corner of the house, and the drip, drip, drip on the window pane. I put my fingers through them. I cannot feel my hand. I cannot see it either.

The clouds are made of a billion silver sparkles, reflecting the light like tiny electric snowflakes, twinkling like stars in the void. There's a ringing in my ears, like the sound you hear just before you pass out.

I can make them stop.

On my way down the stairs, I put my fingers through the dents in the wall and touch Maria Eldridge's foot in tan tights, feel the pain shoot up her leg as her toes break from the impact with the wall and the desperate struggle to bring the oxygen back to her brain in a cold, heaving panic.

Then calm, calm. All is done.

There is a surge of joy as her other body, the one that was big and strong and full of music and poems and love, steps free and smiles at me in serene benediction before disappearing through to the other side of the wall.

128

Below the ridge the river meanders and loses itself in a copse of willow, hawthorn and hazel trees. A giant sycamore stands on the bank, great roots reaching down to the water. Where the roots emerge from its massive trunk there's a hollow, where I can sit with my back against it and watch the river.

In early summer I would see swallows darting and skimming over the surface of the water from this spot. In late summer it would become completely hidden by towering clumps of Indian Balsam and I would be engulfed in their waxy peachy scent, surrounded by the buzzing of bees. In autumn I would spend hours tracking the progress of sycamore seeds as they fluttered down from the branches to be carried away on the rain-swollen current, perhaps to wash up on some distant bank and grow into a tree like mine. Maybe someone somewhere was sitting under a bigger tree upstream, contemplating the fate of all the sycamore seeds they'd ever watched fall and flow away. Someone I'd never know, thinking about my tree and me, the two of us connected by river and earth and seed.

Even autumn seems like a long time ago now. The branches of the trees have been black and bare for so long, it's hard to remember how it looked when all was lush and green, busy with bees and birdsong; or even damp and misty with the musty scent of rotting leaves underfoot.

On this colourless, scentless, black and white morning I sit beneath the tree, looking at the lifeless branches sodden with the moisture of melted snow.

I watch a single droplet form at the tip of a branch overhanging the river. How many melted snowflakes does it take to make one drop? I focus on it, a perfect crystal sphere thrown into relief against a backdrop of river, fields, distant mountains and clouded sky. All is reflected in this single drop, that contains a billion snowflakes, each one unique, an infinite number of reflections of the world.

I watch it, poised above the river.

Across the water a bird flaps its wings once, rises into the air, and is gone. For a moment there is a disturbance in the current. I look at the point where the bird just was and it is as though the space momentarily retains some memory of the bird's presence.

Dents in the wall.

Even in the seeming silence, I can hear the music of the world. The snow melts on the mountains and a hundred tiny rills are born and make their way to the river, dripping over the rocks and gurgling through gullies, joining together and streaming down to add their voices to the raging torrent that my lazy summer river has become.

Sheep bleat on the hillside. A tractor crosses a field. Crows call to one another over the treetops. And the wind.

The sounds blend together, instruments in some great elemental orchestra, weaving a melody underpinned by the rushing river, the howling wind, the hum of blood in my ears... variation upon variation of the same themes, running through spring, summer, autumn and winter, the infinite symphony of the Universe...

I watch the droplet shiver and tremble, hear the music swell to a magnificent, deafening crescendo...

Then all sounds seem to cease. For a moment, I see the clouds reflected in the surface of the water.

All is slow, still, static.

I watch it

drip.

Stalking Hugo McIntyre

by Antony N Britt

'Murder and Mayhem, what a great name for a bookshop. Come on Josie, take a picture of me outside the window.'

'Simon, we're late enough getting into Hay as it is; you don't want to miss your precious Hugo McIntyre at the festival do you?'

'I didn't know it was going to take that long to get here did I?'

'Ha,' she said. 'We very nearly didn't when you tried to jump that level crossing.'

'Oh Jose, but think; it would have been a death worthy of the master McIntyre himself.'

'You're weird,' she said. 'And we're still going to miss him if you're not careful.'

'Relax Jose, we have an hour yet before the show.'

'But Simon, the festival site's half a mile away and I don't think they'll keep the seats empty for too long, even if you have won the competition to sit there.'

I looked at Josie as she searched inside her leopard print shoulder bag for the camera. She was right, we had to get a move on, but we'd catch the shuttle bus at the other end of town in plenty of time. As for the seats, well, they would have to keep them for the winner of the Hugo McIntyre Website Trivia quiz. Not that winning was ever in doubt. I suppose some would call me his number one fan, though Josie says I'm a geek. I don't care; it certainly helped knowing each of his twenty one novels from cover to cover when I had to answer all those questions. Still, it was all worth it. Just think, sitting on the front row of his televised chat in the Sky Arts tent with a chance to meet and talk to him afterwards.

'Come on Jose,' I said turning to look at the books on display in the window of this shop which, apparently, specialised in matters of death on a grand scale. Hugo's work would certainly be at home here. He was at present, the number one writer of his genre and his twisted tales were now legendary to the point of a film being made of *Head Case*, his best-selling novel to date. It wasn't my favourite, but still pretty gut-churning; the way that girl's head is carried about in the suitcase the entire length of the book.

'Simon, turn to face me then,' I heard Josie shout as I looked with widening eyes at the display of books currently being neatly arranged on the shelf in the shop window.

Hugo McIntyre – Signed Copies.

'Quick Jose, just take the shot,' I said turning back to my harassed looking girlfriend.

'Okay,' she said. 'Just stay still for a minute and... there, done it. Hey, where you going?'

'In the shop.'

'But we haven't got time!'

'It's only for a minute.'

'Your choice,' she said. 'He's your bloody hero.'

Too right he was, but to have a selection of autographed books in front of me, well, I couldn't pass that opportunity. I had my own copies in the bag, or rather Josie did, and they were all ready to be signed. Still, he may not have time to do all of the seven that I'd agonised over choosing. It wouldn't hurt to buy some pre-signed ones here and save myself the possible disappointment later.

'How much are the Hugo McIntyres?'

An elderly woman behind the counter smiled at me with an air of smugness. 'Considerably more than they were a few minutes ago, he was just in here signing them.'

'WHAT?'

No! No! No! No no no no! It couldn't be, it wasn't fair. If only Josie hadn't insisted on going to the toilet after the four-hour drive, I'd have met him in person already and got my books signed for sure.

'What, where is he?'

'Oh he's gone now; doing a spot down at the festival in a bit. Talking about his books and all the grisly deaths he writes. You ought to go and see him.'

'Yes, I know; I have tickets, but which way did he go?'

'Well, he went off in that direction,' she said pointing. 'Down Lion Street.'

'Come on, Josie,' I said to my flustered companion, as she finally entered the shop, staring at me in bewilderment. 'We got to go and find Hugo McIntyre.'

I raced toward the door, almost knocking Josie over in the process before I stopped in my tracks and turned back to the woman in the shop. 'How much for all the books?'

'Two hundred and forty quid! TWO HUNDRED AND...'

'Yes Jose, I know,' I said panting as we ran along the country lane, passing a selection of pretty houses, some of whose occupants had taken advantage of the festival and chosen to set up a yard sale. There looked some good stuff actually, and we'd have to have a browse on the way back. There wasn't time now though, and we had to run fast if we weren't to miss Hugo McIntyre. If only we hadn't gone into Booth's bookshop to see if he was in there. He wasn't as it happened, and hadn't been at any time today. That delay made us late, then Josie insisted on dropping the fifteen new signed copies back at her car rather than carry them with the others in her bag. With both the delays combined, we'd missed the bus to the festival site and now had to run.

'Hey Simon,' Josie shouted, lagging behind. 'Look at that antique trunk.'

I stopped in astonishment as Josie stood, panting for breath outside a house selling off many years of accumulated junk, and in particular, a battered storage chest. What the hell was she doing? We were supposed to be in a hurry, and she was... she was... SHOPPING!

'Yes,' I said. 'Make a great place to hide your body. NOW RUN!'

'Oh you're obsessed with death and morbid stuff like that,' she said, huffing to a start again. 'You read too much of that bloody Hugo.'

'Come on,' I shouted, looking back to her as she laboured along with the bag full of unsigned books swinging to and fro on her back. God she looked stunning today, especially the way her breasts bounced up and down inside that tee-shirt as she ran.

'Mind how you cross,' she shouted as I saw the festival entrance on the other side of the road. 'You don't want end up as a McIntyre character, do you.'

'I'd be proud to,' I joked, and set about navigating the danger before heading into the book festival site in front of me.

'What do you mean, I can't go in?'

'I'm sorry,' a rather severe woman in her twenties with glasses and tied-back hair told me. 'We're about to start filming now and everybody's in place.'

'But I'm not. I have reserved seats, at the front.'

I stared, drooling at the décor of the temporary TV studio, set up inside the large tent. The area at the front had been made to look like a graveyard with tombstones and fake grass. In the middle stood a single oak chair on one side and a battered chaise-longue on the other where presumably Hugo McIntyre would be interviewed. In front of these, separating my hero from the audience (which was irritating by the fact that its front row was now all occupied) was a set of fake rusty-looking railings to complete the sinister scene for the show.

'I'm sorry,' the studio technician said as Josie stood at my side, now doubled up and gasping for breath. 'There's really nothing I can do.'

She turned away and gestured to a cameraman as a call from another man with headphones at the front stated, 'Twenty seconds.'

An elderly man, some TV presenter I'd never seen before, entered the arena to a round of applause and seated himself in the oak chair within the artificial graveyard.

I listened with frustration as he entered into his spiel about my hero, the fabulous Hugo McIntyre and how his tales of bizarre death and destruction were about to be turned into films.

'Come on Simon,' Josie panted. 'They say we have to go; there isn't room.'

'No, Jose, I'm not going to be beaten after all this.'

I looked to the front as the presenter stood up and announced to the packed arena, 'Put your hands together, for Hugo McIntyre.'

Everybody cheered; some people even people stood up, and in my desperate state, I clapped too. It was then I realised that nobody was watching me. This was my chance.

'SIMON!' I heard Josie cry as I raced down the side perimeter of the circular tented studio. Here he was, waving to acknowledge the crowd. Hugo McIntyre walked onto the set and... *God, he looks smaller in real life.*

Shit! I realised I'd forgotten the books, and after all my effort bringing them here. Never mind, he'd let me go back and get them once I made contact. Hugo turned to me, taken by surprise as I ran

134

toward him. One of the TV staff noticed too and made a frantic dive to grab me.

'It's okay,' I shouted. 'I'm his number one fan!'

I dodged out of the technician's way only to collide with a large TV camera to my right whose operator had swung it round to film what was happening. As he did, the heavy structure hit me on the shoulder and I staggered to one side, losing my balance in the process. My vision blurred as I flew through the air and everything around me moved with speed. It wasn't the world in motion, it was me, and it only stopped when a searing pain of immeasurable magnitude ripped through my stomach.

Shit! The iron railings, they weren't fake after all. My innards felt like somebody was twisting them with a knife, which I suppose was a pretty accurate supposition. Aware of screaming, I looked up and saw the astonished face of Hugo McIntyre peer down at me.

'Can you sign some books for me?' I asked.

Although the studio was cleared by now, it was still very noisy in the tent. Most of that was due to the fact Josie was still shrieking. She was the only one I think, all the other banshees had been evacuated out of the area. I couldn't feel much pain now, not after all the stuff the medics had pumped into me and it was a real coup to have Hugo McIntyre here holding my hand.

Still, I didn't understand the delay. Why wasn't I being whisked off to hospital? I looked up and saw Josie, who was crying onto the shoulders of the stern looking technician who'd tried to stop me getting in. She looked far to touchy-feely with my girlfriend.

'I'm sorry love,' she said to Josie. 'They say he hasn't got long.'

What the hell did that mean? I wasn't going to die; I'd be out of here in a bit and everything would be okay. Things around me were starting to blur though as Hugo McIntyre turned to speak to somebody behind him.

'A bit ironic really,' I heard Hugo say.

'Yeah,' came an unseen reply. 'A death worthy of one of your novels.'

What the hell do they know? Idiots. I'm fine, or at least I will be in a minute. I'll just shut my eyes for a bit, and then I'll get him to sign my books.

Colin's Tale

by Cedric Fox-Kirk

After a particularly busy year, Saint Peter allowed himself the luxury of leaving the duty at the main Gates of Heaven in the capable hands of lesser angels and martyrs and standing – or in his case, as we find him, sitting – at one of the rarely-used lesser gates.

This was it – Christmas was coming and the blessed Peter saw it as a time to rest, sit back and let the others get on with it. Duty at a gate that saw no traffic was just the ticket. Suddenly there was a distant 'pop' – near enough to be heard but far enough away not to be next to him. Looking down the celestial path, Saint Peter saw a tall figure in a woolly hat walking purposefully towards him. Dressed in a warm shirt, thick casual jacket and jeans the man drew up to the Saint and loomed over him.

'Hullo,' the man said.

'Who are you?' asked Peter, 'I wasn't expecting anyone.'

The man looked around him and up at the gates and replied, 'Colin. Here, are these your actual Pearly Gates?'

'Colin who?' said the Saint, becoming a tad irritated, 'And these are one of the lesser Pearly Gates.'

'I wondered,' said Colin in a friendly, knowing manner, 'because they're looking a bit dingy. I've got just the thing that'll bring them up a treat. Oh, and it's Melnyk – Colin Melnyk.'

'What do you mean 'a bit dingy'?'

'Well, look at 'em, 'said Colin, gesturing with one big hand at the end of a long arm, flashing the gold bracelet that hung loosely around his wrist.

Peter glanced enviously at the bracelet then caught himself. 'That won't do,' he muttered to himself, 'envious thoughts are sinful.' He looked at Colin and something clicked in his celestial brain. 'Hey, did you say Colin Melnyk? But you're not dead.'

'Hope not,' Colin answered with a smile 'But I am Colin Melnyk from Paralimni. That's in Cyprus.'

'Yes, yes, I know where Paralimni is,' Peter said, getting decidedly tetchy now, 'and, for your information, Orthodox adherents have the entrance round the other side.'

'Ah' said Colin, 'I'm an ex-pat, not a native of the Island. Originally from The Fens – well, sort of a bit past King's Lynn and head south.'

The blessed Peter silently counted to ten, reminding himself that patience was a virtue even though his day of rest was rapidly being ruined by this tall stranger who had just shown up out of nowhere.

'Anyway,' the saintly one said, rummaging around at the side of his chair until he produced a large book, 'how did you get here?'

'There are ways,' Colin replied, throwing the Saint a knowing smile.

If he noticed, the Keeper of the Gates of Heaven chose to make no reply but busied himself with the great book. He closed it with a thud and sighed. 'Colin,' he said, 'Colin Melnyk from Paralimni you are definitely not due here for some time yet.' He stood up, wincing at his aching joints, and put his hand up to Colin's shoulder.

'Listen to me, my son; you're not dead and you've found your way here by some means I can't fathom and presumably you will return to Paralimni by the same mysterious method.' He paused as Colin nodded, then continued, 'What I have to ask myself, though, is… why?'

'I can tell you that, mate,' said Colin, glad that the penny had dropped for the old Saint. 'You see, I get to hear things and I hear about the angels and the souls of the saved bathing in the celestial pools. Then I say to myself, 'Hullo, there might be what you'd call an opportunity here,' and I'm always on the look-out for opportunities.'

The Saint was, by now, completely mystified but went along with the conversation in the hope that enlightenment would come. 'What opportunity would that be?' he said.

'Well, someone must have the contract for cleaning them – I can't see all the angels mucking in – and I thought, as I said, got to be an opportunity. After all, I am the best pool cleaner in Paralimni – not cheap but the best.'

'Oh!' Saint Peter said, finally realising what all this was about. 'Well, not my province really, Michael is nominally in charge but I must say they have been looking a bit – well – green, recently.'

'Any chance of a word with this Michael bloke?' said Colin, seeking to press home his advantage.

'Well,' said Peter, 'The Archangel Michael is principally the Smiter of the Enemies of the Lord, and so doesn't give a lot of time to what you might call his ancillary duties.'

'Well he should do,' observed Colin. 'Once green algae gets hold it can be the devil to shift.'

'Yes. Quite. Get your drift with the devil thing.'

They stood together looking through the gate to the towers sparkling through the clouds for a few moments, then Saint Peter turned to Colin and said, 'Look, Colin, you've obviously made the effort to come all the way up here and it's likely you have spotted a problem that your particular skills would be able to help with. No promises, but I will have a word with Mick – that is, I mean, the Archangel Michael – and suggest he gives you a try out.'

'Fair enough,' said Colin. 'Always happy to oblige, tell him. And I've served my time in Her Majesty's armed forces if he needs any help with the other things.'

'Other things?' queried the Saint, looking quizzically at Colin.

'You know – the smiting business.'

'Oh! Yes, yes. But for now I'll just tell him about the pool cleaning.'

'Fair enough,' said Colin. 'You know how to get in touch, I assume.'

'Er – yes,' said Peter. 'Like you, we do have our ways.'

'Rightio,' said Colin. 'I'll be off – catch you later.' And with that he walked a few paces and vanished.

Christine, Colin's wife, was a patient woman: married to Colin she needed to be – a fact that Saint Peter would have readily agreed with. She stood in front of the newest 'Oriental Eating Experience' in Agia Napa, where she was supposed to meet him for a meal out, but couldn't see him anywhere. Then he appeared. 'Oh! There you are – been inside already,' she observed as Colin's tall figure came striding through the 'Gates of Heaven' Chinese restaurant.

Internet Explorer

by Janet H Swinney

'I can't call you that,' said Evelyn.

'Why not?'

'Because we have an equal opportunities policy here. If I'm caught calling you that I'll be for the high jump.'

'But I've always been called Porky.'

Pork. On the other side of the room, a young woman in a black hijab that narrowed her face to a triangular sliver wrinkled her nose in distaste.

'Surely you have another name.'

'I have. But nobody ent gonna call me that. I'm Porky because my old dad had a pork butcher's for years over in Camberwell.'

'Ah well, that's different, I suppose.' Evelyn twiddled her pen nervously on the enrolment form before writing something on the page.

'My brother was called Pinky. And he was an' all. A right ole Pinko. Always out on the picket line, till he didn't have a job no more.'

'Your brother sounds like a very worthy citizen,' ventured a gaunt man with horses' teeth and an elderly blazer. 'I myself was a member of the Indian Workers' Association when I first came to the UK.'

'And you are?' said Evelyn, flicking through her forms.

'Sonny Rosario.'

'Okay, Sonny. Thank you very much.'

Evelyn continued round the group until she had the names of everyone and a little bit of information about each of them. Meanwhile, they were busy sizing her up. She was lanky, with a pastel pale skin, almost flat shoes and a bit of a dark moustache going on. What saved her from drabness were an unruly cascade of black hair, and breasts like globe artichokes slung across a narrow frame. Her deep, dark cleavage was a place where Porky, and probably several other members of the group, lost himself in thought for an unconscionable amount of time.

The course, Evelyn explained, would help them to overcome their fears about IT. She had written what she called the 'intended outcomes' up on the board. They included 'switch on the computer and log-on,' and 'send emails (with and without attachments)', 'perform basic calculations using Excel' and 'carry out an internet search'. Despite her assurances, it all looked pretty daunting. Porky curled his toes in his velcro-fastening shoes. He was beginning to wonder if he'd come to the right place.

Then they all had to say something about why they had signed up. Ursula, in a wheelchair and attended by a carer, was researching her family history. She'd been at it for years, apparently, and had got as far as she could without getting access to some documents on the internet. Ursula had lank grey hair, and one of her spectacle lenses was misted over. She had developed the knack of holding her head on one side so that her decent eye could get a good look at the world. Just how interesting could her family be, Porky wondered.

Shazan, the young woman in the hijab wanted to 'better' herself, and perhaps get a job. Porky didn't think much to her chances – what with the headscarf and that. Hardip, a broad, shy bloke in denims and a checked shirt confessed he was a builder who couldn't keep his books straight. Mabel, a large African-Caribbean woman, wanted to keep in touch with her family. Mabel's hands shook while she rehearsed the whereabouts of her familial diaspora. Obviously, none of the bastards wanted to keep in touch with her. Ephraim, a thin leathery guy who looked as though his shirt was still on the rack, had been sent along by another tutor who was teaching him English. To be able to get a job in the UK he needed to pass a Citizenship test. The English tutor had suggested that learning IT might help him with this.

Then there was Sonny. Negotiating the foibles of his teeth, Sonny carefully explained that he talent-spotted young performers of classical music and launched them on their professional careers. He wanted to be able to use email to keep in touch with orchestral managers and concert venues worldwide. As he finished, he leaned back in his chair, revealing a slight paunch and the piece of hairy string that held his trousers up. It was clear that no-one, not even Evelyn, believed him.

Porky got straight to the point. He told the group he had a growing suspicion that there was a whole world he knew nothing about. 'It's like sitting in the coal hole with the light off,' he said. 'No matter what you watch on telly, it always ends with: "Visit our website, w w w." You can't even give money to charity without doing that.'

By the end of that first session, they had done pretty well. They could all switch their machines on, and use the mouse to get around the screen and open up Internet Explorer. They'd been shown how to conduct a basic search, and had looked up the college website. On the way home on the one five six – he couldn't manage the walk any more – Porky felt well pleased with himself.

Barrie came round that night with a bag of groceries. He went straight into the kitchen with them. 'Did you have them burgers, Dad?' he shouted.

'Yeah,' said Porky without interest.

'What?'

'I said, "Yes!"' yelled Porky.

Barrie came through into the living room, where Porky was sitting in front of the telly with his feet up on a pouffe watching *The Dog Whisperer*. Barrie was a stocky young man with go-faster tattoos on his upper arms, and a fast food belly that loomed above his cargo pants.

'Only, I've just brought some more, but there's still a packet in the freezer.'

'Ah,' said Porky. He was eyeing the Dog Whisperer work his magic on a cross-bred Doberman with teeth in every orifice.

'And there's sausages in there that have seen better days.'

'Is there?' said Porky. He wanted to see what happened when the Doberman got put in with the Whisperer's own pack.

'You have to watch out with these things, Dad. You don't want to end up poisoning yourself.'

'Yeah, yeah. I know.'

Porky really didn't want to debate the pros and cons of sell-by dates. He snapped the television off.

'Whad you do with the kids today?'

'Took 'em up Trafalgar Square.'

'Oh yeah?'

'But it wasn't the same as when you and Mum used to take me. Now the place is full of fucking fencing, and a bloody stupid statue that looks like shelving from IKEA. Not a pigeon in sight. We had to take the kids to an effin ice cream parlour. You should've seen the fancy prices. Me and Tanya couldn't afford nothing for ourselves.'

The next time they met, Evelyn said: 'These are your individual learning plans. You need to write on your form exactly what it is you're here to learn.

'Er,' said Porky, sucking on his biro. 'I don't know exactly what I'm here to learn. I'm waiting to find out.'

'It's like this,' said Evelyn. 'You're all going to do the same basic things, but you'll have your own special reasons for wanting to do some of them. Remember? Sonny said he wanted to be able to email people in the music business. That's the sort of thing.'

It was at this point that it became clear that Mabel couldn't read and write very well. She had started to sweat copiously over her form. Porky took advantage of Evelyn's gentle concern, and the fact that her back was turned to him, to write 'Pigeons' on his form. He then inserted 'Ken Livingstone' and 'pigeons' into his Google search engine and waited to see what would come up.

He sat next to Ephraim during the break. They were in the library's spanking new café with drinks that were made in a machine and piddled into cardboard cups.

'Pigeons sweat on the inside,' said Porky, kicking off the conversation and thinking mildly about Mabel.

Ephraim looked at him without interest. 'Oh?'

'Yeah. They release water vapour into the lungs and expel it to bring their temperature down.'

Ephraim grunted and twiddled his fingers. You could tell he was longing for a cigarette.

'You'd be amazed at the number of diseases pigeons can get – one-eyed cold, canker, feather rot, rickets. It's only feral pigeons you have to worry about infecting humans, though, like the ones that Ken banned from Trafalgar Square.' Porky became aware of Ephraim's boredom.

'Do people race pigeons back home then?' he ventured.

Ephraim shrugged his narrow shoulders inside his dingy polo shirt. 'Nope.'

'What, never?'

'Nope.'

'Ah,' said Porky. He looked at Ephraim thoughtfully. He was very much his own man, what with that distant look and his reluctance to speak. He had dressed in all the right sort of things to pass himself off as an acclimatised westerner – jeans, trainers etcetera – and yet he looked wrong in them.

'How's Citizenship?' asked Porky.

Ephraim shrugged again.

'What's it all about then?'

'We been doin' about Em Pees.'

'Oh yeah? Don't you have them back home, then?'

Ephraim shook his head.

'You ent missing much, mate. Bunch of wankers.' Porky reflected for a minute. Maybe this wasn't the most constructive thing he could have said. 'Whatchyou doin' here, anyway?' he asked.

'War back home,' said Ephraim. 'Many years. The government is weak.'

'Oh,' said Porky. 'What they fighting about?'

'Same as everywhere. Everyone wants to be the big shot.'

'Whad you do back there, then?'

Ephraim scrutinised Porky closely with a mean eye, then looked around cautiously. He lowered his voice. 'Vigilante,' he said.

Porky played with the word slowly in his head, reminding himself of newsreels he'd seen on telly.

'What,' he said eventually, 'You mean you...?'

Ephraim drew his fore-finger across his throat and made a noise with his glottis. 'Yeah,' he sniggered. 'Lots. Dogs didn't go hungry after we bin through a village.'

Porky could think of nothing to say. He felt out of his depth. In silence he followed Ephraim back into the classroom for the second half of the lesson.

Porky had really got the bit between his teeth on the pigeon front. It was a sunny afternoon, and the sunshine dispelled the curious unease he had felt since Ephraim's revelation, so he did something he had

143

never before done in his life: he went and joined the library proper. This meant he could sit at the computer for about forty minutes at a time before it was someone else's turn. During two forty-minute slots he discovered that racing pigeons had been used during both World Wars for carrying messages. The Germans had commandeered over a million from the Belgians in the First World War, as they were the best going. The Americans and the British had their own Pigeon Services. The birds flew all sorts of missions and thirty-one of them ended up getting outstanding service medals.

It was as he had suspected: a whole new world was waiting in the ether. It was like being in a mystery mansion with an infinite number of doors. Every time a page clicked open, more treasure was revealed. Excitedly he pressed on door after door. On he went greedily, page to page, link to link, faster and faster. His craving for door-opening could not be satisfied: he was hooked. By the end of his second session, he was conversant with every detail of basic loft design, and a whole lot more. When the assistant came to tell him his time was up, and that a sixth-form student was waiting for his place, he could barely recognise her as the woman who had given him his log-in details. Outside, the high street looked like a foreign country.

Porky unlocked the door and stepped out onto the minute balcony of his ground floor flat. There was a clothes frame there that he used occasionally and a broken armchair that no-one could be bothered to nick.

Of course he wasn't best placed, being on the ground floor. No-one flew pigeons from the ground floor. He considered the possibility of flying them from the drying area at the top of the building, but it only took a moment to realise that washing and bird droppings don't mix. He wished he could be like the Dutch fanciers, with a house of his own, and a loft built into the er, loft. But the fact was: he hadn't lived in a proper house throughout his entire married life, and he wasn't likely to get one now. No, he thought wistfully, the idea was not a goer.

The group grew into a comfortable accommodation with one another. Porky and Shazan were usually the first to arrive. Sonny could turn up at any time, having walked all the way from his digs in Crystal Palace. Hardip was sometimes delayed by work. Mabel would arrive panting, weighed down by shopping bags. Ephraim slipped in like a shadow and departed the same way. Ursula sometimes didn't arrive at all. If either her taxi or her carer didn't turn up, she was stuck. If they turned up late, she was effing and blinding by the time she was delivered into the room.

They were all pursuing their own line of study now. Evelyn was the guiding presence who moved between them, offering a pertinent question or a piece of useful information. Porky enjoyed the sense of having a woman around the place again, generating a warm scent of cosmetics mixed with body odour as she wafted past you. It reminded him how much he missed Irene. You could tell Hardip felt the same. Every time Evelyn neared him, he stirred uncomfortably on his chair, like a bear on a boulder. It turned out his wife had recently left him with two small kids to look after.

Porky gradually developed an affection for Mabel. It began on the day he clocked that one of her bags was always intended for Shazan, a bag of vegetables that she could take home as proof that she'd spent her morning shopping. Money changed hands of course, but all the same, he was touched. But though he liked Mabel, he didn't fancy her. Mabel was endocrinally challenged. No matter what the task, whether to open a new document, or convert something into a different font, her first response was to sweat. It was not the most attractive of features. Still, Porky contemplated the vaguest possibility that she might be a kindly home-maker who could see him through his later years.

They were all developing talents and skills they didn't know they had. One of these was screen flicking. Porky turned in his chair one day to find Hardip looking at pictures of what he could only describe as totty.

'Whatchyou up to then?'

'It's a matrimonial site,' said Hardip, blushing. 'Look, if you like'. He scrolled through some images:

'Nisha – "I am happy-go-lucky person who loves playing pranks."' 'At thirty-two, I don't think so,' said Hardip. He scrolled on.

'Groovy – "I have a bright personality and live a very modern life style. I seek a like-minded partner who is mentally stimulating, and who can respond to my..." Ball-breaker,' muttered Hardip. He pressed his finger on the mouse again.

'Ooh, what about her?' said Porky. A heavily-kholed woman peered from beneath a curtain of raven black hair. 'Rami – "I am a very social creature, but I very much enjoy my own space as well."'

'Well, she's playing the field, ent she?' said Hardip, 'You can't tell nothing from that.'

'So what are you looking for?' asked Porky.

'None of them says what I want to hear.'

'Which is?'

'I make first class pooris, love kids, like a damn good jiggy-jig and am a grade one accountant,' Hardip tittered.

At this point Evelyn approached. With a flick of his finger, Hardip brought up the inevitable spreadsheet, and Porky returned to his pigeon researches.

'For Chrissake, Dad!'

'What?'

'There's a onion in this freezer!'

'So bloody what?'

'What's a onion doin' in the freezer?'

'I bleedin put it there.'

'What for?'

'I had a plan.'

'What plan?'

'Never you mind. It doesn't matter.'

'Don't let me think you can't look after yourself.'

'Or?'

'We'll have to start thinking about a home.'

Porky felt as chilly as the onion.

They were about half way through the course.

'What we're going to do today,' said Evelyn – it was one of those days when her moustache was absent and her cleavage removed from view, so you began to wonder if you might be dealing with a doppleganger – is have a look at your individual learning plans again and review how far you've got. If you remember, I asked you all to tell us about something you've been working on.'

They turned their chairs into the room and sat facing one another, their arms folded, feeling exposed without their computer terminals.

Shazan went first. She made a brief PowerPoint presentation about the top oil-producing nations worldwide; moved on to a consideration of prices at the pump in the US, the UK and Iraq; made reference in passing to the cartel of oil producers in the States, and concluded with a proposition about British foreign policy. Her slides included snappy bar charts and graphs and a number of colourful maps. When she finished, there was silence.

'Any questions?' asked Evelyn. There were none. 'You've done so well, Shazan, I think you should be preparing to get onto an Access to Higher Education course. Do you know what that means?'

Shazan shook her head.

'It means you should be preparing to go to university.'

Shazan glowed and sat down, Hardip whistled. Ursula said, 'Well done, gel!'

There was no Mabel. She had flu. Sonny was next under the spotlight. He explained that he could now send emails with attachments. He read out an email he had drafted: 'Dear Maestro, I will be arriving in Vienna on thirteenth inst. with an exceptional young violinist who has recently left the Academy with highest distinction. I beg you most ardently to make some space in your schedule to hear her. Yours, most obliged, Sonny Gunaratna Rosario.' Sonny's slightly antique turn of phrase made you wonder if after all he was, as he claimed, descended from a minor Indian royal family.

'So what next?' asked Evelyn. Sonny hadn't thought about that. Evelyn pressed him. Reluctantly he conceded that he might be persuaded to learn how to book tickets on-line, though he was wary about letting blighters of unknown background and dubious credentials have sight of his banking details.

'Good,' said Evelyn, scratching this hastily on his form. 'What about you, Hardip?' Hardip gave a jumbled description of how he had attempted to enter the last six months of his accounts onto a spreadsheet, and how it had all gone badly wrong.

Evelyn rubbed her finger thoughtfully across the place where her moustache had been. 'You're starting to get a hang-up about this, Hardip. What's the problem?'

Hardip shifted uncomfortably on his chair and looked at the floor for a long time. 'I don't like it,' he said at last. 'I'm no good at it.'

'He wants to look for a wife to do it,' chuckled Porky.

Hardip looked at him half in resentment, half in gratitude. And so it was agreed that Hardip would work on drafting a profile of himself that he could post on a matrimonial website.

When it came to Ursula's turn, she proclaimed that she had unearthed a new relative, a great-uncle who'd gone logging in Canada and disappeared without trace, abandoning his family.

'Okay. That's good. Very exciting,' said Evelyn slowly, tapping her pen on Ursula's record sheet. 'But you've spent a lot of time delving into that 1911 census now. I think it's time to move on. What about using Word to keep a learning journal, or..?'

Ursula glared at her with the glittering eye of the obsessive: 'I'm nowhere near ready yet,' she breathed. 'I have to find out what happened to the family.'

Ephraim read out an assignment he'd prepared for his Citizenship course. He'd taken the trouble to print out typed copies, which he passed around the group. It was brief, to the point, and he'd made a stab at getting some punctuation into it. 'In this England,' it went, 'there are; laws to protect people who Have come from Other countries. So we can Get jobs and maybe a flat and Vote. There are laws; for women, as well. So they can get jobs and Divorced. These are Good laws that make everybody equal. But to me women can Never be like men. A man should beat a woman if, She anoys him. So laws the laws are okay but what's the point.'

'Pisshead!' muttered Ursula.

'A sound analysis, my man,' smirked Sonny.

'Get on, there!' said Porky.

'Hmm,' said Evelyn. 'What line of work are you thinking of going into, Ephraim, once you've got your certificate?'

'Care. My tutor says there is always lots of jobs for assistants in care homes.'

'Right. Good choice. But you'd better think carefully about the fact that a lot of the people who live in care homes are elderly women. They're not going to take too kindly to your views.'

'I won't tell them,' said Ephraim.

'Better not,' said Evelyn. 'Okay then, I'll put down that you're progressing on to a Social Care course, and need to learn how to write reports. Next: Porky!'

Porky had made no preparations. He simply opened his mouth and waxed lyrical about pigeons. 'These days people mainly keep three different types of pigeons,' he said, 'long-distance or racers – that's mainly what we have here in the west; high flyers or tipplers – people over in India and Pakistan like them, and fancy pigeons – and that's a case of 'if you fancy them you keep them'! Racers have to be trained before they can do long distances. Some of the best can do about eight hundred miles. One of the biggest races every year is from Barcelona, so if a pigeon went the wrong way, it could end up in North Africa!...'

'Erm,' said Evelyn.

Porky pressed on: 'But I've got to tell you about fancy birds. There's pouters and fantails, and tumblers – they can flip over backwards while they're flying. There's Lahores – they're amazing. They've got these really crazy feet – two fans made up of feathers. And Bokhara trumpeters – they look like two washing up mops having a... I mean, one on top of the other...'

Evelyn cut in: 'That's good, Porky. You've learned an awful lot about pigeons. I think we can safely say you've learned how to do an internet search. Now what about moving on to something else?'

Porky was taken aback. There was still a hell of a lot of ground he had to cover.

'Are you on Direct Payments? You could learn how to use Excel to keep track of your cashflow.'

Oh, no. He was going to head that one off at the pass. He shook his head vigorously. Only last Wednesday he'd come across the website of an Armenian chap, Yovnan, who kept the most spectacular array of fantails and tumblers. He wanted to know a whole lot more about that.

'We have to think about what you're going to go on to after this. We have to think about your progression on to a more advanced course or into something socially useful. What did you have in mind, Porky?'

Porky shrugged. He was sixty-seven. His idea of progression was keep out of the home on Daggert Street that smelled pungently of wee with a none-too-subtle bouquet of Glade.

Evelyn noted his disgruntlement. 'All right,' she said, relenting, 'what about learning how to download pictures of your favourite pigeons, and including them in a presentation that we can all see?'

Porky brightened at once.

'Barrie,' wheedled Porky, the next time Barrie came round. 'I bin thinking.'

'Oh yeah?'

'See your little garden?' Barrie and his family lived in a tiny terraced house at the foot of Runnymede, built in the eighties, all mod cons but no room to swing a cat.

'Yeah.'

'And you know how the kids have always wanted to have a pet, but Tanya wouldn't let them.'

'Yeah, no point with both of us out at work all day.'

'Well, how about we get a few pigeons and build a loft at the end of your garden?'

Barrie was silent.

'I could get fancy birds, white fantails maybe. The kids would love 'em, and they don't need much flying.'

'An' who's going to buy them?'

'I could do that. We only need a pair to start with. I could come over in the mornings to see to 'em after you've gone to work. And I could come over again in the evening, clean them out and...' Porky felt a sudden rush of blood to the head, '...have my tea.'

Barrie thought for a moment. 'Okay,' he said. 'I'll speak to Tanya about it.'

The following week there was still no Mabel and no Shazan either. They'd just got their noses stuck to their screens, when there was a commotion outside the door. A man in a sports jacket and a white, high-collared shirt was thumping on the glass. He was carefully turned out: closely-trimmed hair, neat beard and wire-rimmed specs – to all intents and purposes a reserved-looking man, but on this occasion he appeared to have completely lost his rag. Evelyn unfolded herself from examining Hardip's screen and went out. She attempted to engage the man in conversation, bending towards him – she was taller than him – in a placatory fashion, but he was having none of it, and continued gesticulating. The plate glass was thick and they couldn't hear everything, but phrases like, 'What business..?' '...university..', '...ideas into her head..', '...western values..', '...wife... mother... home..' drifted through. They were clear now that it was Shazan's husband, and that her scheme had been rumbled.

'Poor git,' said Ursula. 'That'll be the last we see of her.'

As the library's security staff bore down on him, the man chose his moment and ricocheted off into the book stacks.

Tanya had said yes. And then added, 'As long as the thing doesn't look a flamin' eyesore.' Gleefully, Porky joined Barrie in his beat-up little car in the evenings and they trundled round the better streets, delving into skips and hauling out bricks, ply, lengths of four-be-two and refrigerator shelves. What was in short supply was sheet metal and tarp. And they needed a strip light, but that would have to come from Wickes. The kids, meantime, were on the lookout for anything that would serve as drinking pots and a nesting bowl.

Porky's preparations of his PowerPoint presentation were well advanced. He'd learned how to do bullet points and fancy scripts and he could make the words appear a line at a time – with sound effects like a Gatling gun if he wanted. Evelyn had shown him how to make the script large and not too fancy, so that everyone would be able to read it. Best of all, he'd learned how to save pictures from the internet and import them into his presentation. He was busy reviewing these during one of their sessions when they got a visitor, a large woman in a light-coloured trouser suit and a bottled tan. A look crossed Evelyn's face that reminded Porky of a cat coughing up a fluff ball.

'Ah...' She got up. 'Remember I told you we may be having a visitor. But she's come to look at me, not at you. Just carry on with what you're doing.'

Of course it was all horseshit. The woman sat at a work station, donned the smallest pair of reading specs that Porky had ever seen, extracted a pen from a handbag the size of a stuffed hog and started scribbling at once on a sheaf of papers. At intervals, her eyes darted rapidly round the room, sizing each of them up, like a hawk on a hunting mission. Evelyn continued discussing with Hardip how best to present himself to a potential bride. Hardip faltered. His suggestions became increasingly lame. A conversation that five minutes ago had entertained them all as they'd eavesdropped on him now sounded completely inane.

The woman summoned Evelyn and, in a stage whisper, requested their individual learning plans. Evelyn handed them over. The woman devoured these with the coruscating vigour of Nitromors stripping paint off doors. Then came more pointed whispering.

'The inspector would like to talk to you now,' Evelyn announced, 'without me present. There's nothing to worry about. Just answer her questions and tell her what you've been doing.'

It was like setting a trap.

'Have you enjoyed your course?' The inspector smiled, peering over the top of her spectacles.

'Yes,' they chorused.

'And how do you like your tutor?'

'Bloody good,' said Ursula. 'Nothing's too much trouble for her,' added Hardip. 'She explains things good,' said Ephraim. 'You're never afraid to ask,' said Sonny.

'And what have you learned while you've been on the course?'

That was harder.

'I have made significant progress,' ventured Sonny. 'I am now able to communicate with distant persons via the medium of email. I find it a considerable boon.'

'And I'm doing Powerpoint,' threw in Porky.

'And what about the rest of you?' the inspector pressed further. 'What would you say you've gained by coming here?'

'Friends,' said Ursula, 'And I've found a second cousin once removed – in Saskatchewan.'

'I've got a meeting to discuss programming at the Cadogan Hall,' said Sonny.

'And I'm getting a pigeon loft,' said Porky.

The woman appeared to weigh this up. Then she fixed her gaze on Hardip. 'Hardip, isn't it? According to your plan, you were working on Excel. Isn't that right? How did you get on with that?'

'I...'

Porky rushed to his rescue: 'Hardip done best of all. He's got a date. With the love of his life.' He managed a camp falsetto: '"Sandip – I can be a bit shy but I'm a loving personality. My interests include Hindi film music and cooking. I am easy to get along with and I'm just glued to family values. My favourite pastime is Excel spreadsheets."'

They all laughed.

'Seriously, though,' The inspector laughed too – she'd got into the spirit of things now, and they were warming to each other a bit – 'Is anyone going on to college, or to a job?'

They all looked at Ephraim. 'Yeah,' he said grudgingly. 'I got a place for that.'

'And there was Shazan,' added Ursula, 'She was bloody brilliant, but she's left.'

The trap shut.

Evelyn was visibly shaken after the session.

'What did the woman say?' they all wanted to know.

'She said not enough of you had achieved all the course outcomes, and not enough of you were going on to further education, training or employment.'

'The woman is deluded,' declared Sonny defiantly. 'Ask the wrong question and you get the wrong answer. The woman is a soulless functionary of a small-minded governing class. The Naxelites were right to dismiss such people.'

'Even if you're right, Sonny,' said Evelyn, 'what she says still matters. Once my bosses find out, the course won't run again, you can be sure of that.'

Porky was very excited, despite the disturbing impact of the inspector's visit. After class, out in the main concourse, Sonny had shown him how to send an email. And so, Porky had sent his first ever message... to Yovnan. He didn't say much, just hello and something about how much he admired his birds. He guessed from the captions on Yovnan's photographs that his grip on English was a bit rudimentary, but if he got a reply – big if – and depending on how intelligible it was, he might ask some questions.

He lay on his back on his orthopaedic bed. He had printed off his favourite pigeon pin-up and stuck it on the wall of his bedroom. It showed a pair of Yovnan's fine white and brown tumblers, elegantly poised in gentle fellowship, in their cage, deep in snow. The two birds bore as much resemblance to London pigeons as Concord did to a Hercules bomber. The light reflected from the snow gave them an ethereal quality, the darker feathers of their mantles and tails softened to the colour of rock rose, their Persil-white breasts suffused with a subtle glow. The pair stood meek, but alert, as if waiting for instruction from one whom they respected. Porky was awed by the beauty of the birds, and struck by the humanity of the man. Someone he didn't know, in a land that he knew nothing about, had taken the trouble to hand rear these birds and care for them, day in day out, no matter how harsh the weather. Surely that was something worth knowing about and understanding?

The group met one more time. Mabel returned, her bouts of perspiration replaced by a chesty cough. Ursula read them a letter she'd just received from her second cousin once removed. She emphasised the bit where he mentioned his jacuzzi. Hardip – in a suit for once – told them he was in with a chance, and would be meeting the lady of his affections for a second time later that day. And Porky gave his presentation. 'Those birds are too good to eat,' said Ephraim, which Porky took as a sign of approval. 'You come a long way, boy,' said Mabel. Porky beamed at her. She was immediately thrown into a fit of wheezing and obliged to look away in confusion.

Even Evelyn, in a demure skirt and waisted jacket, had something to report: she had an interview for another teaching job on the far side of town.

154

As a farewell gesture, Sonny treated them all to a meal at the Officers' Club where they stuffed themselves with naan, chicken makhni, aloo ghobi and several different kinds of chutney even though it was barely twelve o'clock. Sonny himself had bought tickets online, and was off that night to the Verbier Festival.

As Porky plodded across the green from the bus stop to his flat, he felt he was making a new beginning. Tonight, he and Barrie were going to make a start on the foundations for the loft. Then – you never knew – today might just be the day he would hear from Yovnan. Later in the afternoon, he would go back to the library to check. What's more, deep in the pocket of the padded jacket Tanya had got him in the market, was a small slip of paper, and on that slip was Mabel's phone number.

Getting Shot

by Pam Eaves

He can't be out. Not Saturday afternoon with football on TV.

Jane rang the doorbell again, and pressed her nose against the glass in the front door. A shadowy figure hovered at the back of the hall. She bent down, pushed open the letter box and shouted, 'Stop mucking about, Colin, and open the door. My key won't go in. The lock must need oiling.'

There was a muffled, 'Go away,' and the shadow disappeared. Fuming, Jane shoved her finger on the bell push and held it there, the shrill ringing echoing through the house. What the hell's he up to? she thought, banging her other hand on the door. Surely he's not still sulking over that row we had?

The shadow appeared in the hall again and moved towards the front door. Jane took her finger off the bell. At last.

'Piss off,' Colin said.

'Let me in, you idiot. I live here.' Jane was near to tears with fury and frustration. It had been a rotten journey, the flight delayed at Pisa and she was dying for a cup of tea, a shower…

'Not any more, you don't. I've changed the lock.'

'You've what?' Jane's legs gave way and she leaned against the porch, trying not to panic. 'Why? There was nothing wrong with the old one.' Peering through the letter box, she could see the rough, grey cardigan she'd always hated – rotten, shabby, old thing.

'Come on Colin, open the door for pity's sake.' The cardigan retreated, reducing her to impotent fury. She straightened up, hammering on the door and shouting, 'Let me in, bugger you. It's my house. I pay for it. You're only the lodger.'

But there was silence from inside. Jane leant against the porch, trying to make sense of it all. Had Colin gone mad? He'd been acting peculiar before she went…

'Problems?' The quavering voice made Jane jump. She turned and saw her elderly next-door neighbour peering over the fence and her heart sank, but there was no escape. Winnie's thin pink nose was twitching as she asked, 'You bin away?'

Jane stared at the old woman, wondering how to get rid of her. The last thing she needed was Winnie spreading it all round the neighbourhood that she'd been locked out.

'That chap of yours 'as been up to summat,' Winnie said. 'There's bin all sorts of noise coming from the 'ouse; banging all hours. I asked 'im what 'e was doin' but he didn't answer. Gone a bit peculiar if you ask me.'

'What?' Jane stiffened at Winnie's echo of her own thoughts.

'D'you fancy a cup of tea love? Talk about it?' Winnie cocked her head invitingly.

Talk about it? With Winnie? No way, but perhaps she could get in the back door – over the garden wall, and tea? Jane licked dry lips and hesitated, then nodded.

'Yes, please.'

The old lady beamed and held her front door wide open.

'I'll put the kettle on,' she said as Jane trundled her case up the path. 'Dump that in the hall and the bathroom's upstairs if you need it.'

As Winnie shuffled through to the kitchen, Jane ran upstairs to the old-fashioned bathroom, wondering what Colin was up to. 'Banging all hours,' Winnie had said. If he's fixed up that train set – he's a goner.

Jane glanced through at Winnie's sitting room as she came downstairs, and shuddered. Old photographs, ornaments and lamps covered every surface. If Colin had his way my place'd look like that – a mess. Tears pricked her eyes as she thought of her beautiful minimalist room, the pine floor, low sofas and carefully chosen ornaments – before he moved in.

Winnie was in the kitchen hovering over a battered kettle; brown teapot at the ready. Jane took in the ancient gas cooker and old-fashioned kitchen cabinet, her nose wrinkling, but as Winnie poured hot water into the teapot and swilled it round, she suddenly remembered her grannie doing the same.

'How long have you lived here, Winnie?' she asked.

'My Bert bought this house when we was married,' Winnie replied. 'I had to mind me p's and q's in them days 'cos the house were in his name.' She grinned, revealing yellowish false teeth. 'But I got it when Bert pipped it. I always told him it were worth his while to keep me alive if he wanted to eat good and old Bert was right greedy.' She spooned tea into the teapot and poured boiling water over it.

'There,' she said. 'Wait five minutes and that'll be just right. You go through to the lounge and sit down and I'll bring you the best cuppa you've had for ages. Biscuit?'

'No thanks.'

'Dieting?' Winnie sniffed. 'Keep thin to keep your man? You eat what you want, girl. Blokes ain't worth 'anging on to most times. Go and sit down.'

Jane perched on the edge of the dingy sofa, wondering what on earth she was going to do. She looked up as Winnie shuffled in with the tea tray. 'Right,' she said. 'Get this down and then you can tell me all about it.'

Jane sipped silently, feeling calmer in spite of the cluttered room. The ticking of the grandmother clock was soothing and she marvelled at how peaceful it was. No television on. But there was an ancient TV in the corner.

'Can you hear our television, Winnie?'

'Yes. Gets on my nerves sometimes, blaring all hours. I like a bit of quiet.' Winnie, who'd been staring through the window, turned to Jane.

'Sorry. It's Colin. He likes it on, for company he says.'

'If he went to work like other blokes he'd have company,' was the tart reply. 'I see you go off in the morning, but...'

'He's looking for a job,' Jane explained quickly.

'Well, he ain't looking very 'ard.'

'I don't think he's very well. He's been irritable since he was made redundant.' Tears welled and Jane fished down her bag for a tissue. 'In fact I'm wondering if he's gone a bit funny. Colin hates me going away and we had a terrible row just before I left.'

'Business trip?' Winnie enquired, picking up her cup.

'No. Holiday with my girlfriend.'

'Did you get up to mischief?'

'Of course not.' Jane was shocked. 'Annie and I like looking at art, architecture – that sort of thing, but Colin hates all that. He's only interested in sport on television.'

Winnie sipped tea silently.

'Anyway, he's been hard up since he lost his job. It's my house but when Colin and I fell in love I asked him to move in, and we were very....' Jane's voice trailed off.

'You don't sound 'appy to me.' Winnie plonked her cup down in the saucer. 'In fact it don't sound like you've got much in common. More tea?'

Jane nodded and Winnie re-filled her cup.

'What was the row about?'

'Colin's Mum threatened to throw his train set out, so he wanted to set it up in my living room.'

'Bloody cheek. Anyone'd row about that,' Winnie said. 'I bet that's what all that banging was while you were away. I've seen him going in with funny-shaped parcels. You need to tell 'im straight.'

'He won't let me in,' Jane said. 'Can I get over your fence and try getting in the back way when I've finished this, please?'

'What?' Winnie glared at Jane. 'It's your house. You should go in through the front door.'

'He changed the lock while I was away.'

'He's got no right,' Winnie snapped. 'You could have 'im for that.'

'It's not that easy,' Jane said, her eyes filling with tears. 'He's been living with me for over a year now and there's laws protecting tenants. I'll probably have to go to court, prove I own the house. It'll take ages, and he'll argue he's got rights...'

'Rights be blowed,' Winnie exploded, struggling to her feet and moving towards the kitchen with the teapot as Jane dabbed her eyes.

When Winnie returned with the refreshed pot, she poured more tea without asking and stood looking at Jane.

'I bin thinking,' she announced. 'You should be ashamed of yourself, young lady. I see you trottin' off every morning, smart as paint in your nifty trouser suit. A career girl with your own house, all independent, and you let some low life snatch it away because you say he's got 'rights'. He's got no bloody rights at all.' She thudded down in the armchair and glared at Jane.

'Forty years I slaved in this house pandering to a bad-tempered old devil. I 'ad rights – and I saw I got 'em too. And you've got to do the same.'

'I don't think you understand, Winnie,' Jane said, standing up. 'Thanks for the tea, but...'

159

'Sit down,' Winnie growled.

Jane sat.

'Now. I've bin thinkin' how to get round this, this – cheek. What we'll do is....'

Jane listened, inserting the odd doubtful protest, which was quickly brushed aside as Winnie outlined her plan. She ended up, 'So – first things first. You got somewhere to stay tonight? You can stay 'ere if you like.'

'Annie will put me up,' Jane said hurriedly. 'But thanks for the offer.'

Winnie suppressed a grin. 'Right. Ring her first and get yerself fixed up and then I'll make my call. You'd better tell that Annie it could be for a coupla weeks, but that's better than going through all that old malarky you was talking about.'

At least that part of Winnie's idea is sensible, Jane thought as she scrabbled in her bag for her mobile.

'Annie said I can stay as long as I like,' she sniffed when she rang off. 'She's coming to get me right away.'

'Good,' Winnie said briskly. 'Now, don't upset yourself. It's going to be alright. I'll deal with that low-life. He'll be out in no time.'

Three weeks later Jane made a chocolate cake and invited Winnie for tea – proper loose tea, made in her grannie's old brown teapot. The old lady's black eyes twinkled when she scanned the lace-covered table, but she didn't comment.

'Well, you've got yourself sorted out then,' she said as she plonked herself on a chair.

'Thanks to you, Winnie.' Jane poured the strong brew. 'You're a crafty old woman. I had to laugh when I saw the newspaper headline: 'Local Good Neighbour Fears Terrorist Attack.''

'I learned a few tricks in my time with Bert, but I really enjoyed spinning that tale to the police and I got me moment of fame. All over the papers it was. Did you see?'

'Yes, and the photographs; they were good of you, and the photographer got one of Colin being taken away in handcuffs, and all his stuff being carted off by men in white overalls. You must have been quick off the mark – notified the local paper at the same time as the police.'

'Before, actually,' Winnie said, biting greedily into the large slice of cake Jane passed her. 'Wanted to make sure everyone knew I was doing my civic duty. Them parcels your bloke took in could have been guns or bomb-making equipment. I wasn't to know.'

'Were the neighbours frightened?'

'Didn't see much of them. As soon as they heard the sirens they were all at their windows, but when the police shouted warnings about shooting, there wasn't a sign of 'em. All flat on the floor probably.' Winnie grinned as she polished off the cake.

Jane hesitated for a minute, then – 'Winnie,' she said. 'Do you mind if I ask you something? What did your Bert die of?'

Winnie's grin widened. 'I didn't kill 'im, if that's what you think' she said. 'He did it 'imself, being greedy. He got up to twenty-five stone, then dropped orf the twig nice and easy with an 'eart attack, so I got me 'ouse, and a bit of peace and quiet. There's always a way round these little problems.'

Sea God

by Nina Milton

Ari zipped up her jeans. Skin against denim from hip bone to hip bone, tight as a drum, best feeling in fashion-land. Zip flying up, button popping nice n' easy.

No way could she let this change. Graphic pictures in her biology text book. A jelly bean, then a fish, then... then jeans to the back of the wardrobe. She threw on her coat and pushed her feet into black boots.

Outside, wintry air hit her face. The leaves on the row of trees were spinning, hitting the ground and blowing along it like remote-controlled toys. She looked up at the golden branches. 'Easy, ain't it?' she taunted. 'Easy to drop 'em. If you're a fucking tree.'

More like a fish than a leaf. A shrimpy thing you could see right through, swimming in a plastic bucket of seawater. Both hands over the top. Keep it safe.

Ari took the bus past the Next, past Wallis. She got off at the big Boots, two floors of make-up, beauty products and assorted gifts. She joined the queue for the pharmacy. It was long. It was always long in the big Boots. Long equalled anonymous. She was well known in her local chemist, Sally'd been there since GCSEs.

'I want the Morning After Pill, please.'

A woman took her into a little cubicle which smelt of people's feet.

She didn't go into Virgin. Ryan would be at the Pay Here, and one look at her face... she could't risk it.

Besides she had to go home and swallow up this bad boy packet. Teach her to think ahead. Responsibility was something grow-ups did. I *am* a grown-up, she reminded herself. She half believed it. She knew what she wanted. Good exam results – very good. An escape – different... what did careers call it? *Prospects*. Someone smart, in a suit, eventually. Not a mother. Fuck it; mothers were like... *her mother*... unsmart. No suits. Little lives for years, nagging fathers to mow lawns and hitch up caravans until you didn't care any more.

Relief flooded when she felt that sticky warm dampness at the top of her thighs. She phoned in sick to college and told Mum she had free periods. *Periods* was bloody right. *Bloody* was bloody right. She took a shower and stole some of her mother's massive pads because tampons seemed a bit daft in the circumstances. Then she lay on the bed and texted Ryan.

Cant C U 2nite

Y not?

MYOB

U 2

Piss off then

The heaviness of the pain surprised her. Mother of all periods. She locked herself in the loo. She sat on the toilet and let the blood run into the bowl. This was bleeding, proper bleeding. Her whole belly contracted in one long wrenching tear. She gripped the sink and it felt like ice to her hot hand. A sort of groaning scream came out from somewhere in her lungs and her heart thrust in a fast beat she could see through her T-shirt.

Another wave of pain took her over, her mouth rasping in air. Could a jelly bean rip you so bad? Quite suddenly the storm past, and she was passing something biblical… *it came to pass.* A splash against the water in the bowl beneath her. She wiped the blood away with a damp flannel, swilling and swilling it in a sink full of pink water, before she risked a look in the loo.

A sheen of curdled blood and raw tissue floated on the water. A packet of soft redness. She'd heard about sponges, what women used to use. It looked like one of those, how she imagined it. It floated. Like a bad egg. Inside, baby thing. Hidden, as if it were rejecting her.

Not baby. When you do the morning after pill, there's no baby. You are swilling away the natural products of your own body.

She pulled at the flush. The water flooded the bowl. For a moment Ari thought that the huge clot of her blood was going to block the S bend. The water swirled to the very top.

'Get away,' she yelled. 'Get away!' She thrust her whole arm into the toilet, pushing the clots down to the bottom. The water swirled away, taking everything into a subterranean place.

The sea, Ari thought. Everything is swept out into the deep sea. It will become a fish, after all.

That night, she dreamed of waves and deep water, azure blue right to the bottom. A naked baby boy swam, plump with a shock of golden, curly hair. Bubbles of air floated from his mouth. He somersaulted in the water, moving between jutting rocks and swaying weed. She couldn't cry out because she was also under the water and was afraid of drowning. When she woke, it was early, still dark. She got up and checked her pad. No more bleeding. It was over. Thank the fuck for that.

Dylan had been going to uni to study music technology, but instead he got a job serving in Virgin. He was supposed to be forming a band, but the trouble there was he didn't know anybody who could play an instrument well enough. Ari would have liked to say, oh, you can talk, but she couldn't because he could…talk…play keyboard, guitar…he was good, when he wanted to be.

Her jeans' zip flew up. She caught the bus and hung around Pay Here. They didn't talk about anything much. She recognised how *slight* the things she talked about were. She was burning to disclose the secret. But Ryan mustn't know about this. She wondered if it ran in the family – keeping secrets was what Mum did.

'What shall we do tonight?'

'Not busy tonight then?'

'I was feeling lousy yesterday.'

'Aw…' He pecked at her lips with his. 'Ne'mind.'

She had the dream again. The child swam like a merboy, born to the seas. His hair had darkened and grown, lifting from his head like seaweed in the gentle movement of the water. In the bubbles from his lips she thought she caught a fleeting sound. A baby's first word? Mama? Papa?

'I'm sorry,' she said to him.

He laughed, happy here in his water-world. She reached out and felt the softness of his baby limbs. He kicked with his feet and was gone.

'I'm moving into a flat.' They were lying on Ryan's bed in his parents house.

'What, can you afford that?'

'Yeah, like, I've got promotion.'

'What you?'

'Trainee assistant floor manager.'

She snorted. 'Only the four words? Not 'junior deputy under-floor assistant sub-manager's trainee?'

He batted her arm. 'You could move in.'

'What with you?'

'No, with Mighty Mouse, stupid.'

'That is you, ain't it?'

'Yeah, my alter-ego.'

Ari got off the bed and started to dress. 'I'm going to York. You know that. Conditional place.'

'That's months away.'

'True.'

The denim of her jeans rasped against her skin. The zip was sticky. The button wasn't popping easy. She hardly noticed.

Ryan snored next to her. They didn't make love as often, because there was no urgency to do it. They were like an old married couple, snug in their own little flat. But last night, he'd held her close as if she'd suddenly grown precious to him and they'd fallen asleep like that, him first, Ari a long time later, almost anticipating the dream, which came more often.

'You understand, don't you,' she told her son. 'Why I did it? Anyway, you're happy. Look – you're a natural here.' In the dream, she almost considered the merboy as her elder, someone who would understand and look after her. Encourage her. He was like a young god of the sea; he would know everything. He knew she'd taken oaths, silent but intent, never to be her mother; to get her A grades; to wear a suit one day.

In the curtained morning light, the dream felt as amorphous and abandoned as an old DVD. She lay on her back, feeling the bubbles from the fish-child's mouth erupt in her stomach.

'It's wind,' she said aloud.

'What?'

'It's eight o'clock.'

'Get the kettle on, Ari.'

'Don't for godsake say that, it's what my dad says to my mum.'
In the kitchen, as the kettle fizzed, she threw up into the sink.

'Oh, Christ,' she said, wiping her mouth. 'F.H. Christ.'

'Can I call you Arianrod?' said the sonographer, not waiting for an answer. 'Can you make out the image on the screen?'

He was running the probe over Ari's stomach. She was reminded of her dad, mowing the grass at the front of the house. Don't miss out any bits, impress the passers-by.

She tossed her head on the flat pillow with its industrial-strength plastic lining. 'I thought I'd got rid of it? But the doctor says there must have been two.'

'That is possible,' said the sonographer. 'Not common, but non-identical twins have separate placentas. The weaker one can be lost.'

'Weaker?'

'If it was deformed, or if its placenta was not doing the job. But this one's doing fine. Looks perfect.'

'In case you haven't guessed, I don't want a baby.'

'Sometimes, seeing it move on the screen is the first time the baby feels real... alive. See that? Definitely a limb.'

'Not... no, I can't see.'

'It's often hard to discern the baby at this stage...looks to me like fourteen weeks...'

'What?'

The back of her eyes burnt, a furnace lit in her brain. She lowered the lids, but the sonographer was looking, saw the water squeezing out from under them. She was surprised it didn't steam. Six weeks back, she took the morning after pill. She must've been eight weeks pregnant. Having twins.

'Okay, Arianrod. Take your time.'

'It's none of your business.' She flicked her hands. 'Get that fucking thing off me.'

Instantly, he lifted the probe from her stomach and took a step back. 'We don't tolerate swearing in the hospital. There's a policy.'

'Don't worry, I'm going.'

She covered her stomach to stop him getting at her with his probe. With the downward pressure, she felt the tiny kick of fragile knee, heel or elbow. The child rolling in water, in tune with its brother.

'Okay... why don't you take this with you?' He was printing off the image she had seen on the screen. It had moved in grey jerks like an old silent movie. Now it was a photo in her hand. Her second child. Possibly a boy.

Two eggs planted inside her, putting out shoots. One so firm it held on as the boat rocked. The other... perhaps he'd been ready for a dream life in the sea. She was damn sure her young sea god knew about its twin. It had been trying to tell her for weeks. *Look after my brother.*

She was running. Up the hill from the hospital. Perfect blue winter sky. A single gull wheeling inland. Too cold at sea for it. Her dad had driven the car, towing the caravan behind. Her mum had packed bacon and cheap Tesco scones and her yellow swim suit although it would be too cold to bathe. Her brother had a blue bucket. Hers had been red. He liked the sand, she liked the sea. The gull had hovered, soaring in a circle above her. He'd wanted what she had. She put her hand over the bucket.

Ryan wouldn't be home until gone midnight. He was in Chad's garage where Chad kept his drum kit. There were three of them, Philippe on guitar, and Ryan alternating; bass, vocals, keyboard. She was exhausted by the time Eastenders was over. She flipped through her coursework and tried to get into a text book. It was useless.

'Listen,' she said to herself. She flicked the remote, so her voice would sound stronger. In the silence, she could believe her sea god might listen. 'It's got to go. I've got York. I've got suits to wear.' She panted for a while as the words...*fourteen weeks*...spun round her head. Then she yelled, spittle flying over the carpet. 'Fuck *you!*'

Ryan woke her up as he came in. She sat up on the sofa and rubbed her eyes.

'How was practice?'
'Cool. Did you go?'

'Yes. Of course I went.'

'And?'

She saw his face in profile in the muted TV light, lean cheeks, the slight curl to his hair. The words got stuck inside her throat. She'd already surfed the net, she knew what they did when you were this late; you had to sit with a drip, sort of baby poison, and give birth. Well, she'd done it one once. Killed the child then watch it swim away. And it had been perfectly all right.

'It's a boy,' she said at last.

'Bloody hell!' His eyes actually shone. 'I reckon Philip. It's my Grandad's name?'

'God, Ryan, not yet. No names yet.'

She saw the sea god's smile. Smirk, actually.

Look after my brother better'n you looked after me...

He was getting older, strong in his limbs, ribs showing through but arms already muscled, the spit of his father. As if, between the dreams, he was living a life without the measure of time, racing through the promised Ryan life. A famous, talented guitarist, leader of an underwater pop group.

He wasn't the weaker one. He was the first born, who had made his own mind up about where he wanted to be. He was the fit and healthy one, the one she'd allowed to swim away.

She closed her eyes, imagined herself running. Wide street like the one on holiday that went up a hill so that you only saw puffy clouds and the seagulls flashing silver until you got to the top. The bucket was tight in her hand, but she never liked sandcastles, she liked going out into the sea and coming back with the bucket full to brimming so that it slopped over her bare feet, fizzing with froth. She would happily fill her brother's moat with water, while he made turrets and pushed ice-lolly sticks into them. She would run back and forth, bucket on bucket poured into the channels, breathless but laughing, because it felt like freedom, this running, dipping, running, pouring and watching everything but the brine seep away.

When she found the tiny creature, curled and whiskered, transparent as breath, she stared as it circled the seawater in her bucket for a long time. In harmony the gull circled above. She'd heard of them swooping for battered cod. She didn't want to lose it. But she couldn't keep it in the bucket. It deserved its own life. She went out into the sea in her yellow costume. It was Easter – bitter

168

cold water. She was shivering before she tipped the bucket. It swam into the deep, where her baby's twin danced now, growing into a naked god so strong that she fancied if she took the wrong turning in her life, she'd feel his gentle nudging action, moving her back the right way, or if she walked too soon, he'd change the lights to red, so she could safely cross over.

Ryan was already asleep as she got undressed for bed. His lips puckered with each breath.

She went over to the wardrobe and chucked her jeans into the back.

The Invitation

by Joanna Campbell

Ruby were right excited that she were coming home with me. Mostly she kept herself all calm, floated along like a coot on a pond, but today she clapped her light hands and jumped three times on the spot. I was smiling, but there were a squirming inside me. Like on Big Dipper. Like those mornings when you wake up and know something's happening, but not if it's good or bad. Like a bit of birthday and a bit of dentist rolled up together.

She asked me questions all day. Loved it, I did. I told her about my bedroom with the yellow cupboard built-in and my puppies on the wall. She asked if we had a real puppy, kept asking if we had things we didn't have. I had to keep disappointing her.

'Have you got tropical fish?'

'I won a goldfish at the fair. Fetched him home in a plastic bag.'

'We have seven angelfish.'

'Oh.'

'What's your goldfish called?'

'He were dead by the time I got home.'

'Oh.'

Her school dress was the proper one for summer. Her Mam made it from the special green daisy material at Bradshaw's. It had that zig-zag stuff round the armpits and a little silver charm hanging off the zipper. It were a different charm every day. I liked the curly snail and Ruby's favourite was the prancing pony with his front legs up. My wrong dress were Alice Bagstaff's and before that it were Sharon Clitheroe's and before that it were Sharon's Mam's. It came from the Home Stores and flitted all the way down our terrace. It'll be Emmy Wainwright's next.

The sun were boiling our heads on the long walk home. The others stared and shouted, 'Why is she going to yours then?' The worst thing was, 'Did your Mam say she could?'

Ruby kept watching me with that hard face she had sometimes, making me say, 'Yeah, course it's all right.' I screwed my eyes up against the sun to look at her. Her hair shone like the polished black tiles in my auntie's privvy. I glared at the others and jerked up my sock.

The ice-cream money were sweating in my fist. I'd saved it for weeks for this day. Wrapped the coins in a strip of tissue and wound it round and round. It spent the day in my shoe and burned up a blister. I'd unravelled it a few times to look at the pennies. One were right black and I were worried that Mr Beavis would shake his head at it. I stroked my thumb over the bumps of Her Majesty's head so many times, it were in danger of being rubbed out. Then Beavis would really have summat to shake his fat head about. But it's not that easy to wipe heads off. The great lady were safe with me.

Beavis had put the prices up. So I bought Ruby her Witch's Hat and kept the halfpenny that wouldn't buy anything. I reckoned on getting a lick, but she was a bit tight-lipped again.

'Why can't the cornet be a Ninety-Nine?' She asked that ninety-nine times.

''Cause the Flakes are another bloody penny, Ruby.'

Mr Beavis tried to reach across his cones to clip me round the ear. Couldn't get me, though. He might tell me dad at the Lamb and Flag. I'll pray he forgets. Mam and Dad listen to me pray every night, but they don't get to hear my secrets. I add them on in the two minutes for silent confessing.

Like, 'Please can I have a nicer Mam and Dad?' Or 'I wish you were dead.'

The other thing is that I talk to Jesus, not God. God is a scary old git in a white dress, but Jesus is quite a lot nicer. He fetched up with a lot of bad friends and I felt sorry for him screwed onto cross at the end.

Ruby was still moaning at Rochester Drive and sulking by Cemetery Row.

'Fancy you not knowing what a Witch's Hat is.'

'I bloody do! It's a cornet with a lolly stuck head-first in the ice-cream. Everyone knows that.'

'But it should have the Flake. Our ice-cream man always pops one in. Sometimes two. My father once had three, actually.'

I felt sick. I bet her mam's sink didn't have big chips out of it. I didn't want Dad eating slices of Sunblest rolled up from the packet on the table. Ruby would stare at the hairs bushing out of the holes in his vest. I hoped and prayed we had a bit of toilet paper left. Couldn't have her wiping on her bum on the Express, could we?

171

She dropped the ice-lolly. A rare purple one it were. Beavis usually had yellow or green. She squealed and stood there like a right lemon. I picked it up, but she wouldn't touch it.

'Lick it for me.'

'You what?'

'Lick the gravel off. I can't. And I don't want to waste your money.'

Her face were crumpling. Like my sock this morning. Had a slapped leg for gabbing in assembly. It weren't bad, but the teacher yanked the sock down and it wouldn't pull up again. He'd snapped me garter. The others pointed at the red finger marks all day. He did the same to Eunice, but she had her sister Stella to wait for her and link arms. I saw Ruby watching all the slaps, but she ran off after.

It were still a good day because I had Ruby coming home, but I had to spend it holding me sock up and now I had to stop Ruby from going to pieces too. I couldn't take a misery-guts home now, could I?

I licked the lolly, then she made me wipe it with me best hanky so she wouldn't get my germs. Then I rammed the bloody thing back in her cornet. I had bits in me mouth from the pavement, so I spat them out and the others made disgusted noises from behind the pillar box. They couldn't fetch their eyes off me and my new friend and her Witch's hat. I pretended they weren't there. I melted them away with that hot bit in my head that stops up tears.

Didn't stop me feeling sick, though. There were frothing in my belly and my throat filled with sour stuff. That started as we turned the corner into our road. I'd have traded my Bunty for another taste of blackcurrant ice. Even if it turned bitter after one second, I would have still liked it, I was that dry. Tongue too big for my mouth.

I could see our gate. I could see our Mam with pegs in her mouth. She had that short dress on so you could see the knotted blue strings in her legs. And the see-through scarf on her head, all hedgehoggy with curlers. I had prayed to that Jesus for this not to happen. I had prayed for the cornflower skirt and a smile. But they were just for picnics. I could see the frown carved into the space between her eyebrows from as far back as the Tanners' gate.

'Let's walk really slow, Ruby.'

'Why? I want to get out of the sun now. And I need to wash my hands. They're sticky from that stupid ice-cream. And I want to be in time to watch Blue Peter.'

We didn't have telly. I couldn't say. I told her about cutting out and sticking with gum. I said she could have her own page in my scrapbook. I told her about Ludo and how I was allowed to get that out on the dinner table if I were careful. I even told her about the secret game with Belinda, my doll with no head. It were a hospital game and you could choose to be the nurse, the doctor or Belinda's Upset Mam. Ruby looked quite interested then. I was winning again.

She pulled a face when I said it might be pilchard salad for tea. I reckon she wouldn't know a pilchard if one fetched up and played hopscotch with us. She cheered up when I said we'd have iced buns after, but that was a lie. Just to soften up her gob like.

'Do you have a paddling pool? Ours is red. It was the biggest in the shop.'

'Hose might be mended.'

We reached the gate.

I didn't breathe while we waited, me and Ruby together. Mam was crouched by the laundry basket with her knees splayed out, dark stains under her arms. The sick feeling was like a big fist in a boxing glove jabbing at me insides. Faster and faster it banged, as Mam started to heave herself up, cigarette yellowing the whites. It quivered on her bottom lip when her mouth dropped open.

She wouldn't let us in. She stood blocking our gate. I couldn't look at Ruby. I had to fix my eyes on a little tuft of brown grass trying to grow by the gate-post where next-door's cat piddles. If you stare hard without blinking, the tears don't come.

I tried my small polite voice. 'Can Ruby play, please?'

I don't think she heard, she were that vexed. Just kept pointing. I'm not sure where. Just in the direction of the other end of town where all the flats are. And the new parades of shops with the silky stuff and the spicy smells. And the restaurants called Curry Houses. Me dad always said, 'Those sort smell out of their skin, they do. Bloody spices. It's not natural, it's not.' Me mam would say 'Ugh!' and shudder. 'Not just their breath, but their skin is filled with it.' Told me to hold me breath if I walked past one of them sort. But not make it obvious like. Said summat about letting too many in and Eeknock Power being right about them Rivers of Blood.

I did think they'd like Ruby though. Her skin didn't smell and it were the colour of creamy coffee. I've seen pictures of coffee in cups. Pale milky brown. And she said 'scones' properly.

173

Mam told me to get in now or else. I watched Ruby walk away. She went backwards for the first few steps. She shrugged a tiny bit and then turned as if it didn't matter. She can be right hard.

But I wanted her as my friend such a lot. I had prayed for that. It was after she told me she were having a party. I might get an invitation, she said, if she could play at ours first.

I prayed hard for that. Never had one before. People don't have parties round here. Sharon had shrimp-paste-baps and tinned-pear-flan when she turned seven and I was told to come for that and a game of Blind Man's Buff, with her dad in his vest, cheating with his blindfold and grabbing our legs. But it weren't a party.

Ruby was having a real Party with things in pastry. And purses with sequins all over to give as prizes. I prayed for one of them. I even asked God as well as Jesus. Her mother were going to stick balloons on the front door.

Anyhow, I watched Ruby go and Mam growled at me to get in. She squeezed my arm so tight it were like a Chinese burn. I didn't have sleeves on account of it being summer, so it were extra hard. She didn't speak a word, just looked right mad. I didn't cry all the way upstairs, all the way across the landing and into me room. Only when I lay on my bed. That's when these right hot tears kept on coming. I kept them silent though. And I did a lot of praying.

Next day she gave me the invitation. Thanked me for the Witch's Hat. It was like this happened all the time. She weren't even surprised. Happen she knew her colour upset some folk. So she set her face hard. Inside she was as sad as me.

The invitation was on this card with jagged edges and a scrap of bright red ribbon threaded along the top. The party was on Wednesday. Two days away. The writing was small and neat. Her real name was Rubaida. I loved it. She had done a proper signature. Rubaida. And it said RSVP. That could be her other name. Don't know how you blinking well say it.

But it was in pencil. She said to bring it back if Mam said No. Then she'd rub my name out and try another girl. I looked hard at my name. There were lots of little pencil-dents already there.

I did pray extra that night, but I still weren't brave enough to ask Mam and Dad, so it didn't do nowt anyway. Then there were no time left. I gave her back the card. Rubbed me name out for her, I did. I unravelled the bit of ribbon. Kept it. Tied it on Belinda's wrist. A little river of blood.

I walked the long way home past her house on the day of the party, but there were no balloons on the door.

Rabbit Punch

by Stephen Atkinson

The girl stood in the driveway for a moment, staring at the house. She was pushing a bicycle, sky blue, its front wheel completely buckled and the mudguards and chain dangling uselessly onto the gravel. She was badly bruised down one arm and stood there forlornly with a black eye which extended to a gash in one corner. Barely out of her teens, she was wearing a red summer dress and sported a matching ribbon in her hair which appeared to have been knocked crooked.

After a moment or two she walked on, her trainers crunching in the driveway gravel and the front wheel of the bicycle wobbling comically. She walked past the parked silver Mercedes and on towards the front door of the secluded and expensive-looking house, standing alone in the quiet, tree-lined country lane.

Jack Dawkins and his wife Doris were reading their gardening magazines in the front lounge when Doris looked up to spot the girl through the window.

'Jack – look,' she implored, replacing Home and Garden on the coffee table and hurrying to the front door.

Jack turned around in his armchair and peered over his glasses at the sorry-looking sight outside.

'Good lord,' he mumbled and chased his wife out to the front.

'Whatever happened to you, sweetheart?' Doris put her arm around the clearly dazed girl and led her inside while Jack took the bike.

'I... I suppose I had a bit of an accident,' the girl started. 'Round the corner near the shop. A cat – I swerved and...'

'Never mind about that now,' said Doris softly. 'Sit down here and I'll make you some tea. Would you like that?'

'Perhaps she'd like to clean herself up,' said Jack as he followed them into the front room. 'Mud all over your nice dress. Bike's a bit of a write-off, I'm afraid.'

The girl didn't answer but stared vacantly at her hands, resting on her lap. She seemed mesmerised by the long red scratches on the backs of each.

'Sugar and milk?' asked Doris on her way to the kitchen. The girl nodded.

Jack did his best to console her as they waited for Doris to return. He looked uncomfortable as he fussed and dithered, fluffing up her cushions and tidying the magazines on the table.

'Are you badly hurt? You should get those cuts looked at by the hospital, you know. I'll run you up there when you've had your tea. It's only a mile or so.'

'No need, really,' she replied. 'I'm fine. Just a little dazed maybe.'

'It could be concussion, dear,' worried Doris as she returned with a tray and put it down on the coffee table. 'Looks like you had a really nasty little scrape.'

'If I could just use your phone? I'll ring my friend. He's not far away. I'm afraid I haven't got my mobile with me.'

'Of course, of course,' replied Doris and Jack almost in unison.

'Drink your tea,' said Doris, pouring. 'Then you can ring your friend. Phone's in the hall. But Jack will run you anywhere you want to go, won't you, Jack? It's no problem.'

The girl smiled gratefully but shook her head to decline. 'I'm not badly hurt. I don't think I struck my head. It's just that I swerved to miss this cat...'

'Damned cats,' muttered Jack unnecessarily.

'I lost control, I suppose. Went flying into a ditch. Stupid really.'

'Nonsense,' cooed Doris. 'You were just trying to avoid the stupid cat. Anyone would have done it.'

'I wouldn't,' said Jack petulantly.

'I'm fine. Really,' said the girl, sipping her tea. 'May I have a little more sugar?'

'Of course, dear.' Doris pushed the bowl forward. 'Then go right ahead and ring your friend. The bathroom is further down the hall if you want to clean up. I think you ought.'

'Thank you,' said the girl, taking the sugar and finishing her tea. 'Would it be OK to leave the bike here until tomorrow? My friend has a small car but I can return with another friend. He's got a van.'

'Of course,' said Jack, pushing his slipped glasses back up on the bridge of his nose. 'But I could run you and the bike home if you like. I presume you must be local? I could manage it in the Merc. But anyway we have the wife's hatchback behind the garage.'

Again the girl smiled sweetly. 'I wouldn't dream of it. If I could just leave it here overnight...?' Her voice trailed off as she waited politely for his permission.

'Of course,' said Jack. 'I'll go and put it in the garage for you. Then I'd best put the Merc away too, if you don't want to be run to hospital.'

'Thanks so much,' said the girl. 'You've been quite kind enough already, Mister...?'

'Dawkins. Jack and Doris Dawkins. This is The Laurels, Bailey Farm Road in case you forget where you left the bike.' He grinned sheepishly.

'No chance of that,' she smiled and she got up to follow him out on the driveway where she watched him pick up the bike and carry it to the garage.

At the sound of Doris's voice she went back indoors just as Jack climbed into his car.

'Such a lovely bike. I hope you can get it mended,' said Doris consolingly.

The girl continued to smile. 'I hope so. I feel stronger now. May I use the phone now, please?'

Doris gestured to the hall table and left her to it, busying herself in the kitchen. A few minutes later Jack returned just as the girl was finishing her conversation. She turned to him as she replaced the receiver.

'He's going to meet me at the shop around the corner. He'll only be a few minutes. Can I pay you for the phone call?'

Jack waved his hand dismissively. 'Don't be silly,' he said, feigning offence.

'Well, my name's Tracy. Tracy Scott. I can't tell you how grateful I am for your kindness. If I can just go back out to the bike I've got a card in the saddle bag. I'll leave my numbers by your phone just in case. But I'll be back tomorrow.'

'Of course,' said Jack. 'The garage door is shut but there's a pedestrian door. It's unlocked.'

The girl stepped out through the front door to head outside. 'You don't think you should at least wash up before you go?' called Doris after her from the kitchen.

178

'I'm fine,' she replied.

Jack joined his wife in the kitchen, to see a worried frown on her face. 'I really think we ought to insist she goes to the hospital,' she said.

'She's a grown girl. She knows if she's fine or not.' Jack was adamant.

'Concussion can be a strange thing. People sometimes don't know they have it,' Doris insisted.

'She sounds coherent enough to me,' said Jack. 'Besides, her friend will take care of her now.'

Presently the girl was back at their side. 'I've left my name, address and telephone numbers by your phone. You've even got my email address.'

For the first time since she arrived, she managed a small girly giggle.

'There – what did I tell you? She's feeling much better.' Jack turned triumphantly to his wife, who still looked concerned as she wiped her hands on a tea towel.

'Well, thanks again for everything.' The girl sounded decisive, a different person to the wretched little rag doll who had first appeared on their driveway.

'John will be there by the time I've walked around the corner.'

They waved goodbye and stood arm in arm to watch her as she walked back across the gravel.

'She's still got a slight limp,' said Doris quietly.

'She's fine,' Jack assured her, and as she disappeared up the lane they returned gratefully to their gardening magazines.

'Lovely girl,' said Jack.

'I hope she'll be alright,' insisted Doris.

'She'll be back tomorrow. Right as rain. You'll see.'

Around the corner at the Eight-Til-Late mini supermarket, the girl in the red dress was climbing into a silver Merc, identical to the one parked at The Laurels, Bailey Farm Road. She and the young man at the driving wheel exchanged a brief meaningful glance as she slid gracefully into the passenger seat, but at first they said nothing.

'You OK?' he asked at length, and when she nodded he slammed the big powerful car into gear and tore off at high speed down the country lane away from The Laurels and the sky blue bicycle.

Unnoticed by them, a young rabbit was left squashed by their wheels at the side of the road. The shattered bundle of fur shuddered once or twice more before stiffening and finally laying still.

Things were busier than usual at Whaplode-St-Mary police station. Desk Sergeant Paul Gracechild was rubbing his massive chin as he read yet again the typewritten RTA report in his hand.

He was about due for retirement, and today more than ever, he looked it. Heavy on his mind was the tragic death of a young girl cyclist, found sprawled in the road after an apparent hit-and-run accident. Sadly, Sgt Gracechild thought of his own granddaughter, of similar age, as he mulled over the facts. Which just didn't make sense. The young girl's distraught parents had identified her broken body, her red summer dress stained a darker shade of burgundy by the blood, but had earlier mentioned a matching red ribbon. Strangely, there was no ribbon, possibly lost in the wind before the accident, he thought. But more eerily yet, there was no sign of her bicycle either. It had just vanished.

Sgt Gracechild cast a glance at the picture on his desk of his pretty grand-daughter. He sighed. Only one lead – a 999 call to report a speeding black BMW shortly after the accident.

The call came from a Mrs Dawkins. Mrs Doris Dawkins of The Laurels, Bailey Farm Road.

Forty minutes later Detective Inspector Paul Jacob, accompanied by a uniformed patrol officer, drew up on the driveway of The Laurels in an unmarked car.

Jack and Doris were immediately at the door to greet them, their faces creased in consternation.

'It's not the girl, is it? ' Doris pleaded. 'Tell me she's OK.'

The officers briefly exchanged a baffled look and then turned back to the couple. 'Can we come in?'

They settled awkwardly in armchairs in the front lounge, but Doris was too agitated even to take a seat.

'She's dead, isn't she?' Doris reached down to her husband's shoulder. He stood and wrapped a comforting arm around her.

DI Jacob lowered his gaze to the floor. 'Yes, I'm afraid she is. Perhaps you can tell us how you knew about it?'

Jack Dawkins tried to take command of the situation. 'She seemed fine when she left here. A little shaken perhaps, but we had no idea...'

'What do you mean "left here?",'persisted the detective, even more confused. Then: 'We're here to ask your wife about the BMW,' he added. 'Are you saying you talked to the deceased girl?'

DI Jacob waited for someone to reply, but found himself faced instead with an implacable wall of non-comprehension.

'...The black BMW that you reported speeding,' he prompted.

'I'm sorry....?' Jack started ineffectually.

The DI consulted his notebook. 'According to police switchboard records Mrs Dawkins made a 999 call from this address this afternoon at 5.40pm. She reported a black BMW, being driven dangerously at high speed in the area. Thirty minutes earlier at around 5.10pm a young girl was killed on her bike not far from here. I want to know how it is that you already seemed to know about it.'

'But my wife made no such phone call,' insisted Jack, his composure fast slipping away despite all his best efforts. 'We haven't been out all day. Your switchboard must be mistaken. We made no such call.'

'Jack! The girl.' Doris gently nudged him to remind him of the afternoon visitor.

'Yes, of course,' said Jack, excitedly waving his finger. 'She was wearing a red dress. Turned up wheeling her wrecked bike. All scratched and bruised she was. Bike was a worse mess than she was. She said she had fallen off. '

Dubiously DI Jacob interjected, looking at his notes: 'A bright blue bike? Sky blue?'

'Yes, yes,' said Jack and his wife nodded energetically in agreement. 'That's it. It's in the garage right now. She was going to pick it up tomorrow.'

DI Jacob shot a look at the uniformed officer who jumped up and made for the front door.

'You'll need the key,' said Jack and hurried to the sideboard to retrieve it.

As the officer left, Jack and Doris sensed DI Jacob's attitude was more than a little hostile. 'And the 999 call?' he persisted.

'We let the girl use the phone. She wanted to call a friend to come and fetch her,' explained Jack.

They were alarmed to see that the detective didn't look at all convinced.

'She left her card, her name with all her details, by the phone,' stammered Doris nervously.

DI Jacob rose from his seat: 'Show me?'

Jack and Doris led the way back out to the hallway where the white telephone sat on a low table. Next to it lay a completely blank piece of paper. On top, a crumpled, red ribbon.

'I don't understand. She insisted on leaving her name and address,' said Jack as the detective picked up the ribbon on the end of his pencil as if it were deadly poison.

As the detective studied his clue, Jack pressed 'redial' and it was clear from the expression on his face what he was hearing.

'Sorry. Dialled in error,' he mumbled as he hung up.

Just at that moment the uniformed officer stepped back in through the front door. 'No bike,' he said. 'But you'd better come and look at this, sir.'

They all stood at the garage entrance, Jack turning on the light for a better view. He and Doris looked stunned and scared, their mouths dropped open in shock, for the gleaming silver Mercedes boasted two ugly gashes right across the gleaming bodywork of its lower bonnet. They were sky blue with ragged, sharp edges like a contorted saw blade.

'Been in an accident, sir?' PC Davies studied the scratches and then leaned down for a closer look at a piece of broken plastic mudguard jammed behind the front bumper.

'Don't touch it! That's evidence,' barked DI Jacob.

'I don't understand,' said Jack as Doris began sniffling uncontrollably against his shoulder.

'Well I'm very much afraid that we do,' said the detective curtly. 'I'm going to have to ask you to accompany us down to the station. I must warn you that anything you may say will be taken down and may be used in evidence against you.'

The uniformed officer had wandered to the back of the garage where he found a large sheet of tarpaulin concealing something underneath.

'Sir! It's here,' he called, lifting the edge. 'Looks like they've tried to hide the bike under this.'

DI Jacob looked solemn as he turned to the distraught couple standing beside him.

'We haven't tried to hide anything,' said Jack desperately. 'The girl must have done it. And the scratches on my car.'

'You expect me to believe a dead girl did all this?' asked the detective incredulously. 'What time did this visitation take place?'

Jack and Doris looked at each other. 'Around 5.30 I suppose,' said Jack and his wife nodded.

The detective raised his eyebrow and his voice was slow, deliberate. 'The girl was found dead in the road two miles from here at 5.20pm. The pathologist thinks she had been dead for 10 minutes at that time. Are you seriously trying to suggest you're being framed by a ghost?'

Meanwhile some miles away a flash of silver sped across the country bound for the safety of crowded London, a smug looking young girl and her boyfriend inside.

The girl, peering into the sun visor mirror to remove the make-up and mascara 'wounds' from her face, arms and hands, was Kay Wesley. She and her boyfriend Marc Jessup had come to the Fens looking for burn-up thrills. They were both speed freaks, and found the long, straight lanes hugging the dykes and canals irresistible in a fast car. And, unlike the motorways, there were few police and no cameras.

She had been at the wheel when they first saw the girl in red on her bright blue bicycle. She had loomed up from nowhere, a sudden splash of red and blue against the green bushes at the side of the road.

The Merc was touching eighty and at that speed she was impossible to miss. The short, truncated scream and the heavy thump as her fragile body was sent hurtling across the tarmac rudely shattered the Fenland peace.

They'd got out and examined her sprawled, broken body but she was already dead. They looked around and were relieved that they could see nobody across the flat miles of uninterrupted terrain all around.

'What do we do?' said Kay, sheer panic etched in her face. 'She was wearing a red dress just like mine. It was such a shock. I couldn't avoid her.'

He didn't say a word. His mind was racing as fast as the car had been moments before. He remembered another silver Mercedes he had seen parked on a driveway maybe a mile or two back.

Silently and mysteriously he had picked up the ribbon lying on the road and handed it to Kay.

'Take this,' he said. 'I've got an idea.'

Kay looked on utterly baffled as he bundled the smashed bike into the back of the car.

Later, as they sped towards the safe anonymity of the capital, she sat back in her seat, relaxed.

'Thank you, darling,' she said to his handsome profile. 'I guess I should just stick to the motorways.' There was not a hint of remorse in her lighthearted banter.

'Can't have you facing jail just because some yokel can't ride a bike, can we?' he smiled back.

In answer, she pecked his cheek playfully between her fingers. 'You clever thing,' she purred. 'The 999 call from the Dawkins house was an inspiration. When the police called to investigate, it would look as if they were deliberately trying to throw them off the scent with the story of the speeding black BMW.'

Marc grinned triumphantly. 'And all the time those naughty Dawkins were 'hiding' the bike and the scratched Merc in their garage. You did a good job there. If anyone had spotted our car – well, there it was! '

As they raced along the long, straight roads they were just a speeding blur – no eyes quick enough to spot the bright blue scrapes on their front bumper. Sky blue with just a sinister hint of blood red.

'We're home free,' said the girl, exultant, tossing back the hair from her face. 'I'm all cleaned up – all we have to do now is sort out the car when we get back to Chelsea. Presumably the Dawkins will manage to talk their way out of it. But while they are all tied up in knots we get clean away.'

The pair laughed, an evil, uncaring sound that gradually became one with the roar of their racing, three litre engine.

Back in the Fenlands, near the Eight-Til-Late store, little seven-year-old Rupert Wilson was still fighting back the tears after seeing his escaped pet rabbit crushed to death by the big silver car. He'd gone straight inside to ask the shop owner Mr Jenkins to write the car's registration number down for him.

He was good at remembering number plates, was Rupert. He just wasn't so good at writing them down.

Many Happy Returns

by Annette Keen

The problem with deceit is that you have to see it through right to the end. Any successful liar, and those who have most to lose from detection, will tell you that you haven't a hope of getting away with it unless you can do that.

Mother understood this.

When we were children Carole was the only one of us who regularly told lies – and I don't just mean the odd fib, which all children indulge in from time to time. Carole's were real whoppers, but she always trapped herself by forgetting to keep it up. Mother's exasperation with her was most often expressed in the form of a rhetorical question, 'Whatever would Daddy have said?'

This gave her an unfair advantage over Carole since she was born after the accident which took the real Daddy out of our lives, leaving behind the shadowy one whose thoughts, deeds and opinions were all filtered down to us through Mother. I would have been able to answer the question myself only from hearsay, as I was little more than four when he died and up till then had never done much to cause the sort of reaction which Mother was clearly aiming at. Colin, two years older than me, was in only a slightly stronger position.

Many years later, when she had learned much more about life and lies, Carole became a journalist.

'We ought to start thinking about what we're going to do for Mother's birthday. It's less than a month away.'

Carole and I don't often meet up at lunchtimes. She's successful and busy and I'm too lazy to make the effort as a rule, but with Mother's seventieth coming up I really felt we should get down to some arrangements. It was no good leaving it to the others – Colin had enough trouble organising himself to visit her on a regular basis, without being expected to do anything else and Robbie was impossible to get hold of. If it was to be done, I'd have to do it. My family are hopeless.

'It falls on a Saturday so we could all go round for tea, or something,' Carole said, swigging back her gin with an eye on the clock.

'It still needs discussing,' I said, exasperated at her lack of interest. A colleague of hers arrived and I was introduced. He looked from one of us to the other, comparing our features and colouring, our build and expressions.

It's true that we look alike, we're both like Mother. Carole takes after her in most other ways too, but I resemble her only in looks. I'm like Daddy.

Once the interruption was over we got down to some basics, starting with the whereabouts of Robbie. Neither Carole nor I had any idea where he was living at the time.

'...but I can tell you where to find him most evenings.' Carole said. 'Our London Diary did a club review and turned him up in Greenwich. The reporter who went over to hear him was very flattering.'

Robbie is a musician and the odd one out. He's nothing like the rest of us, not even Colin, who has Daddy's looks. Especially not Colin.

'I went over home last weekend, Susie. First time for ages,' said Carole, knocking back another gin.

'And Mother had all your favourite things for lunch, I'll bet.'

'No, it was a surprise visit. She was messing about with bits of material. They were all over the floor.'

Eventually it was decided that I should order the cake and flowers, do the other shopping and contact the boys. I knew I'd have to.

Apart from the four of us, and Colin's wife, there were no other relatives or close friends to invite to Mother's party. Her only grandchild was working abroad and Carole and myself have both divorced, twice in Carole's case. Robbie has had a succession of women in and out of his life and bed over the years, which leaves only dear old dependable Colin with a relationship that has lasted. When you see them together you can tell why. Neither of them would spoil a couple.

On my way home from seeing Carole I popped in on Mother. Apart from the occasional bit of decorating, the house is just as it was when we were children. It's a large Victorian town villa, three floors and lots of high-ceilinged rooms. It had been Grandpa and Grandma's house and when my parents married they took over the top floor. In time the house passed to my mother, although that was after Daddy had died. The house and Mother suit each other well – they both have style.

I remember my grandparents quite clearly, but my father hardly at all. It's strange how we all refer to him as Daddy, but to her as Mother. I suppose it's partly because we had no adult relationship with him - no relationship at all in the case of the twins – but also because that's what Mother has always called him. That's how she has perpetuated him for us, for the last forty-two years.

When I arrived it was just as Carole had found the previous week. Mother was messing about with bits of material. When we were children she made all our clothes and hers, and a couple of trunks in the attic were filled with remnants. And now there they were again, scattered about on the floor and the dining room table.

'I'm making a patchwork quilt, dear, for the best of all possible reasons. It's a very thrifty thing to do.'

She looked around her at the scraps and sighed.

'There'll be my whole life sewn into this quilt, Susie. Your school dresses, the boys' pyjamas, part of a shirt of Daddy's...'

'You kept his clothes? All these years?'

'Only one or two things that were nearly new. Now dear, shall we have some tea?'

I'd been experiencing the most curious feeling lately on visits to Mother, almost as if we were taking part in rehearsals for a play. I'd let myself in and straight away feel as if I had just stepped onto stage and given her a cue line. On more than one occasion she was in the same place as when I'd arrived the time before, which reinforced the idea that we were in rehearsal – going through it again until we got it right. Everyday items – the photo frames, the empty cigarette box and redundant table lighter – started to look like props on the set and I began to think if I moved something there would be a chalk mark underneath.

On that day it happened again. Mother was standing behind her favourite chair when I opened the sitting room door. She came forward to kiss me but instead of going the obvious way, past the coffee table, she started on that route, stopped and then walked back behind the chair to come round the other side. This made it necessary for her to step over all the remnants of fabric and the sewing box. It gave her the lead-in to her opening line –

'I'm making a patchwork quilt dear...'

She had sewn about a dozen squares together and she talked me through the completed block while we had tea.

'...made this up into a maternity smock... Colin and Rowena's bridesmaids...'

I stayed for a couple of hours then made my exit, stage left.

Colin and Rowena still live in the house they bought when they were first married. It's a semi-detached 1980s estate house, with a silver birch and an open plan lawn for a front garden, and they're the last remaining original owners in their close. Colin is a bursar and Rowena a librarian in the same college. They're not ambitious people.

On the following Saturday I drove across London to see them and they seemed pleased to see me in a fairly inert way. Rowena is a bit of a mouse and Colin is not exactly effusive either. It beats me how they ever got a relationship started in the first place.

'Mother phoned yesterday,' said Colin. 'She said she'd seen both you and Carole recently.'

'How did she seem to you?'

'Fine, fine. She wanted a bit of Rowena's wedding dress for some reason.'

We talked about the impending birthday celebrations and they fell in with my suggestions, relieved, I suspect, that they were not being called upon to do more than buy a present and turn up on the appointed day. The responsibility of taking a hand in the organising was probably more than their combined talents could bear.

'Colin, I wanted to ask you... has Mother been doing things lately that appeared in any way odd to you?'

'Odd? How do you mean, odd?'

'You know... unusual, quirky... odd.'

Rowena fled to the kitchen, no doubt thinking that she shouldn't get involved in a family discussion. They've only been married for twenty-seven years, after all.

'There are no longer any pictures of Daddy around at home,' I went on. 'Plenty of us, but none of him... and I have the strangest feeling when I go to see her that all is not as it appears...'

'Fancy you only just noticing – the photos were put away years ago.'

I was a little taken aback by this, mostly because I'd failed to notice something that had been obvious to him. I'd never thought of Colin as perceptive.

'Did you ever ask her why?'

'No, maybe she didn't need them any more, once we were grown up. It probably seemed unnecessary to keep on dusting them.'

'Can you remember him, Colin? Other than what Mother has told us, I mean.'

'Not a lot. I was only six when he died and he'd worked away from home a lot of the time. I can remember the solemn atmosphere at home after the accident happened and wondering if I'd done something to cause it. But what sticks in my mind most are the arguments.'

'Arguments? Who argued? She's never mentioned that.'

'Mother and Daddy. Loud, shouting matches that used to frighten me. Sometimes Grandma and Grandpa got involved too. We used to put our heads under the bedclothes and sing to block it out. Fancy you not remembering.'

'You've never said anything before,' I said, as if that somehow made it all his fault.

'Why would I? I sometimes thought I'd got it wrong, you know, the old memory playing tricks. She brought us all up on the idea of their wedded bliss.'

'What did they argue about?'

Colin shrugged. 'I've no idea. Probably nothing much. When you're a child things can seem out of proportion. I expect they were really close, in their own way.'

He said it as though to pacify me, then sat forward in his armchair and reached across to squeeze my hand. It was typical of Colin that he'd kept this to himself all those years, never challenging her once.

'Doesn't really matter now in any case, does it,' he said. 'He's been dead over forty years and we all grew up with good and decent ideals, if a little inaccurate so far as they were concerned.'

Rowena came in at that moment with a tray of tea, having first knocked on the door of her own lounge.

Running round my head was the thought, this was more than inaccurate, these were downright lies. And then I thought, why?

Seeing as I was already south of the river that evening I took a homeward route back through Greenwich and tracked down Robbie. The club was more sophisticated than the sort he'd been playing in the last time I heard him and he had headline billing outside. It probably meant little in financial terms, but that wasn't top of Robbie's priorities, whose cornet and other less important worldly goods could be packed into whichever beat-up car he was currently driving and still leave room for passengers. This arrangement was handy for him since he's lived in a state of no fixed abode for years.

As a teenager, Robbie gave Mother more trouble than any of the rest of us. He took to music quite early on, to the detriment of everything else at school that might conceivably have been of some use in later life. And whilst Mother had no objections to him playing the cornet as a hobby she couldn't come to terms with the idea of it as a profession. He left home at seventeen determined to pursue a career in music and, in his terms at least, made it.

The band was taking a break when I arrived and we went off to the bar for a chat. Needless to say, he'd forgotten that Mother's birthday was coming up and had no idea she would be seventy. I filled him in on the plans and even found myself offering to shop for his present. Somehow, Robbie and I have always been the closest of the four of us.

We gave each other the usual grilling about our love lives.

'Anyone special at the moment, Robbie?'

'No, current live-in girlfriend's on the way out I think.'

'I presume that means you'll be the one moving out. Or do you have an address of your own now?'

'Not yet, I'm working on it though. How about you?'

'What do you think? All the decent men are already fixed up. I've given up on love.'

It was a variation on the same conversation we'd been having for years.

I stayed at the club for a while and Robbie and the band were still playing when I got up to go. He stopped in the middle of his solo to blow me a kiss and as the saxophonist filled the gap he told the audience, 'That's my favourite sister.'

They loved him for it. So did I.

Mother's seventieth birthday was bright blue and sunny, the kind of late September day that seems like an extra treat before autumn takes a real hold and starts flinging rain and dead leaves about.

To my relief, everyone turned up on the right afternoon and at the right time. Mother pretended it was all a huge surprise and squeezed out a tear or two before opening her presents. Colin had brought his camera, and Rowena, who had no false hopes about ever making it into our inner circle, took photos of the family group.

Act One finished with the arrival of the Interflora bouquet and a few more tears. It sounds ridiculous but I still couldn't shake off the idea that we were all acting out our roles within the theatre that Mother's house had become.

At about four o'clock, just as Carole and I were thinking about setting out the tea things, there was a ring at the front doorbell. We were not expecting anyone, since there was no-one else not already present in the house. Robbie went out to answer it and was gone some little while. When he came back he had an old man with a suitcase in tow. The room fell silent. We had to wait for the newcomer to speak, since he was a stranger to us all.

'Hello, Ruby. It's me Stan. I've come back.' Then as if he were just returning from a fortnight's holiday he added, 'I've missed you all.'

Mother pressed a hand to her mouth. Nobody else moved a muscle. When she finally found her voice it came out small and feeble. 'Get out of my house – my house.'

Stan put his suitcase down. 'Ah yes,' he said quietly, 'of course it was always your house. Even when your mum and dad were alive I was never allowed to forget that.'

From the corner of my eye I saw Colin jerk forward as if he had just been shot in the back of the head.

Mother seemed to have forgotten we were all there. For a woman who must have been writing variations on this scene for more than forty years she was surprisingly lost for words. Stan, on the other hand, seemed quite relaxed and perfectly at home. He looked around at us all.

'Colin,' he said pointing firmly at him. 'Susie,' pointing at me, then his attention drifted past Rowena, who looked terrified, and fixed on Carole.

'Just like your mum,' he said.

Robbie went over to Mother's side and knelt down by her chair.

'What's going on here Mother? Dad died, you said. So who's this guy who seems to know all about us?'

'Aha!' said Stan, swinging our attention back to him. 'Twins? Yes, that would make it right.'

'This has gone far enough,' said Carole in the sort of voice that meant business. 'I want to know who you think you are, bursting in here like you have the right to.'

Before he had a chance to reply Mother pulled the action back to her corner of the room.

'This,' she said quietly, 'is your Daddy.'

She stood up and took hold of Robbie's hand. 'And I did what I thought was best for you all.'

Gaining a little of her old confidence she turned to Robbie. 'Show him out will you, dear? He's ruining my birthday.'

'I'm not sure I can just do that Mother... we need to know...'

Then the most remarkable thing happened. Colin got up from his chair and took Stan by the arm.

'We don't need to know,' he said, crisply. 'Not now and possibly not ever. You went out of our lives forty-odd years ago. Mother was here, you weren't, and the rest no longer matters. If she wants you to leave I think she has the right to insist on it.'

Colin steered Stan to the door, but he shook his arm free and turned round to face Mother.

'How could you have lied to them for all those years?'

'Because I had to. And whose was the greatest lie? You said you'd never come back. It was all right until now.'

Stan left the room, followed closely by Colin, and we sat in silence until we heard the sound of the front door closing. Rowena made a dash for the kitchen.

193

'I'll make some tea,' she said over her shoulder.

Colin came back into the room and tripped over Stan's suitcase as he did so. We all focused on it, a battered reminder that what had just taken place was not in our collective imagination.

'I'll go,' I said, and took hold of it firmly.

I caught up with Stan by the gate. He was looking up and down the street as if trying to decide which way to go. He seemed neither surprised nor gratified by my sudden appearance at his elbow following our complete rejection of him, and didn't seem to have noticed that he'd left his case behind. We wandered slowly in the direction of the town.

'Did you know it was her birthday?'

'I knew it was something but I wasn't sure what. No grandchildren present at the celebration?' he asked.

'There's only my daughter Karen and she lives in the States. We're not very good at relationships in this family, it was too much of a responsibility for us all trying to live up to the role model. Robbie daren't try, for fear of failing and Carole and I expected too much of our men. Colin has managed a successful marriage though.'

'Yes, well maybe he was old enough to have had an image in his own mind.' Stan sighed. 'That was unfair of her. There were faults on both sides.'

I remembered Colin's surprising revelations about the arguments they'd had.

'Then why? She took an awful risk lying.'

'Not really. Like she said, I was never coming back. And why do most people lie, eh? Ask yourself that.'

I didn't need to ask myself for very long. 'Guilt?'

'You're a smart girl.'

We looked at each other awkwardly as the first rush of conversation died away, facing each other like two strangers searching for something in common and finding nothing. Stan broke the silence.

'Maybe I did you all a favour then, coming back today? Lowered your expectations a bit.'

'I don't think you did Mother a favour.'

He sighed. 'No, it wasn't what I'd hoped.'

'Tell me something... Who was the twin's father?'

194

He looked for a moment as though he wasn't sure how to play that one, then made a sudden decision.

'Eddie something – I can't remember his name now. He was a right layabout, never had a proper job as far as I recall. Well, unless you count the tea dances as being work.'

'Tea dances? What was he, a gigolo?'

'In a way I suppose he was. He played the piano, "music for dancing" they called it. It was a good way to get to know who all the lonely women in town were. You don't seem surprised.'

'I'm a smart girl.'

There was another pause and then I thought of the suitcase.

'Where will you go now?'

'Oh, I'll find somewhere for the night, then move on tomorrow. There's the YMCA in Station Road.'

'Not any more there isn't. They pulled it down about twenty years ago.'

'Well never mind, I'll be okay. You'd better get back to the others now.'

We looked at each other for a moment. A hug seemed to be out of the question, and we'd run out of things to say at the very moment when we should have been saying so much.

'Goodbye, Susie. Look after your mum.'

And with that, he carried on up the road without a backward glance.

'Goodbye, Stan.'

When I got back to the house Mother had them all gathered together admiring her growing piece of patchwork. Even Robbie was showing an interest and Rowena was positively pink with what I imagine was a mixture of enthusiasm and relief. They looked up at me as I shut the sitting room door, closing ranks around Mother with me on the outside.

'I wanted to make sure he'd be all right,' I said.

'He will be, don't you worry,' said Mother. Her confidence had returned. 'Anything to report back?'

'No nothing. Nothing at all.'

Colin moved back to let me through.

'Look at this Susie – a bit of our nursery curtains. Remember?' he said.

'Yes,' I lied. 'And this was left over from Robbie's costume for a school musical... '

'My whole life,' said Mother. 'Well, the best bits, anyway. Now Carole, perhaps we can have that cake you sneaked into the kitchen when you arrived. And if any of you brought anything stronger than tea we could do worse than open it now, don't you think?'

She blew out her birthday candles, we cut the cake and drank champagne, kissed and hugged each other. All things considered, Mother had a lovely day and I don't think she would have wished for anything more.

I spent a while trying to find Stan the next day, but he'd disappeared. I could have made some effort to look further afield but there didn't seem to be a good enough reason for doing so.

Mother finished her patchwork quilt. Once the centre panel was completed she decided she didn't want to use any more old fabrics, so I went with her to choose some new pieces to finish it off. At her suggestion, the remaining old clothes and bits of material went up to the tip.

And because there is no longer any need to do so, Mother never mentions Daddy any more. When she talks about him now, she calls him Stan.

Our James Says He's a Christian

by Adam E Smith

If James had not met Becky he would still be on the phone to his mam, listening to her reports of old friends being caught speeding or committing benefit fraud. His first few weeks in Sheffield were filled with such conversations. Then Becky sat next to him on a bench midway between the university and the building site where he worked. As if she knew him already, Becky talked about a concert she was organising with her friends and family.

James extended his arm underneath the duvet to the cold patch and imagined Becky there. Before he could think more, the alarm sounded. Stretching one final time before righting himself and standing up, he was already thankful for the day ahead. Holding back a curtain, James noticed a man carrying a newspaper and a girl on a mobile phone. For most people it was a normal Saturday. For James, the day held excitement. He knew that his dad would want to hear all about the Sheffield Wednesday match and that his mam would ask an endless spiral of questions. James hoped he would get to speak to Wes alone, but realised that this would not be easy with Becky along. He could not just go out with his brother, leaving her with his mam and dad.

For Becky, the day would already be difficult. James had warned her that his family were not Christians. When he'd told his dad that Becky went to church and believed in god, the phone line went quiet. His dad's excruciating silence unsettled James. Becky had shrugged it off but it occupied James's thoughts for days. He'd called Wes, who was watching a football match. His brother had said quickly that Becky being Christian wasn't a big deal. 'It's not like we're Muslims,' he'd chimed.

Now, as he let the curtain fall closed, James smiled through his unease. Following Becky's advice, he bowed his head to ask for the weekend to go smoothly. When nothing else came to mind, he shrugged his shoulders and whispered, 'Amen.'

Becky's housemates were still in bed when James arrived to pick her up so she opened the front door only a crack and crept round it, meeting James in the car. The gear stick pressed into James's thigh as he leant over and hugged her. Becky clicked her seatbelt into place, which reminded him that he had moved the passenger seat for her. When they arrived home, James would have to readjust it into Wes's position.

'Are you nervous?' he asked, not yet starting the engine.

Becky nodded. 'But I'm looking forward to meeting them. It's like getting new family members.'

'But it's not as if you've got a shortage of them,' James replied.

'I know. You collect more and more family and friends as you go through life,' she said rapidly. 'It's brilliant. By the time I'm eighty I'll have a huge family.'

His first girlfriend had wanted the same. 'Seven kids,' declared Chantelle, who chewed gum constantly and smelled of hairspray. They were only fifteen years old; she had pushed her tongue in James's mouth and James asked immediately if she wanted to be his girlfriend. When he brought her home, his mother, over sausages and chips, asked: 'Are you going to want to sleep together tonight?'

Chantelle's bemusement was outdone only by James's embarrassment. He stared at his mother in horror, before dropping his gaze to the food and muttering a negative. James's mother looked around the living room at the other silent diners, applause on the television mocking them all. Then she said, 'I just wondered if Chantelly would – '

'No, Mam,' Wes interrupted calmly. 'And you say it, "Shantell".' He smiled sympathetically at this little brother, whose appetite had evaporated. James could not hold on to Wes's gaze: he was too flushed with a blend of humiliation, love and gratitude that he understood only now. Later, his mam told him that she considered Chantelle a lovely girl. She had even taken her shopping when James went to the football with Wes, their dad and Chantelle's brother.

It had now been almost a year since he'd seen Sunderland play at home.

Becky placed her hand on his and squeezed a little. Her touch aroused him, slightly at first (the shock of it) and then, after a while, deeply. He pulled his seatbelt across with his other hand and shifted a little.

'It'll be fine,' he spluttered, not feeling confident at all. At least his mam had known Chantelle's mam. This time his girlfriend would be someone completely new. She didn't even sound like anyone in

198

his family. They might consider her Kent accent to be posh. After one parents' evening at school, James's dad had made fun of Ms Dunant, the snobby art teacher nobody liked. It was a tradition after parents' evening to mock the most eccentric teacher. But James remembered that both his mam and dad, after deriding Ms Dunant, had said that she was a kind lady and a good teacher. Hadn't she helped James, inspiring him to work with his hands at the potter's wheel rather than try to draw?

Becky looked through the car window, watching the tall, stone houses slide away downhill. The city gradually grew sparse, the houses farther apart from one another, and after a short time they had made it on to the motorway, flanked on both sides by other roads and then fields. She took a deep breath. It was the kind of breath one took in preparation for a dive from the highest board; or, James knew, the kind Becky made as she began a prayer. James could not tell whether she was praying now: she looked contemplative but her hands were not clasped together. That was another thing he had to confirm: did you have to hold your hands together when praying? Did it amplify your thoughts to god? Surely god could hear them anyway?

Not for the first time, he tried to picture god, listening in. As usual he had trouble conjuring god's image. Becky had said that god looked like a man. This offered so many possibilities that James could not even begin to imagine what god looked like. He tried to think of him as a long-lost grandfather, part of James but distinct also. It helped a little but whenever James felt close, the image vanished, depressing him.

Becky, on the other hand, could easily imagine god. She explained that it was because she had been raised with him. God had always been there, a third parent who understood when she'd slumped into childish moods and forgave her when she behaved recklessly as a teenager. James envied Becky's church upbringing; he had to build his relationship with god from scratch. It would have been much easier to do so as a boy. But his parents had never been religious. Nor were they likely to see the benefit of it now. Although they rejected religion, today it would enter their home. His soul was filled with the hope that his family would not reject Becky as they did god. They would enjoy Becky's character and listen to her thoughts. As with Ms Dunant, if necessary they would then mock her privately.

199

Wes might not be so tactful. He had once laughed at James when the younger boy asked him whether god existed. If Becky even mentioned religion to him, Wes would probably not react with an immature outburst like that. But he would easily tell her that it was all a load of rubbish. One of Becky's housemates had temporarily crushed her spirit by saying that. James had felt unqualified to stand up for his girlfriend. Although he would have more confidence with Wes, he would not want to argue. In their childhood quarrels, James always refused to fight: usually he just walked away. 'It's in 'is nature, son,' their dad had replied when Wes complained.

Once, James had been playing football in the street with some other boys when he heard Wes and another lad picking a fight with a smaller boy a few doors down. 'Haway!' James said, just as Wes grabbed the boy and started yelling at him. Upon seeing his brother, Wes's voice floundered. Humiliated, Wes let go of the boy's jacket, spitting, 'Piss off.' The boy pelted up the road. While his friend laughed, Wes looked thoughtful. Privately, Wes told James that the boy had been too cocky. James did not mention the incident to their parents, but it made him feel that they were dissimilar. Instances, it seemed, could divide them. James kept his thoughts close, while Wes had remained outspoken ever since. James could only hope that, on matters of religion, his brother would keep his mouth shut.

He doubted that religion would even enter the conversation. If it did, James was sure his dad would dismiss it immediately. Wes had never raised the topic with their parents, who did not answer the door to Jehovah's Witnesses. But when James asked his dad what religion was, he had said, 'Magic,' shifting in his seat and taking a sip of beer. 'It's nothing, son. It's people believing in something that doesn't exist, and then fighting wars over it.'

His mother had taken a more explanatory approach. 'It's where some people go to church on Sundays,' she said, closing a kitchen cupboard door and looking down at him. 'It just what they do, like you play football.'

These responses from childhood returned to James like an undelivered letter. Now that he knew more about religion, the memories made him cringe. He found it surprising that his parents knew so little about something so significant. Especially considering that their love and kindness would flourish if they accepted god's embrace.

200

'You're thinking very hard about something,' said Becky, sweetly.

James shook his head, glancing at her for a split second. 'Just about me mam and dad. About today.'

'Let's have some music.' Becky switched on the radio, disapproved of the first station, tuned it straight past the second and then landed on a song she recognised.

'It sounds like one Wes would listen to,' said James.

'Is this what you used to listen to?'

'When I used to go out. With Wes. I never really paid much attention to it. Wes plays dance music at home – me mam and dad hate it.' James smiled. 'Don't really know what music they like. Old stuff probably.'

'We always had music on in the house,' said Becky. 'Or Dad would be at the piano, playing.'

James had never seen a piano in someone's house. In his mind, a piano was something from school. It reminded him of assembly and, now, church. It was not something fun, like how Becky described it.

'... so good,' she was saying. 'Mainly jazz... and I can't play jazz.'

'I'd still love to hear you.'

'Maybe,' she murmured coyly. 'I haven't played since last summer. And I can't play jazz.'

'I don't care.'

'Didn't you want to learn a musical instrument when you were a kid? I thought everyone learnt something.'

'Nope.' He shook his head. 'I played football. All the time. Every break, every lunch, after school.'

Becky laughed. 'So why aren't you playing for Newcastle?'

'Sunderland!' he shouted. 'There's no way I'd play for Newcastle!'

Becky jeered, 'Your face!'

He shook his head. 'It's not something you should joke about.'

Becky switched radio station again and watched James drive.

'Wes had trials for the youth team, you know.'

'Really?'

'Yep. Didn't get in, though. We played in the field next to school. Wes used to take over. He'd go, 'I'll go in goal. No defenders. Come on, pussies!' And we'd have, like, three or four

201

balls, right? So we'd just pound him. But he saved quite a few. More than anyone else could've. We used to get home late – especially in the summer. You had to walk right across the field to the gate that was nearest our road and when it was dark you couldn't really see where you were going. So Mam used to send me to my room and get Wes to stay behind so she could have a go at him.'

'Why?'

'Because he was older. He had to look after me, Mam said.'

'And did he?'

'Yeah, he was a good brother in that way. He didn't want me to hang round him too much, y'know, it's a bit embarrassing. But he looked out for me, like.'

'Do you think I'll get on with him?'

'Yeah,' said James, confidently. 'You don't need his approval, though. You know. But I reckon he'll like you.'

Becky just nodded, taking it in, and looking at James, who kept his eyes on the road.

'He'll probably fancy you,' he joked.

Becky's head dropped. James knew he'd said the wrong thing. He opened his mouth to say something else but couldn't think of anything. Disappointed, Becky looked out of the passenger-side window. James felt guilty: it was just a joke, he thought, the kind that Wes would pull.

Maybe later the pair of them would laugh about it privately, like schoolchildren ridiculing a teacher on the way home. It would be good to hear obscenities from Wes again, he thought. The other men on the site could be crude but they simply were not as funny as Wes. This was especially the case when they had had a drink. James went out with the other labourers after finishing his first week. Quiet and unable to drink as much as them, James had withdrawn and never gone out with them since. Without Wes, it wasn't worth it. James's colleagues just didn't know him like Wes did. So he spent his evenings during those first few weeks looking at the television. Since meeting Becky, however, he had barely turned it on. He had even missed two football matches because he'd been at church events with Becky. Sunday was especially busy: first the service, and then the Sunday lunch, cooked in the cafeteria by the university's Christian group.

Although James enjoyed getting to know everyone at the Sunday lunches, he had skipped it when his brother came down one weekend. James took Wes for a roast at an establishment which he described to his brother as a 'proper working-class pub'.

'We're middle class, aren't we?' Wes asked honestly.

'No,' James laughed. 'We're very working class.'

'But I'm not working, though.'

James shook his head. 'And Mam says you're a fat lot of good at home.'

James could have been wrong but he felt something else in Wes's expression in the pub that afternoon. Perhaps it was just because he was in a new place, but his brother seemed adrift and confused, like a lost child in a supermarket. He did not start a conversation, and rarely passed judgement on James's stories. When James had stood to buy more drinks sometime after their meals, Wes said, 'Nah, let's just go back to your flat, ay?'

James realised now that he had chosen to forget that day. The memory's return brought with it the guilt James felt at having left home. Sadly, he pictured Wes walking across the field besides their old school because he had nothing else to do. Wes's face was frozen with an expression James would never forget: it was the same as that which he'd had when their mam presented James with a kettle she'd bought him from Asda just before he moved.

It was this haunting image that came to him frequently, especially after an evening with Becky and their friends. They were all so kind: James smiled at them politely and hoped that they didn't ask him anything intelligent. It was at these moments when James wanted to see Wes most. At the same time, he didn't want his brother around. Wes's presence in Sheffield would make James feel like even more of an outsider than when Becky's friend Kerry asked him lots of questions about the north-east.

'She wanted to know everything,' he'd told Becky. 'She was like me mam.'

'I bet your mum doesn't wear crazy neon trainers.'

'I don't think you can even buy them in South Shields.'

Becky pulled down the sunshade, which creaked.

'Is Sheffield different to Canterbury?' James asked.

Becky considered the question only briefly. 'Totally. Sheffield's much cooler. Canterbury's a dump, to be honest. I really wanted to leave. There's nothing to do.'

'Shields is the same,' said James. 'Half the shops are boarded up. The seafront used to be nice, but now it's pretty horrible.'

'What did you used to do?'

'Apart from football?'

'Apart from football.' She grinned, watching him.

'Nothin'. Walk around, down the front. There was nothing to do, like. And I didn't want to go and get pissed outside the slotties. Used to stay at home a lot and watch telly with me mam and dad. Didn't even think about leaving until me dad said that Pete asked if I wanted to work.'

'We might never have met,' said Becky.

James felt honestly that they would have. He couldn't explain why so he said nothing, but his silence left him with an unexpected melancholy.

She looked out of the window. 'In Canterbury, it's always the same old people doing the same old stuff. Lizzy, who didn't come to uni, she still goes to the same pub that we used to when we were at sixth form. It's really only for sixth-formers. I just think it's a little sad. It makes sense to move away when you're our age because otherwise you don't change, you don't see anything.'

James moved the car out into the right-hand lane and overtook a lorry. Becky watched his manoeuvre carefully, with interest.

'I had a calm childhood,' she continued. 'No major arguments in the house. If I needed a new pair of trainers, Mum would buy me some. I had nothing to run away from. But I definitely wanted to be independent.'

'If I needed new trainers, me mam would make sure I'd worn out me old ones first. You had to have holes in the bottom before you got a new pair. Same for smart shoes, too, which was annoying because they lasted longer.' Becky had commented on his current pair of smart shoes when they went to a restaurant that had waiters and cloth serviettes. James told her that his old shoes didn't matter; they were under the table the whole night.

Remembering the conversation, James said: 'My childhood was pretty boring. Football was the only thing that kept me awake.'

Things got a little more colourful when Wes started to smoke dope, because the pair of them would have to hide round the corner between the off licence and the footbridge. Wes would draw heavily on the joint, and then look at his fingertips. James, who abhorred the taste, kept guard. This nightly episode soon became banal.

Now, with Becky, his job, Sheffield and church, everything was remarkable.

'Me life's definitely changed since I moved away,' James proclaimed. 'Everything's changed. Even just going to church.'

'I can't imagine never going to church. It was always just part of my childhood. What was it like the first time you came with me?'

'Weird,' he answered.

Becky laughed.

'It was. Now that I know everyone it's OK. Like, me, Paul and Chris are off to the footy next week.'

'What did your mum and dad say when you told them you went to church?'

'Not sure, I couldn't really tell on the phone. I only told Mam, she probably told Dad. But she just went quiet and then said, 'Oh OK, that's nice,' or something. She knew I was going with you so I think she probably thought that was it, that I wasn't interested meself, but.' And James realised now in telling the story that he had not put his mother right.

'I think me mam asked about communion. Like, do I drink the communion wine or whatever. Because they know I don't drink much – especially compared to Wes. I think she had spoken to a family friend. Wes overheard them and told me. She said, 'Our James says he's a Christian,' or something. And they'd had a laugh about me spitting out communion wine.'

'Your mum sounds funny,' she giggled. 'I'm looking forward to meeting her. Is Wes going to be at home too?'

'I hope so. Think Mam said he'll be around for Sunday lunch tomorrow. Tonight he'll be out.'

'Clubbing?'

'Aye, pretty much,' replied James. 'I used to go but I'm not really that bothered about it. I don't enjoy it like he does, with the pills and all that.'

Because nothing else came to mind, his final words hung incongruously between them. It was as if he'd just thrown a dead pig onto a coffee table. As James's unease grew, he realised that he had never acknowledged Wes's habits. It was the knowing that saddened him; if he didn't know about them then perhaps he wouldn't feel so strongly that Wes needed him.

'Does he go out every Saturday night?'

'Think so. There's more chance of scoring on a Saturday.'

Becky, who had been watching James from the side, turned away. Finally, she mumbled, 'Marriage is the goal.'

There was an edge to Becky's tone that made James uneasy. 'Not for Wes,' he joked. 'Not yet anyway.'

'He's probably happy,' Becky said sadly.

'"Probably"?'

'I don't know him well enough to say for definite, but I assume he's happy if that's what he's doing.'

'Becky, you don't know my brother at all,' James kept his eyes on the road. 'But you seemed to have judged him.'

'That's not what I meant.'

'It's not easy for everyone.'

Becky exhaled at James's implication. But he could not think of anything to add that was honest and kind at the same time. Becky had been lucky to be raised the way she had. He could see that now. She'd had a clear, moral path laid out for her. With James and Wes, the path was blurry, cobbled together reactively by their parents, who had done a much better job than those of James's old friends.

For the first time, he admired his family. It was the same feeling he sensed, but could not yet grasp, at church: the sense of being together through a shared ordeal. He'd connected with Becky and her friends through sobriety and grace, but still felt on the outside.

It was exactly how he felt now, driving along the seafront of his hometown, not glancing out at the grey sea or the shabby buildings along the promenade. He connected with this place and understood how it worked. But he did not live here any more. In fact, now that he passed the indifferent sea-view B&Bs he had never before noticed, James felt that every day since he'd been in Sheffield, the distance between that city and South Shields had grown. The essence of his hometown had vanished.

He felt a similar notion of lack when he thought about church – that it attracted him, yet he'd never known why. And now, after

206

months of answers, James still could not pinpoint its central bind. He could not say that god existed.

James pulled up outside his house and turned off the engine. He could feel Becky's curious gaze on him, and knew that he must have an odd expression on his face, but he could not move. Finally he looked at the little house and saw his mam in the window, waving happily. Love and admiration flooded his heart and yet he just could not turn around to share it with Becky. He could not show her his face, because he knew that it was drawn with panic.

~~ The End ~~

About Earlyworks Press

Books

Earlyworks Press lists contain popular and contemporary poetry books and literary and genre short fiction, including science fiction and fantasy. All our books can be ordered from libraries, independent bookshops, by post or direct from our website. The following pages carry details of some of the anthologies we have published in recent years.

Club

The website is also the home of the Writers' and Reviewers' Club – a private, online forum where members can develop and polish their work and help each other to find markets for it. The club promotes members' fiction and non-fiction books and artwork on the website, on independent review sites such as **www.booksy.co.uk** and around the country at book fairs, readings, workshops and festivals.

Competitions

The press does not accept unsolicited work from non-members but if you are a writer and would like to submit work for the next book, you can do so via our regular open competitions and events. There are also regular web-based competitions for fiction, micro fiction, poetry and non-fiction writing. The competitions, and the content of our books, are international, often including work from Europe, Australia, the USA and elsewhere but Earlyworks Press is based in Hastings, Sussex and runs one or two projects a year especially for Hastings and the surrounding towns. For details, go to the competitions page on the website or write, including an SAE, to…

> Kay Green
> Earlyworks Press
> The Creative Media Centre
> 45 Robertson St
> Hastings
> Sussex TN34 1HL

If you would like to join in our online workshops, use our services to writers or have space on our website or at our events to promote your own writing or artwork, please visit the Club and Stepping Stones pages at…

www.earlyworkspress.co.uk

Tasters from **RECOGNITON**

From **Flashpoint** by Judy Walker

... It's dark so she doesn't see me at first. When she does, she jumps.
   "Oh, it's you. You gave me a right fright."
   "What did you do that for, in there?" I ask her.
   "I don't like trouble, that's all."
   I offer her a fag and she takes it, comes closer while I light it from mine, then stands next to me and leans her head on the wall. I haven't been close to a woman for years. She's nothing to look at – mid forties, dyed blond hair, running to fat, and when she lifts her arm, I can smell sour sweat.
   "Just out of prison, are you?" she says.
   "Shows, does it?"...

~~

From **Ossie's Circus** by K S Dearsley

...Karina watched him with hands on hips. "And when we're too old? Or when the Protection League finally gets us shut down?"
   Ossie made a rude noise. "Protectionists!"
   "You can't brush them off so easily. There're more of them all the time. There's even one outside the arena now."
   Ossie had seen her: a thin-faced woman who patrolled the entrance with a placard, like a wading bird stalking the shallows, shrieking dire prophecies in a voice to rival the parakeets...

~~

From **White Snow Like Santa Marta** by Peter Webb

On the street the taxi was running, its cab was musty and warm. How strange that on this fine, clear morning, our world was at its end. Then the demented cockerel in the neighbours' property cried out. And my last thought before the crack of the rifles was of my treachery. Darkness fell around...

from **Memoryfest** by Martin Badger

...I'm told I'm not at all religious but passing the church, St Michael's, not far from the hospital where I'm now only an outpatient, I've several times pulled up and stared at it, as if it were significant. This puzzles Maddie – she says she can't remember me ever going inside.

As for what happened before the accident... I can scarcely remember a thing. It's as if my mind were an iceberg and the tip is after the accident but all else is submerged...

~~

21 STORIES TO KEEP YOU AWAKE

How do you know – anything?

Ancestors linger in darkness, held by the attentions of the living; a monk prepares to answer the eternal question; an accident victim loses his memory, another loses something less tangible; one artist dreams of snow, another of the sea – but what do their artefacts dream of? The last performing tiger in the world meets the mob... and then there are the crocodiles...

In these shape-shifting stories murderers, sleuths, monks and marketing wonderboys all battle with their unique visions of the world – but who wins, and how will they recognise victory when it comes?

RECOGNITION cover image by Jim Littlejohn
Published by Earlyworks Press ISBN 978 1 906451 22 6
£8.99 + £1.50 towards p&p to UK addresses

Tasters from **Loretta's Parrot** and other stories

From **Loretta's Parrot** by Ronnie Nixon

'Well, Bukowski, pleased to meet you. I'm James. I'll get you something to drink.'

James shut the window, made sure his bedroom door was properly closed, and, so as not to disturb Bobby, his flatmate, who was watching morning television, tiptoed through the hall to the kitchen. He got a saucer from the pile of unwashed crockery in the sink, gave it a wipe on his t-shirt, poured in some water and carried it through to the desk in the corner of his bedroom. 'There you go Bukowski.' James sat on his bed sucking his parrot wound, watching Bukowski's head bobbing up and down as he drank.

The parrot finished the water...

...'C'mon, Loretta,' she said putting a comforting arm around her and patting her back. 'You never know, maybe someone's taken him in.' Julie fished a crumpled handkerchief out of her skirt pocket and stuffed it in Loretta's hand.

Loretta wiped her eyes and blew her nose loudly.

A bemused customer, who had been standing at the counter for quite some time, staring at his shoes, eventually plucked up the courage to speak. 'Excuse me ladies, sorry to interrupt, but do you happen to have a copy of Mockingbird Wish Me Luck, by Charles Bukowski? Can't see it on the shelf.'

Loretta fled to the toilet.

~~

From **Hostage** by Sarah Evans

'So as Julia's partner...' Rebecca starts.

'Friend,' he corrects. She must have known he would say this.

'Okay. As Julia's friend...'

She proceeds to ask the routine questions. The answers are ones he's given before. She's less assured than the professional journalists he's dealt with, she twiddles with the ends of her hair, glances anxiously at the tape recorder.

'Well,' she says eventually. 'Thanks for your time.'

'No problem. What will you do with the interview?'

'It's for the website. We highlight a hostage a month.' She grimaces, as if realising it sounds like a supermarket promotion. 'I should be going.'

His heart thuds uncomfortably; the intention and voicing it present themselves simultaneously....

...In Starbucks she orders a Strawberry Frappuccino. They always look sickly to him, but he likes the way she chooses something without hesitation, immediately knowing what she wants. The fact she doesn't insist on paying for hers is somehow reassuring.

'So,' she leans over the table towards him. 'Tell me off the record. What does this stuff about only a friend mean?' ...

An escaped parrot changes lives on the streets of Glasgow

An art historian finds a young lover too much to handle

A big-game hunter meets an unexpected nemesis

– and that's just the first three stories.

This colourful and varied anthology offers a window onto the lives of amnesty activists and kidnappers, soldiers and aid workers, jazzers, photographers, Irish dancers and taxi-drivers – through stories fizzing with love, laughter fear and revenge, fairytales, dreams and nightmares.

Cover art by Catherine Edmunds Published by Earlyworks Press
ISBN 978 1 906451 14 1 £9.95 + £1.50 towards p&p to UK addresses

Tasters from **The Road Unravelled**

From **Chucking Out Time** by R D Gardner

"Matt, what would I have to do?"

"Have another beer, and shut your eyes: this has to go in your spinal cord."

"Er, Matt, how much have you had?"

"Relax, I've never impaled a rat yet."

The needle went into the back of my neck.

I don't remember to this day what we did then, or how I got home: the students next door assured me I came home at sunrise, singing:

Never get bombed with a boffin, you never know where it might end,
Don't get laboratory ratted, and do what you didn't intend...

From **Catherine and the God Market** by Sheila Adamson

On Tuesday night Catherine answered the doorbell to find two aliens outside. It took her a while to work out how to react to that.

"Hallo!" said the alien on the left. "Can we interest you in a message of hope and gladness?"

"Uh?" she said.

The alien smiled brightly. At least, she thought it was smiling. It had a huge lipless mouth, which it was stretching widely; and huge owl eyes which it was blinking enthusiastically. It also had three arms, three legs and rather scaly grey skin. Presumably in an attempt to blend in, it was wearing a dark business suit. "Are you happy?" it enquired.

"Em…"

"Truly happy?"

Catherine felt herself edging backwards. Strangers weren't supposed to ask you questions like that. Of course she wasn't happy. What business was it of anyone else's, human or not?

"We'd like to tell you about true happiness," said the second, smaller alien.

"And eternal life."

"May we come in?"

From **The Beautiful Mind of Samuel Bland Arnold**

by David Dennis

I will tell you why I cannot reveal my love for Patty. There is only one phrase for it: fear of rejection. How can you continue to command a ship this size when your deputy has told you she does not reciprocate your love and yet you are both immortal? You would have to live with your shame and embarrassment forever. ... If I were wrong it would stain my memory with ugliness and breach the Arcado Doctrine.

The Road Unravelled

Birth and death, genetics, evolution and intelligence – natural, artificial and divine: With each new announcement from the world of science shattering more of our traditional assumptions, we asked our writers to look into the future and answer the eternal question of science fiction:

What if...?

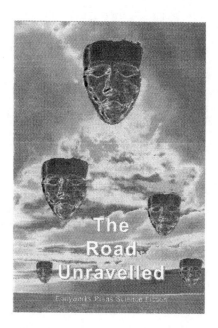

Their answers tell us that far out in the star-fields or here on earth, creatures human and otherwise face life-changing dilemmas; souls and systems, organic and inorganic, must lay aside everything we thought we knew and take an unmapped way forward.

Published by Earlyworks Press
ISBN 978 09553429 98
£9.75 + £1.50 towards p&p to UK addresses

Poetry and Flash Fiction from Earlyworks Press

Do you know why the sky is blue?

Really know?

Within these pages you will dream of peacocks and learn what happens when barnacles march across rocks, then pause for breath as the sea gathers the next breaker. But be sure to watch out for the angels – angels of the dung, grotesques, gargoyles, 'step on a crack, break your mother's back' - and welcome the gentler kind; clouded yellow butterflies and girls with pony-tails.

Sky Breakers[*] is the latest title in the series of poetry and flash fiction titles available from Earlyworks Press. To View the full list of titles and read extracts and reviews, please visit the website

www.earlyworkspress.co.uk

Earlyworks Press books can be ordered from your library, your local independent bookshop or purchased online. Please use the Paypal buttons on the website at www.earlyworkspress.co.uk or email services@earlyworkspress.co.uk

To order by post, please write to Earlyworks Press, Creative Media Centre, 45 Robertson Street, Hastings, Sussex TN34 1HL cheques should be made out to Kay Green.

Discounted copies of back list titles are usually available for Earlyworks Press published authors. Please email us for details.

---

[*] ISBN 978 1 906451 29 5 £6.99 + £1.50 p&p to UK addresses